The Great
White Queen

The Great White Queen

William Le Queux

MINT EDITIONS

The Great White Queen was first published in 1896.

This edition published by Mint Editions 2021.

ISBN 9781513280868 | E-ISBN 9781513285887

Published by Mint Editions®

 MINT
EDITIONS

minteditionbooks.com

Publishing Director: Jennifer Newens
Design & Production: Rachel Lopez Metzger
Project Manager: Micaela Clark
Typesetting: Westchester Publishing Services

Contents

I. A Romance!   7

II. Omar's Slave   12

III. Outward Bound   19

IV. A Strange Promise   24

V. The Giant's Finger   29

VI. The Royal Jujus   34

VII. Samory's Stronghold   39

VIII. The Secret of the Queen   44

IX. Condemned to the Torture   49

X. Zomara   54

XI. The Human Sacrifice   59

XII. In the Sacred Grove   65

XIII. The Way of the Thousand Steps   70

XIV. Foes   76

XV. A Natural Grave   81

XVI. Words of Fire   88

XVII. A Salute of Bullets   96

XVIII. The Mysterious Realm   102

XIX. The City in the Clouds   107

XX. The Great White Queen   111

XXI. A Figure in the Shadow   118

XXII. To the Unknown   124

XXIII. Under the Vampire's Wing   129

XXIV. The Flaming Mouth   137

XXV. Liola   145

XXVI. The First Blow   152

XXVII. By the Naya's Orders   157

XXVIII. The Fight for the Emerald Throne   164

XXIX. A Mystery   171

XXX. Treasure and Treason   180

XXXI. A Spy's Startling Story   189

XXXII. War   195

XXXIII. The Harem Slave   200

XXXIV. Liola's Discovery   211

XXXV. Into the Mist   222

Conclusion   226

I

A Romance!

It is a curious story, full of exciting adventures, extraordinary discoveries, and mysteries amazing.

Strange, too, that I, Richard Scarsmere, who, when at school hated geography as bitterly as I did algebraic problems, should even now, while just out of my teens, be thus enabled to write down this record of a perilous journey through a land known only by name to geographers, a vast region wherein no stranger had ever before set foot.

The face of the earth is well explored now-a-days, yet it has remained for me to discover and traverse one of the very few unknown countries, and to give the bald-headed old fogies of the Royal Geographical Society a lesson in the science that I once abominated.

I have witnessed with my own eyes the mysteries of Mo. I have seen the Great White Queen!

Three years ago I had as little expectation of emulating the intrepidity of Stanley as I had of usurping the throne of England. An orphan, both of whose parents had been drowned in a yachting accident in the Solent and whose elder brother succeeded to the estate, I was left in the care of a maternal uncle, a regular martinet, who sent me for several long and dreary years to Dr. Tregear's well-known Grammar-school at Eastbourne, and had given me to understand that I should eventually enter his office in London. Briefly, I was, when old enough, to follow the prosaic and ill-paid avocation of clerk. But for a combination of circumstances, I should have, by this time, budded into one of those silk-hatted, patent-booted, milk-and-bun lunchers who sit on their high perches and drive a pen from ten till four at a salary of sixteen shillings weekly. Such was the calling my relative thought good enough for me, although his own sons were being trained for professional careers. In his own estimation all his ideas were noble and his generosity unbounded; but not in mine.

But this is not a school story, although its preparatory scenes take place at school. Some preparatory scenes must take place at school; but the drama generally terminates on the broader stage of the world. Who cares for a rehearsal, save those who have taken part in it? I vow, if I had never been at Tregear's I would skip the very mention of his name. As it is, however, I often sigh to see the shadow of the elms clustering around the playground, to watch the moonbeans illumine the ivied wall opposite the dormitory window. I often dream that I am back again, a Cæsar-hating pupil.

Dr. Tregear, commonly called "Old Trigger," lived at Upperton, a suburb of Eastbourne, and had accommodation for seventy boys, but during the whole time I remained there we never had more than fifty. His advertisements in local and London papers offering "Commercial training for thirty guineas including laundress and books. Bracing air, gravel soil, diet best and unlimited. Reduction for brothers," were glowing enough, but they never whipped up business sufficiently to attract the required number of boarders. Nevertheless, I must admit that old Trigger, with all his faults and severity, was really good-hearted. He was a little sniffing, rasping man, with small, spare, feeble, bent figure; mean irregular features badly arranged round a formidable bent, broken red nose; thin straggling grey hair and long grey mutton-chop whiskers; constantly blinking little eyes and very assertive, energetic manners. He had a constant air of objecting to everything and everybody on principle. Knowing that I was an orphan he sometimes took me aside and gave me sound fatherly advice which I have since remembered, and am now beginning to appreciate. His wife, too, was a kindly motherly woman who, because being practically homeless I was often compelled to spend my holidays at school, seemed better disposed towards me than to the majority of the other fellows.

Yes, I got on famously at Trigger's. Known by the abbreviated appellation of "Scars," I enjoyed a popularity that was gratifying, and, bar one or two sneaks, there was not one who would not do me a good turn when I wanted it. The sneaks were outsiders, and although we did not reckon them when we spoke of "the school," it must not be imagined that we forgot to bring them into our calculations in each conspiracy of devilment, nor to fasten upon them the consequences of our practical jokes.

My best friend was a mystery. His name was Omar Sanom, a thin spare chap with black piercing eyes set rather closely together, short crisp hair and a complexion of a slightly yellowish hue. I had been at Trigger's about twelve months and was thirteen when he arrived. I well remember that day. Accompanied by a tall, dark-faced man of decided negroid type who appeared to be ill at ease in European clothes, he was shown into the Doctor's study, where a long consultation took place.

　　　　　　　　　　　　　　　　　　　　　　　　　　WILLIAM LE QUEUX

Meanwhile among the fellows much speculation was rife as to who the stranger was, the popular opinion being that Trigger should not open his place to "savages," and that if he came we would at once conspire to make his life unbearable and send him to Coventry.

An hour passed and listeners at the keyhole of the Doctor's door could only hear mumbling, as if the negotiations were being carried on in the strictest secrecy. Presently, however, the black man wished Trigger good-day, and much to everyone's disgust and annoyance the yellow-faced stranger was brought in and introduced to us as Omar Sanom, the new boy.

The mystery surrounding him was inscrutable. About my own age, he spoke very little English and would, in conversation, often drop unconsciously into his own language, a strange one which none of the masters understood or even knew its name. It seemed to me composed mainly of p's and l's. To all our inquiries as to the place of his birth or nationality he remained dumb. Whence he had come we knew not; we were only anxious to get rid of him.

I do not think Trigger knew very much about him. That he paid very handsomely for his education I do not doubt, for he was allowed privileges accorded to no one else, one of which was that on Sundays when we were marched to church he was allowed to go for a walk instead, and during prayers he always stood aside and looked on with superior air, as if pitying our simplicity. His religion was not ours.

For quite a month it was a subject of much discussion as to which of the five continents Omar came from, until one day, while giving a geography lesson the master, who had taken the West Coast of Africa as his subject, asked:

"Where does the Volta River empty itself?"

There was a dead silence that confessed ignorance. We had heard of the Russian Volga, but never of the Volta. Suddenly Omar, who stood next me, exclaimed in his broken English:

"The Volta empties itself into the Gulf of Guinea. I've been there."

"Quite correct," nodded the master approvingly, while Baynes, the fellow on my left, whispered:—

"Yellow-Face has been there! He's a Guinea Pig—see?"

I laughed and was punished in consequence, but the suggestion of the witty Baynes being whispered round the school was effective. From that moment the yellow-faced mysterious foreigner was commonly known as "the Guinea Pig."

We did our best to pump him and ascertain whether he had been born in Guinea, but he carefully avoided the subject. The information that he came from the West Coast of Africa had evidently been given us quite involuntarily. He had been asked a question about a spot he knew intimately, and the temptation to exhibit his superiority over us had proved too great.

Not only was his nationality a secret, but many of his actions puzzled us considerably. As an instance, whenever he drank anything, water, tea, or coffee, he never lifted his cup to his lips before spilling a small quantity upon the floor. If we had done this punishment would promptly have descended upon us, but the masters looked on at his curious antics in silence.

Around his neck beneath his clothes he wore a sort of necklet composed of a string of tiny bags of leather, in which were sewn certain hard substances that could be felt inside. Even in the dormitory he never removed this, although plenty of chaff was directed towards him in consequence of this extraordinary ornament. It was popularly supposed that he came from some savage land, and that when at home this string of leather bags was about the only article of dress he wore.

If rather dull at school, he very soon picked up our language with all its slang, and quickly came to the fore in athletics. In running, swimming and rowing no one could keep pace with him. On foot he was fleet as a deer, and in the water could swim like a fish, while at archery he was a dead shot. Within three months he had lived down all the prejudices that had been engendered by reason of his colour, and I confess that I myself, who had at first regarded him with gravest suspicion, now began to feel a friendliness towards him. Once or twice, at considerable inconvenience to himself he rendered me valuable services, and on one occasion got me out of a serious scrape by taking the blame himself, therefore within six months of his arrival we became the firmest of chums. At work, as at play, we were always together, and notwithstanding the popular feeling being antagonistic to my close acquaintance with the "Guinea Pig," I nevertheless knew from my own careful observations that although a foreigner, half-savage he might be, he was certainly true and loyal to his friends.

Once he fought. It was soon after we became chums that he had a quarrel with the bully Baynes over the ownership of a catapult. Baynes, who was three years older, heavier built and much taller, threatened to thrash him. This threat was sufficient. Omar at once challenged him, and the fight took place down in the paddock behind a hedge, secure from Trigger's argus eye. As the pair took off their coats one of the fellows jokingly said—

"The Guinea Pig's a cannibal. He'll eat you, Baynes."

Everybody laughed, but to their astonishment within five minutes our champion pugilist lay on the ground with swollen eye and sanguinary nose, imploring for mercy. That he could fight Omar quickly showed us, and as he released the bully after giving him a sound dressing as a cat would shake a rat, he turned to us and with a laugh observed—

"My people are neither cowards nor cannibals. We never fight unless threatened, but we never decline to meet our enemies."

No one spoke. I helped him on with his coat, and together we left the ground, while the partisans of Baynes picked up their fallen champion and proceeded to make him presentable.

Like myself, Omar seemed friendless, for when the summer holidays came round both of us remained with the Doctor and his wife, while the more fortunate ones always went away to their homes. At first he seemed downcast, but we spent all our time together, and Mrs. Tregear, it must be admitted, did her best to make us comfortable, allowing us to ramble where we felt inclined, even surreptitiously supplying us with pocket-money.

It was strange, however, that I never could get Omar to talk of himself. Confidential friends that we were, in possession of each other's secrets, he spoke freely of everything except his past. That some remarkable romance enveloped him I felt certain, yet by no endeavour could I fathom the mystery.

Twice or thrice each year the elderly negro who had first brought him to the school visited him, and they were usually closeted a long time together. Perhaps his sable-faced guardian on those occasions told him news of his relatives; perhaps he gave him good advice. Which, I know not. The man, known as Mr. Makhana, was always very pleasant towards me, but never communicative. Yet he made up for that defect by once or twice leaving half-a-sovereign within my ready palm. He appeared suddenly without warning, and left again, even Omar himself being unaware where he dwelt.

Truly my friend was a mystery. Who he was, or whence he had come, was a secret.

II

OMAR'S SLAVE

O mar had been at Trigger's a little over two years when a strange incident occurred. We were then both aged about sixteen, he a few months older than myself. The summer holidays had come round again. I had a month ago visited my uncle in London, and he had given me to understand that after next term I should leave school and commence life in the City. He took me to his warehouse in Thames Street and showed me the gas-lit cellar wherein his clerks were busy entering goods and calling out long columns of amounts. The prospect was certainly not inviting, for I was never good at arithmetic, and to spend one's days in a place wherein never a ray of sunshine entered was to my mind the worst existence to which one could be condemned.

When I returned I confessed my misgivings to Omar, who sympathised with me, and we had many long chats upon the situation as during the six weeks we wandered daily by the sea. We cared little for the Grand Parade, with its line of garish hotels, tawdry boarding-houses and stucco-fronted villas, and the crowd of promenaders did not interest us. Seldom even we went on the pier, except to swim. Our favourite walks were away in the country through Willingdon to Polegate, over Beachy Head, returning through East Dean to Litlington and its famed tea-garden, or across Pevensey Levels to Wartling, for we always preferred the more unfrequented ways. One day, when I was more than usually gloomy over the prospect of drudgery under my close-fisted relative, my friend said to me cheerfully:

"Come, Scars, don't make yourself miserable about it. My people have a saying that a smile is the only weapon one can use to combat misfortune, and I think it's true. We have yet a few months more together before you leave. In life our ways will lie a long way apart. You will become a trader in your great city, while I shall leave soon, I expect, to—" and he paused.

"To do what?" I inquired.

"To go back to my own people, perhaps," he answered mechanically. "Perhaps I shall remain here and wait, I know not."

"Wait for what?"

"Wait until I receive orders to return," he answered. "Ah, you don't know what a strange life mine has been, Scars," he added a moment later in a confidential tone. "I have never told you of myself for the simple reason that silence is best. We are friends; I hope we shall be friends always, even though my enemies seek to despise me because I am not quite white like them. But loyalty is one of the cherished traditions of my people, and now that during two years our friendship has been firmly established I trust nothing will ever occur to interrupt it."

"I take no heed of your enemies, Omar," I said. "You have proved yourself genuine, and the question of colour, race, or creed has nothing to do with it."

"Perhaps creed has," he exclaimed rather sadly. "But I make no pretence of being what I am not. Your religion interests me, although, as you know, I have never been taught the belief you have. My gods are in the air, in the trees, in the sky. I believe what I have been taught; I pray in silence and the great god Zomara hears me even though I am separated from my race by yonder great ocean. Yet I sometimes think I cannot act as you white people do, that, after all, what my enemies say is true. I am still what you term a savage, although wearing the clothes of your civilization."

"Though a man be a pagan he may still be a friend," I said.

"Yes, I am at least your friend," he said. "My only regret is that your uncle will part us in a few months. Still, in years to come we shall remember each other, and you will at least have a passing thought for Omar, the Guinea Pig," he added, laughing.

I smiled too, but I noticed that although he endeavoured to appear gay, his happiness was feigned, and there was in his dark eyes a look of unutterable sadness. Our conversation drifted to a local cricket match that was to be played on the morrow, and soon the gloomy thoughts that seemed to possess him were dispelled.

It was on the same sunny afternoon, however, that a curious incident occurred which was responsible for altering the steady prosaic course of our lives. The most trifling incidents change the current of a life, and the smallest events are sufficient to alter history altogether. Through the blazing August afternoon we had walked beyond Meads, mounted Beachy Head, passed the lighthouse at Belle Tout and descended to the beach at a point known as the Seven Sisters. The sky was cloudless, the sea like glass, and during that long walk without shelter from the sun's rays I had been compelled to halt once or twice and mop my face with my handkerchief. Yet without fatigue, without the slightest apparent effort, and still feeling cool, Omar walked on, smiling at the manner in which the unusual heat affected me, saying:

"Ah! It is not hot here. You might grumble at the heat if the sun were as powerful as it is in my country."

When we descended to the beach and threw ourselves down under the shadow of the high white cliffs to rest, I saw there was no one about and suggested a swim. It was against old Trigger's orders, nevertheless the calm, cool water as it lazily lapped the sand proved too tempting, and very shortly we had plunged in and were enjoying ourselves. Omar left the water first, and presently I saw while he was dressing the figure of a tallish, muscular man attired in black and wearing a silk hat approaching him. As I watched, wondering what business the stranger could have with my companion, I saw that when they met Omar greeted him in native fashion by snapping fingers, as he had often done playfully to me. Whoever he might be, the stranger was unexpected, and judging from the manner in which he had been received, a welcome visitor. I was not near enough to distinguish the features of the newcomer, but remembering that I had been in the water long enough, I struck out for the shore, and presently walked up the beach towards them.

Omar had dressed, and was in earnest conversation with a gigantic negro of even darker complexion than Mr. Makhana. Unconscious of my approach, for my feet fell noiselessly upon the sand, he was speaking rapidly in his own language, while the man who had approached him stood listening in meek, submissive attitude. Then, for the first time, I noticed that my friend held in his hand a grotesquely carved stick that had apparently been presented by the new-comer as his credential, together with a scrap of parchment whereon some curious signs, something like Arabic, were written. While Omar addressed him he bowed low from time to time, murmuring some strange words that I could not catch, but which were evidently intended to assure my friend that he was his humble servant.

In spare moments Omar had taught me a good deal of his language. Indeed, such a ready pupil had I been that frequently when we did not desire the other fellows to understand our conversation we spoke in his tongue. But of what he was saying to this stranger, I could only understand one or two words and they conveyed to me no meaning. The negro was a veritable giant in stature, showily dressed, with one of those gaudily-coloured neckties that delight the heart of Africans, while on his fat brown hand was a large ring of very light-coloured metal that looked suspiciously like brass. His boots were new, and of enormous size, but as he stood he shifted uneasily from one foot to the other, showing that he was far from comfortable in his civilized habiliments.

Without approaching closer I picked up my things and dressed rapidly, then walked forward to join my companion.

"Scars!" he cried, as soon as I stood before him. "I had quite forgotten you. This is my mother's confidential adviser, Kouaga."

Then, turning to the grinning ebon-faced giant he uttered some rapid words in his own language and told him my name, whereupon he snapped fingers in true native fashion, the negro showing an even set of white teeth as an expression of pleasure passed over his countenance.

"We little thought that we were being watched this afternoon," Omar said to me, smiling and throwing himself down upon the sand, an example followed by the negro and myself. "It seems that Kouaga arrived in Eastbourne this morning, but there are strong reasons why none should know that he has seen me. Therefore he followed me here to hold palaver at a spot where we should not be observed."

"You have a letter, I see."

"Yes," he said slowly, re-reading the strange lines of hieroglyphics. "The news it contains necessitates me leaving for Africa immediately."

"For Africa!" I cried dismayed. "Are you going?"

"Yes, I must. It is imperative."

"Then I shall lose you earlier than I anticipated," I observed with heart-felt sorrow at the prospect of parting with my only chum. "It is true, as you predicted, our lives lie very far apart."

The negro lifted his hat from his brow as if its weight oppressed him, then turning to me, said slowly and with distinctness in his own tongue:

"I bring the words of the mighty Naya unto her son. None dare disobey her commands on pain of death. She is a ruler above all rulers; before her armed men monarchs bow the knee, at her frown nations tremble. In order to bring the palaver she would make with her son I have journeyed for three moons by land and sea to reach him and deliver the royal staff in secret. I have done my duty. It is for Omar to obey. Kouaga has spoken."

"Let me briefly explain, Scarsmere," my friend interrupted. "Until the present I have been compelled to keep my identity a secret, for truth to tell, there is a plot against our dynasty, and I fear assassination."

"Your dynasty!" I cried amazed. "Are your people kings and queens?"

"They are," he answered. "I am the last descendant of the great Sanoms of Mo, the powerful rulers who for a thousand years have held our country against all its enemies, Mahommedan, Pagan or Christian. I am the Prince of Mo."

"But where is Mo?" I asked. "I have never heard of it."

"I am not surprised," he said. "No stranger has entered it, or ever will, for it is unapproachable and well-guarded. One intrepid white man ventured a year ago to ascend to the grass plateau that forms its southern boundary, but he was expelled immediately on pain of death. My country, known to the neighbouring tribes as the Land Beyond the Clouds, lies many weeks' journey from the sea in the vast region within the bend of the great Niger river, north of Upper Guinea, and is coterminous with the states of Gurunsi and Kipirsi on the west, with Yatenga on the north-west, with Jilgodi, Aribinda, and Libtako on the north, with Gurma on the east, and with the Nampursi district of Gurunsi on the south."

"The names have no meaning for me," I said. "But the fact that you are an actual Prince is astounding."

With his hands clasped behind his head, he flung himself back upon the sand, laughing heartily.

"Well," he said, "I didn't want to parade my royal ancestry, neither do I want to now. I only tell you in confidence, and in order that you shall understand why I am compelled to return. During the past ten years there have been many dissensions among the people, fostered by the enemies of our country, with a view to depose the reigning dynasty. Three years ago a dastardly plot was discovered to murder my mother and myself, seize the palace, and massacre its inmates. Fortunately it was frustrated, but my mother deemed it best to send me secretly out of the country, for I am sole heir to the throne, and if the conspirators killed me, our dynasty must end. Therefore Makhana, my mother's secret agent, who purchases our arms and ammunition in England and conducts all trade we have with civilized countries, brought me hither, and I have since been in hiding."

"But Makhana has been bribed by our enemies," exclaimed the big negro, who had been eagerly listening to our conversation, but understanding no word of it save the mention of Makhana's name. Turning to Omar he added: "Makhana will, if he obtains a chance, kill you. Be warned in time against him. It has been ascertained that he supplied the men of Moloto with forty cases of rifles, and that he has given his pledge that you shall never return to Africa. Therefore obey the injunction of my royal mistress, the great Naya, and leave with me secretly."

"Without seeing Makhana?" asked Omar.

"Yes," the black-faced man replied. "He must not know, or the plans of the Naya may be thwarted. Our enemies have arranged to strike their blow three moons from now, but ere that we shall be back in Mo, and they will find that they go only to their graves. Kouaga has made fetish for the son of his royal mistress, and has come to him bearing the stick."

"What does the letter say?" I asked Omar, noticing him reading it again.

"It is brief enough, and reads as follows," he said:

> Know, O my son Omar, that I send my stick unto thee by
> our trusty Kouaga. Return unto Mo on the wings of haste,
> for our throne is threatened and thy presence can avert our
> overthrow. Tarry not in the country of the white men, but
> let thy face illuminate the darkness of my life ere I go to the
> tomb of my ancestors.
>
> Naya

I glanced at the scrap of parchment, and saw appended a truly regal seal.

"And shall you go?" I asked with sorrow.

"Yes—if you will accompany me."

"Accompany you!" I cried. "How can I? I have no money to go to Africa, besides—"

"Besides what?" he answered smiling. "Kouaga has money sufficient to pay both our passages. Remember, I am Prince of Mo, and this man is my slave. If I command him to take you with me he will obey. Will you go?"

The prospect of adventure in an unknown land was indeed enticing. In a few brief words he recalled my dismal forebodings of the life in an underground office in London, and contrasted it with a free existence in a fertile and abundant land, where I should be the guest and perhaps an official of its ruler. He urged me most strongly to go as his companion, and in conclusion said:

"Your presence in Mo will be unique, for you will be the first stranger who has ever set foot within its capital."

"But your mother may object to me, as she did to the entrance of the white man of whom you just now spoke."

"Ah! he came to make trade palaver. You are my friend and confidant," he said.

"Then you suggest that we should both leave Eastbourne at once, travel with Kouaga to Liverpool and embark for Africa without returning to Trigger's, or saying a word to anyone?"

"We must. If we announce our intention of going we are certain to be delayed, and as the steamers leave only once a month, delay may be fatal to my mother's plans."

As he briefly explained to Kouaga that he had invited me to accompany him I saw that companion to an African prince would be a much more genial occupation than calculating sums in a gas-lit cellar; therefore, fired by the pleasant picture he placed before me, I resolved to accept his invitation.

"Very well, Omar," I said, trying to suppress the excitement that rose within me. "We are friends, and where you go I will go also."

Delighted at my decision my friend sprang to his feet with a cry of joy, and we all three snapped fingers, after which we each took a handful of dry sand and by Omar's instructions placed it in one heap upon a rock. Then, having first mumbled something over his amulets, he quickly stirred the heap of sand with his finger, saying:

"As these grains of sand cannot be divided, so cannot the bonds of friendship uniting Omar, Prince of Mo, with Scarsmere and Kouaga, be rent asunder. Omar has spoken."

III

Outward Bound

How, trembling lest we should be discovered, we left Eastbourne by train two hours later—Kouaga joining the train at Polegate so as to avoid notice—how the Grand Vizier of Mo purchased our travelling necessities in London; how we travelled to Liverpool by the night mail, and how we embarked upon the steamer *Gambia*, it is unnecessary to relate in detail. Suffice it to say that within twenty-four hours of meeting the big negro we were safely on board the splendid mail-steamer where everything was spick and span. Kouaga had engaged a cabin for our exclusive use, and the captain himself had evidently ascertained that Omar was a person of importance, for in passing us on deck he paused to chat affably, and express a hope that we should find the voyage a pleasant one.

"Your coloured servant has told me your destination," he said, addressing Omar. "We can't land you there on account of the surf, but I understand a boat from shore will be on the look-out. If it isn't, well, you'll have to go on to Cape Coast Castle."

"The boat will be in readiness," Omar said smiling. "If it isn't, those in charge will pay dearly for it. You know what I mean."

The Captain laughed, drew his finger across his throat, and nodded.

"Yes," he said. "I've heard that in your country life is held cheap. I fancy I'd rather be on my bridge than a resident in the Naya's capital. But I see I'm wanted. Good-bye," and he hurried away to shout some order to the men who were busy stowing the last portion of the cargo.

As we leaned over the rail watching the bustle on board the steam tender that lay bobbing up and down at our side, we contemplated the consternation of old Trigger when he found us missing. No doubt a hue and cry would be at once raised, but as several persons we knew had seen us walking towards the Belle Tout, it would, without a doubt, be surmised that we had been drowned while bathing. The only thing we regretted was that we had not left some portion of our clothing on the beach to give verisimilitude to the suggestion. However, we troubled ourselves not one whit about the past. I was glad to escape from the doom of the gas-lit cellar, and was looking forward with keen anticipation to a new life in that mystic country, Africa.

At last there was shouting from the bridge, the tender cast off, the bell in the engine-room gave four strokes, the signal for full-speed ahead, and ere long we were steaming past that clanging beacon the Bell Buoy, and heading for the open sea. The breeze began to whistle around us, the keen-eyed old pilot tightened his scarf around his throat, and carefully we sped along past the Skerries until we slowed off Holyhead, where he shook hands with the captain, and with a hearty "good-bye" swung himself over the bulwarks into the heavy old boat that had come alongside. Thus was severed the last link that bound us to England.

Standing up in his boat he waved us a farewell, while our captain, his hands behind him, took charge of the ship and shouted an order.

Ting-ting-ting-ting sounded the bell below, and a moment later we were moving away into the fast falling night. For a long time we remained on deck with Kouaga, watching the distant shore of Wales fade into the banks of mist, while now and then a brilliant light would flash its warning to us and then die out again as suddenly as it had appeared. We had plenty of passengers on board, mostly merchants and their families going out to the "Coast," one or two Government officials, engineers and prospectors, and during the first night all seemed bustle and confusion. Stewards were ordered here and there, loud complaints were heard on every side, threats were made to report trivialities to the captain, and altogether there was plenty to amuse us.

Next day, however, when we began to bow gracefully to the heavy swell of the Atlantic the majority of the grumblers were glad enough to seek the comfort and privacy of their berths and to remain there, for during the two days that followed the waves ran mountains high, the wind howled, the bulkheads creaked and the vessel made plunges so unexpectedly that to stand was almost impossible. The great waves seemed to rush upon us as we ploughed our way through them, sometimes burying our bows in foam and at others striking us and lifting us high up, the shock almost causing us to stop. The roar of the tempest seemed deafening, the ship's bell tolled with regularity, but no one appeared in the saloon, and it seemed as if the cook in his galley had little, if anything, to do.

"Never mind," I heard one officer say to another, as they lounged outside their cabins off duty. "It'll give 'em their sea legs, and the weather will be all right the other side of the Bay."

Both laughed. Sailors seem to enjoy the discomforts of passengers.

During those two days I think we were the only passengers who spent the whole day on deck. Kouaga was a poor sailor and was in his bunk horribly bad. When we visited him the whites of his eyes seemed perfectly green.

This was my first taste of a storm, and I must confess that I did not enjoy it. I was not ill, but experienced a feeling the reverse of comfortable. Through all, however, I congratulated myself that I had actually left England, and was about to commence life in a new land. The officer whose words I had overheard proved a prophet, for after three days of bad weather we ran into blue water, calm as a mill-pond, the sun shone out warm and bright, as quickly as the spirits of the passengers had fallen they rose again, and a round of gaiety commenced that continued unbroken until we left the vessel.

We touched at Funchal, a pretty town of white villas half hidden by the surrounding greenery, and with others went ashore, but we were not there more than a couple of hours, for soon the Blue-Peter was run to our masthead as signal that the ship was about to sail, and we were compelled to re-embark. Then a gun was fired on board, the crowd of small craft around us that had put out for the purpose of selling the passengers bananas, live birds, etc., sheered off, and very soon we had restarted on our southward voyage.

Ere long, having passed the snow-capped peak of Teneriffe of which we had heard so much at Trigger's, we entered the region of the trade-winds, and the steamer, aided by its sails that were now spread, held rapidly on its course rounding Cape Verd. For a day we anchored off Bathurst, then steamed away past the many rocky islands off the coast of Guinea until we touched Free Town, the capital of that unhealthy British colony Sierra Leone. Anchoring there, we discharged some cargo, resuming our voyage in a calm sea and perfect weather, and carefully avoiding the dangerous shoals of St. Ann, we passed within sight of Sherboro Island, a British possession, and also sighted Cape Mount, which Omar told me was in the independent republic of Liberia. For several days after this we remained out of sight of land until one afternoon, just about tea-time, the captain came up to us, saying—

"We shall make the mouth of the Lahou River in about two hours, so you'd better be prepared to leave. I'll keep a good look-out for your boat. Have you had a pleasant voyage?"

"Very," we both replied in one voice.

"Glad of that," he said, and turning to Omar added, "you'll look after me if ever I get up country as far as Mo, won't you?"

"Of course," my friend answered laughing. "If you come you shall have a right royal welcome. Come at any time. You'll have nothing to fear when once inside the borders of my mother's country."

"Ah, well. Perhaps I'll come some day, when I retire on my pension and set up as an African chief—eh?"

We all laughed, and he ascended the steps again to the bridge.

Kouaga, in the meantime, was busy collecting our things, giving gratuities to the stewards, and otherwise making preparations to leave. For over two hours we eagerly watched in the direction of the shore, being assisted by a crowd of passengers who had by this time learnt that we were to be taken off.

The shore which slowly came into view as our eager eyes scanned the horizon was the Ivory Coast, but the sun sank in a glorious blaze of crimson, and dusk crept on, yet the captain, whose glasses continually swept the sea, could distinguish no boat approaching us.

"I'm afraid," he shouted to us from the bridge, "their look-out is not well kept. We'll have to take you along to Cape Coast, after all."

"Why not fire a gun, Captain?" suggested Kouaga, his words being interpreted by Omar.

"Very well," he answered, and turning to the officer, he gave orders that the signal gun should be fired three times at intervals.

Presently there was a puff of white smoke and the first loud report rang out, making the vessel quiver beneath us. We waited, listening, but there was no response. The light quickly faded, night cast her veil of darkness over the sea, but we still stood in for the coast.

Again, about half-past nine, the gun belched forth a tongue of flame, and the report sounded far over the silent waters. All was excitement on deck, for it was a matter of speculation whether an answering shout or gunshot could be heard above the roar and throbbing of the engines. Ten, eleven o'clock passed, and presently the third gun was exploded so suddenly that the ladies were startled. Again we listened, but could hear nothing. Kouaga fumed and cursed the evil-spirit for our misfortune, while Omar, finding that we were to be taken to Cape Coast Castle, imparted to me his fear that the fortnight's delay it must necessarily entail, would be fatal to his mother's plans.

We were hanging over the taffrail together gazing moodily into the darkness, having given up all hope of getting ashore at the Lahou River,

WILLIAM LE QUEUX

when suddenly about half a mile from us we saw a flash, and the report of a rifle reached us quite distinctly, followed by distant shouting.

"There they are!" cried Omar excitedly. "They've hailed us at last!"

But ere the words had fallen from his lips we heard the bell in the engine-room ringing, and next second the steam was shut off and we gradually hove to.

Kouaga was at our side almost immediately, and we found ourselves surrounded by passengers taking leave of us. Our boxes were brought up by a couple of sailors, and after about a quarter of an hour's wait, during which time the vessel rose and fell with the swell, the craft that had hailed us loomed up slowly in the darkness, amid the excited jabber of her demoniac-looking crew.

She was a large native vessel, brig-rigged, and as dirty and forbidding-looking a craft as you could well see anywhere. Kouaga hailed one of the black, half-clad men on board, receiving a cheery answer, and presently, having taken leave of the captain and those around us, we climbed over the bulwarks and sprang upon the deck of the mysterious ship.

As Omar alighted the whole crew made obeisance to him, afterwards crowding around me, examining me by the lurid light of the torches they had ignited.

Very quickly, however, several boxes belonging to Kouaga were lowered, the moorings were cast off, and slowly the great mail steamer with its long line of brilliantly-lit ports looking picturesque in the night, moved onward.

"Good-bye," shouted a voice from the steamer.

"Good-bye," I responded, and as the steamer's bell again rang out, "full speed ahead," I knew that the last tie that bound us to European civilization was severed.

IV

A Strange Promise

By the light of the flambeaux the sleek, black, oily-looking natives managed their clumsy craft, which, dipping suddenly now and then, shipped great seas, compelling us to hang on for life. The sails creaked and groaned as they bent to the wind, speeding on in the darkness towards the mainland of Africa. To be transferred to such a ship, which I more than suspected was a slaver, was a complete change after the clean, well-ordered Liverpool liner, and I must confess that, had we not been in charge of Kouaga, I should have feared to trust myself among that shouting cut-throat crew of grinning blacks. Clinging to a rope I stood watching the strange scene, rendered more weird by the flickering uncertain light of the torches falling upon the swarm of natives who manned the craft.

"Are these your mother's people?" I inquired of Omar.

"Some are. I recognize several as our slaves, the remainder are Sanwi, or natives of the coast. Our slaves, I suppose, have been sent down to be our carriers."

"Judging from the manner in which they crawl about this is, I should think, their first experience of the sea," I said.

"No doubt. Over a thousand English miles of desert and almost impenetrable bush separates the sea from our kingdom, therefore few, very few of our people have seen it."

"They'll go back with some wonderful tales, I suppose."

"Yes. They will, on their return, be considered heroes of travel, and their friends will hold feasts in their honour."

As he finished speaking, however, our cumbrous craft seemed suddenly to be lifted high out of the water, and amid the unearthly yells of the whole crew we were swept through a belt of foaming surf, until in a few moments our keel slid upon the sand.

I prepared to leap down upon the beach, but in a second half-a-dozen willing pairs of arms were ready to assist me, and I alighted in the midst of a swarm of half-clad, jabbering natives.

One of them, elbowing his way towards me, asked in broken English: "Massa have good voyage—eh?" whereupon the others laughed heartily at hearing one of their number speak the language of the white men. But Kouaga approached uttering angry words, and from that moment the same respect was paid to me as to Omar.

We found there was a small village where we landed, otherwise the coast was wild and desolate. In an uncleanly little hut to which we were taken when our boxes were landed and the excitement had subsided, we were regaled with various African delicacies, which at first I did not find palatable, but which Omar devoured with a relish, declaring that he had not enjoyed a meal so much since he had left "the Coast" for England. But I did not care for yams, and the stewed monkey looked suspiciously like a cooked human specimen. My geographical knowledge was not so extensive as it might have been, and I was not certain whether these natives were not cannibals. Therefore I only made a pretence of eating, and sat silently contemplating the strange scene as we all sat upon the floor and took up our food with our fingers. When we had concluded the feast a native woman served Omar with some palm wine, which, however, he did not drink, but poured it upon the ground as an offering to the fetish for his safe return, and then we threw ourselves upon the skins stretched out for us and slept till dawn.

At sunrise I got up and went out. The place was, I discovered, even more desolate than I had imagined. Nothing met the eye in every direction but vast plains of interminable sand, with hillocks here and there, also of sand; no trees were to be seen, not even a shrub; all was arid, dry and parched up with heat. The village was merely an assemblage of a dozen miserable mud huts, and so great was the monotony of the scene, that the eye rested with positive pleasure on the dirty, yellow-coloured craft in which we had landed during the night. It had apparently once been whitewashed, but had gradually assumed that tawny hue that always characterises the African wilderness.

Again Omar and I were surrounded by the crowd of fierce-looking barbarians, but the twenty stalwart carriers sent down from Mo, apparently considering themselves a superior race to these coast-dwellers, ordered them away from our vicinity, at the same time preparing to start for the interior. Under the direction of Kouaga, who had already abandoned his European attire and now wore an Arab haick and white burnouse, the gang of chattering men soon got their loads of food and merchandise together—for the Grand Vizier had apparently been purchasing a quantity of guns and ammunition in England—

hammocks were provided for all three of us if we required them, and after a good meal we at length set out, turning our backs upon the sea.

After descending the crest of a sand-hill we found ourselves fairly in the desert. As far as we could see away to the limitless horizon was sand—arid, parched red-brown sand without a vestige of herbage. The wind that was blowing carried grains of it, which filled one's mouth and tasted hot and gritty; again, impalpable atoms of sand were blown into the corners of one's eyes, and, besides, this injury inflicted on the organ of vision was calculated by no means to improve one's temper. However, Omar told me that a beautiful and fruitful land lay beyond, therefore we made light of these discomforts, and, after a march of three days, during which time we were baked by day by the merciless sun and chilled at night by the heavy dews, we at last came to the edge of the waterless wilderness, and remained for some hours to rest.

My first glimpse of the "Dark Continent" was not a rosy one. As a well-known writer has already pointed out, life with a band of native carriers might for a few days be a diverting experience if the climate were good and if there was no immediate necessity for hurry. But as things were it proved a powerful exercise, especially when we commenced to traverse the almost impenetrable bush by the native path, so narrow that two men could not walk abreast.

Across a great dismal swamp where high trees and rank vegetation grew in wondrous profusion we wended our way, day by day, amid the thick white mist that seemed to continually envelop us. But it required a little more than persuasion to make our carriers travel as quickly as Kouaga liked. At early dawn while the hush of night yet hung above the forest, our guide would rise, stretch his giant limbs and kick up a sleeping trumpeter. Then the tall, dark forest would echo with the boom of an elephant-tusk horn, whose sound was all the more weird since it came from between human jaws with which the instrument was decorated. The crowd of blacks got up readily enough, but it was merely in order to light their fires and to settle down to eat plantains. At length the horn would sound again, but produce no result. The whole company still squatted, eating and jabbering away, indifferent to every other sound. The head man would be called for by Kouaga. "Why are your men not ready? Know you not that the son of the great Naya is with us?" With a deprecatory smile the head-man would make some excuse. He had hurt his foot, or had rheumatism, and therefore he, and consequently his men, would be compelled to rest that day.

WILLIAM LE QUEUX

He would then be warned that if not ready to march in five minutes, he would be carried captive into Mo for the Great White Queen herself to deal with. In five minutes he would return to Kouaga, saying that if the Grand Vizier would only give the men a little more salt with their "chop" (food) that evening, they would march.

Kouaga would then become furious, soundly rating everybody, and declare that the Naya herself should deal with the whole lot as mutineers; whereupon, seeing all excuses for further halt unavailing, loads would be taken up, and within a few moments the whole string of half-clad natives would go laughing and singing on the forward path.

The first belt of forest passed we entered a vast level land covered with scrub, which Omar informed me was the border of the Debendu territory. Proceeding down a wide valley we came at length to the first inhabited region. Every three or four miles we passed through a native village—usually a single street of thirty or forty houses. Each house consisted, as a rule, of three or four small sheds, facing inwards, and forming a tiny courtyard. The huts were on built-up platforms, with hard walls of mud, and roofs thatched with palm-leaves, while the front steps were faced with a kind of red cement. In the middle of each centre of habitation we found a tree with seats around it formed of untrimmed logs, on which the elders and head-men of the village would sit, smoke, and gravely discuss events. As we left each village to plunge boldly onward through the bush we would pass the village fetish ground, well defined by the decaying bodies of lizards and birds, a grinning human skull or two, broken pots and pieces of rag fluttering in the wind, all offered as propitiation to the presiding demon of the place, while away in the bush, behind the houses, we saw the giant leaves of the plantain groves that yielded the staple food of this primitive people.

Deeper and deeper we proceeded until we came into regular forest scenery, where day after day we pushed our way through solemn shady aisles of forest giants, whose upper parts gleamed far above the dense undergrowth in white pillars against the grey-blue sky. Sometimes we strode down a picturesque sunny glade, and at others struggled through deep dark crypts of massive bamboo clumps. Here the noisome smell of decaying vegetation nauseated us, for the air in those forest depths is deadly. Beautiful scarlet wax-flowers would gleam high among the dark-green foliage of the giant cotton-tree, whose stem would be covered with orchids and ferns and dense wreaths of creeper, while many other beautiful blossoms flourished and faded unseen. In that dark dismal place there was an absence of animal life. Sometimes, however, by day we would hear the tuneful wail of the finger-glass bird or an occasional robin would chirrup, while at night great frogs croaked gloomily and the sloth would shriek at our approach.

It was truly a toilsome, dispiriting march, as in single file we pushed our way forward into the interior, and I confess I soon began to tire of the monotony of the terrible gloom. But to all my questions Omar would reply:

"Patience. In Africa we have violent contrasts always. To-day we are toiling onward through a region of eternal night, but when we have traversed the barrier that shuts out our country from the influence of yours—then you shall see. What you shall witness will amaze you."

V

The Giant's Finger

For quite three weeks we pushed forward through the interminable forest until one day we came to a small village beyond which lay a great broad river glistening in the noon-day sun. It was the mighty Comoe. We had entered the kingdom of Anno. In the village I saw traces of human sacrifices, and Omar, in reply to a question, told me that although these happy-looking natives were very skilful weavers and dyers who did a brisk trade in *fu*, a bark cloth of excellent quality—which I found afterwards they manufactured from the bark of a tree apparently of the same species as the much-talked-of *rokko* of Uganda—they nevertheless at the death of a chief sacrificed some of his slaves to "water the grave," while the memory of the departed was also honoured with gross orgies which lasted till everything eatable or drinkable in the village was consumed.

We only remained there a few hours, then embarked in three large canoes that were moored to the bank awaiting us. The chief of the village came to pay his respects to Omar, as the son of a ruling monarch, and presented us with food according to the usual custom.

Soon, amid the shouts of the excited villagers who had all come down to see us start, our canoes were pushed off, and the carriers, glad to be relieved of their packs, took the paddles, and away we went gaily up the centre of the winding river. Emerging as suddenly as we had from the gloomy forest depths where no warmth penetrated, into the blazing tropical sun was a sudden change that almost overcame me, for as we rowed along without shelter the rays beat down upon us mercilessly.

The banks were for the most part low, although it was impossible to say what height they were because of the lofty hedges of creeping plants which covered every inch of ground from the water's edge to as high as fifty feet above in some places, while behind them towered the black-green forest with here and there bunches of brilliant flowers or glimpses of countless grey trunks. Sometimes these trees, pressing right up to the edge of the warm sluggish water, grew horizontally to the length of fifty feet over the river. Creepers, vines, whip-like calamus, twisting lianes and great serpent-like convolvuli grew in profusion over everything, while the eye caught glimpses everywhere of gorgeous clouds of insects, gaily-plumaged birds, paraquets, and monkeys swinging in their shaded bowers.

Basking on the banks were crocodiles and hippopotami, while the river itself swarmed with fish and water-snakes. And over all rose the mist caused by heat and moisture, the death-dealing miasma of that tropic world.

But all were in good spirits, for rowing was more pleasurable than tramping in that dismal monotonous primeval forest that rose on either side, therefore against the broad, slowly-flowing waters our carriers bent to their paddles, grinning and joking the while.

Throughout that day Kouaga sat near us, smoking and thinking. Perhaps the responsibilities of State weighed heavily upon him; perhaps he was contemplating with trepidation the passage that would be necessary through a country held by the enemies of Mo; at all events he was morose and taciturn, his dark face bearing a strange, stern look such as I had never before noticed.

During the weeks I had been travelling up country I had embraced every opportunity of improving my knowledge of the curious language spoken by Omar and his mother's subjects, until I found I could understand a large portion of a conversation and could even give directions to our carriers in their own tongue.

Omar was in high spirits, eager, it seemed, to return to his own people. He took a gun and some ammunition from one of the cases that Kouaga had conveyed from England and gave us an exhibition of his skill with the rifle. He was a dead shot. I had no idea he could aim so true. As we sped past in our canoe he would raise his weapon from time to time and pick off a bird upon the wing, or fire directly into the eye of some basking animal, causing it to utter a roar, lash its tail and disappear to die. He seldom missed, and the accuracy of his aim elicited from the sable rowers low grunts of admiration.

A lazy and enjoyable week we thus spent in the ascent of the Comoe, mostly through forest scenery or undulating grass-lands. By day our rowers bent with rhythmic music to their paddles, and at evening we would disembark, cook our food, and afterwards with Kouaga and my friend I would sleep in our canoe upon the heap of leopard skins that formed our couches. Here we were free from the pest of the myriad insects we had encountered in the forest; and at night, under the brilliant moon, the noble river and giant trees presented a fine picture of solitary grandeur. Onward we pressed through the flourishing country of the Jimini, where we saw many prosperous villages of large roomy houses of rectangular form and reed thatched, wide tracts under cultivation with well-kept crops of cotton and rice. Everywhere we passed, without opposition, and with expressions of good-will from the natives.

One evening when the blood-red sun had sunk low in the water behind us, we suddenly rounded a sharp bend of the river and there burst upon us, rising on our right high into the clouds, the great snow-capped crest of Mount Komono. Near its base it was hidden by a bank of cloud, but above all was clear and bright, so that the summit had the appearance of being suspended in mid-air.

"The Giant's Finger at last!" cried Omar, jumping up excitedly and pointing at the mountain. "We leave the river a little higher up, and push again across the bush a twelve days' journey until we come to the Volta, which will take us forward to the boundary of Mo."

"The Volta!" I cried, remembering the incident at school when he had answered correctly the master's question as to the estuary of that river, and had been dubbed "the Guinea Pig." "Why could we not have ascended it from the sea?"

"Because we should, by so doing, pass nearly the whole distance through the country of Prempeh, of Ashanti, one of our bitter foes. The Adoo, the Anno, and the Jimini kings have long ago made blood-brotherhood with our chiefs, therefore we are enabled to pass in peace by this route alone."

Before darkness fell we disembarked at a small village on the left bank, the name of which I learnt was Tomboura, and after our evening meal were given a hut in which to spend the night. Soon after dawn, however, we heard Kouaga astir, giving rapid orders to the carriers, and when we went out to go down to the canoes they were nowhere to be seen. We noticed, however, that the carriers were preparing their loads which they had no doubt landed during the night, and Omar, advancing towards the Grand Vizier, asked:

"Why do we not ascend the river further? We must cross to the other side if we would join the Great Salt Road."

"Dangers lurk there, O my Master," the negro answered, hitching his burnouse about his shoulders. "We must travel by a circuitous route."

"Did not my mother command me to speed unto her?" Omar asked, puzzled. "Is it not necessary that we should travel by the shortest path?"

"The safest is the shortest," Kouaga answered with a frown.

"But by following this bank we are turning our backs upon Mo. See!" and he produced from his pocket an instrument which I did not know he possessed, a cheap mariner's compass.

"Bah!" cried Kouaga in anger, after he had looked at it a long time. "That clock of the white men has an evil spirit within. See! its trembling finger points always in the direction of the Great Evil. It is bewitched. Cast it away. Kouaga has already made fetish for this journey."

"But why should we travel in an entirely opposite direction to Mo?" I argued, seeing that a crowd of grinning impish-looking carriers had gathered around us, enjoying our controversy.

"For three-score years Kouaga has lived in the forest and on the plains," he answered, turning to me. "He knows the direction of Mo."

"Oh, let him have his own way," Omar cried at last, finding persuasion of no avail. Then turning to the Grand Vizier he said in a firm tone: "Listen, Kouaga. If by your obstinacy we are delayed one single day, I shall inform my mother of that fact, and you will assuredly lose your office and most likely your head also. Therefore act as you think fit. Omar, Prince of Mo, has spoken."

"Kouaga bore the staff of the Great White Queen unto thee. He is the trusted of the Naya, if not of her son," the negro answered, turning away. But in that brief instant I noticed an expression on his face of relentless cruelty. An expression such as one might expect to see upon the face of a murderer.

Truth to tell, I had never liked Kouaga; now I instinctively hated him. But ere he had strode a dozen paces he turned back smiling, saying:

"I mean no defiance to the Son of my Queen. He is in my charge, and I will take him safely back unto Mo, the city with walls unbreakable, the capital of the kingdom unconquerable."

"I shall act as I have decided," Omar answered with true princely hauteur. "The rulers of Mo never depart from their word."

"Very well," the other answered laughing, at the same time lighting his pipe with cool indifference. Then, glancing round to see that all was ready, he shouted an order to the head-man and the string of carriers moved away, jabbering and shouting, down the path into the dark gloomy forest depths.

In ill-humour we followed. I must confess that towards Kouaga I entertained an ill-defined feeling of distrust. Once or twice during that day's march in the dull dispiriting gloom, almost every ray of daylight being shut out by the thick canopy of creepers spreading from tree to

WILLIAM LE QUEUX

tree, I had caught Omar surreptitiously consulting his pocket compass, and saw upon his face a look of anxiety. Yet, on the other hand, Kouaga had become particularly jocular, and the carriers were now singing snatches of songs, joking, and laughing good-humouredly at each other's misfortunes, whereas on our journey from the coast to the river they had generally preserved a sullen silence.

No. Try how I would I could not rid myself of the thought that there was something very mysterious in Kouaga's actions.

VI

The Royal Jujus

On the fifth day after we had left our canoes the Grand Vizier of Mo had gone far forward along the line of carriers to speak with the head-man, and Omar was walking immediately before me at the rear of the procession.

As I pulled him by the sleeve he halted, and when the last carrier had got out of hearing I confided to my friend my misgivings.

"Have you not noticed of late a change in Kouaga's manner towards us?" I asked him. "At first he was deferential and submissive to your every wish, but it occurs to me that of late his manner is overbearing, and he watches us closely, as if fearing we might escape."

"Curiously enough," my friend replied, "I have for some days past had similar thoughts. If he's playing any double game his life won't be worth a moment's purchase when once we enter our own land."

"But you had perfect confidence in him," I observed.

"Yes. If my mother trusts him as her chief adviser I have no right to entertain any suspicion of his fidelity," he said.

"True, but, after all, you are the Prince and heir. Surely he ought to have followed your desire as to the route we should take."

"The route!" he cried. "Since we left the river we have travelled in these cross-paths in such an amazing manner that at present I have no idea where we are."

"The carriers have, or they would not be in such high spirits," I observed.

"Yes, but the strangest part of the affair is that every man among them fears to tell us anything. I have secretly questioned most of them as to Kouaga's motive, and all I can glean is that the fetish-man at Tomboura gathered them together and, after performing some of the usual rites and sacrificing to our Crocodile-god Zomara, told them if a word were spoken to us regarding our route or destination the dread god will meet us in the forest path and devour all of us. Not one shall survive."

"And you believe this pagan humbug?" I exclaimed, in disgust.

He opened his dark eyes wide, regarding me in astonishment. I had never before ridiculed his religion.

"The jujus around my neck preserve me from every evil, except those worked by Zomara. He is the great god whose power only the fetish-man can withstand. Slaves, princes, kings, all sacrifice to him. If we offend him death or torture is inevitably our punishment."

"Do you think you've offended him?" I inquired.

"I know not," he sighed with a serious look. "If I have, then nothing can save me; the fetish-man of Tomboura has worked evil against me."

"Well," I said, "this is my first experience of Africa, but it strikes me very forcibly that these fetish-men of yours will do anything they are paid to do. What was there to prevent Kouaga paying that hideous old demon at Tomboura to utter his horrible incantations and so frighten our carriers into silence?"

"Zomara is a terrible god. None dare tamper with him, or utter his name in vain threats," Omar answered.

"Well, whoever he is I still stick to my opinion," I said. "Depend upon it Kouaga is at the bottom of this conspiracy of silence."

Just at that moment the black face of that worthy, rendered darker by the snow-white haick that surrounded it, appeared among the tangled bamboos. He had missed us, and had come back to search. Yes, my surmise seemed correct. He was watching us closely and trying to understand our conversation.

That evening when we halted and the natives went into the bush to collect fuel for the fire, I managed to take one or two of them aside and secretly inquire our destination. But I got the same answer always.

"Zomara has tied our tongues. He commands us to be mute, or we shall be destroyed to the last one."

To endeavour to learn anything from these simple-minded blacks seemed useless. They would speak freely on every subject, indeed they seemed fond of talking with one whose face was white, yet regarding our journey they obeyed the command of the fetish-man to the very letter. It is the same everywhere in West and Central Africa; the fetish-man rules. What he says is more law than the word of kings. If he declares a man or woman bewitched that person will assuredly be murdered before the sun sets; if he orders the people of the village to perform a certain action they will do it, even if death stares them in the face. They blindly believe that the fetish is all-powerful, and that the half naked dancing savages who administer it are endowed with supernatural powers.

That night, feeling tired out I threw myself down early near the camp fire and slept soundly for several hours. But at length some unusual sound awoke me, and when I opened my eyes I saw that the fire had died down to one single flickering ember, which still blazing cast a fitful light upon the boles of the forest giants around.

Scarcely had I opened my eyes when I became conscious of low whispering in my vicinity. This thoroughly aroused me, and without stirring my body I slowly turned my head, when to my astonishment I beheld Kouaga, standing erect with arms folded beneath his white burnouse, talking in an undertone to a dark-bearded stranger who also wore flowing Arab garments and bore in his hand a long-barrelled flint-lock gun with quaintly-inlaid stock. The man seemed older than the Grand Vizier of Mo, for his beard was tinged with grey, and the brown hand that held the gun was lean and bony.

I strained my ears to catch the drift of their earnest conversation, but could not. It was tantalizing that they spoke in so low a tone, for the stranger seemed to mumble into his beard, while Kouaga whispered with his mouth turned from me. The presence of a stranger in our camp was, to say the least, strange, for through those gloomy forest glades no single traveller could journey. Omar had told me that for a person to attempt to traverse that region alone would be merely suicide. My friend was sleeping soundly at some distance from me, therefore I could not awaken him without attracting attention. If only he would open his eyes, I thought, he might recognize the new comer, either as friend or foe.

But no, he slept on as peacefully as if he were still in the cosy dormitory at old Trigger's, with its blue and white counterpanes and windows commanding a wide sweep of distant sea.

While I lay gazing upon my friend and hoping that he might open his eyes, I suddenly heard the stranger raise his voice louder than before. It was only for an instant, but in that moment upon my ear there fell three words the English equivalents of which I understood.

They were "Seek the treasure!"

But I could distinguish nothing more, and in a few moments the two men hurriedly snapped fingers, and the mysterious stranger disappeared noiselessly into the dark silent bush.

When the loud blasts from the ivory-horn, with its hideous ornamentation of human teeth, proclaimed the advent of another day I took Omar aside and told him of what I had witnessed and overheard. After I had described the stranger he said:

"I know not who he may be. It is evident, however, we are travelling in the opposite direction to Mo, therefore we will go no further. I will command Kouaga to return to Tomboura, cross the river, and press forward over the hills of Dabagakha to the Black Volta."

"And if he refuses?"

"Then we will go alone."

An hour later, when we had eaten our plantains and the usual babel was proceeding which was always precursory of a start being made, my companion strode up to Kouaga with a look of fierce determination upon his face, saying:

"Give ear to my words. I am Omar, son of the Naya, the Great White Queen, before whose wrath all nations tremble."

"Speak. I listen," answered the giant negro, with a look of surprise upon his ugly countenance.

"I will go no further along this path. You, the head-man and the carriers shall return with me to the bank of the Comoe, otherwise my mother shall punish you for disobeying my orders. All who dare go forward from this moment shall be sacrificed at the yam feast and the dogs shall eat their entrails. These are my words."

"Then whither would you go from Tomboura?" asked Kouaga, apparently astonished at Omar's sudden decision.

"I will only approach Mo by the Great Salt Road."

"It is impossible. There is fighting in the hills, for the Karaboro and the Dagari are at war."

"And what matters, pray, since they are both our allies?" Omar asked.

For a moment the negro was nonplussed, but with a broad grin showing his even row of teeth, he said:

"The bird goes not into the serpent's lair, neither does the son of the Queen enter the country of her enemies."

"I have already given tongue to my decision," my friend replied. "Advance, and each of your heads shall fall beneath the keen *doka* of Gankoma, the executioner."

Kouaga, hearing these words, set his teeth fiercely, and glancing at us with his fiery eyes, the whites of which were bloodshot, retorted:

"Recede, and we will carry you forward, bound as a slave."

"This is a threat!" cried Omar, drawing himself up to his full height and stretching forth his arm. "You, whom my mother raised from a palace-slave, thus threaten me! Let it be thus, but I warn you that if you ever set foot across the borders of Mo, your head shall be set upon the palace wall as a warning to disobedient slaves." Then, turning to me, and waving back the crowd of carriers who had collected and stood open-mouthed around us, he said, "Come, Scars, we will return. I have thrice traversed the path from Tomboura to the Great Salt Road, and can follow it without a guide."

Then, calling down the curse of Zomara, the dreaded, upon them all, he turned on his heel and walked down the narrow path we had traversed on the previous night, while, with a final glance of triumph at the irate negro, I followed.

Scarcely had we gone fifty yards, however, before a dozen carriers, acting upon orders from Kouaga, had rushed after us, seized us, and dragged us back to him despite our desperate struggles.

"So you defy me!" the negro cried in a paroxysm of rage, as Omar was brought up. "This is because I was fool enough to allow your white-faced friend to accompany you. Our country is no place for whites, but he will make a good sacrifice to Zomara when our journey is ended. You have both refused to accompany us, therefore we must use force." Then, turning to the half-naked savages who held us, he said: "Bind them, and tie them in their hammocks. Let not their bonds be loosened until our march be ended, for both are my prisoners." And he laughed triumphantly at our discomfiture.

"You shall pay for this insult with your life," Omar cried angrily.

"Take off his European clothes, and let his string of royal jujus be burned. Henceforth he is a slave, as also is his white companion."

Next moment twenty ready hands tore from Omar most of his well-worn clothes, and although he fought with all the strength of which he was capable, his necklet of jujus, the magical charms that protected the Queen's son from every evil, was ruthlessly spat upon and destroyed by the excited natives, together with his clothes.

Then, after each of us had been tied in a hammock with our hands behind our backs, we were lifted by four stalwart bearers and carried forward at a brisk pace towards an unknown bourne.

It was evident that we were not going to Mo, and it was equally evident too, that Kouaga, whom we had trusted implicitly, was our bitter enemy.

VII

Samory's Stronghold

Through dense dark forests and over great open grass-lands, passing several villages, we were carried forward many days, still bound and never allowed to have our hands free except during our meals.

The face of Kouaga grew more brutal and fierce as we proceeded, and he urged on the carriers until we found ourselves travelling at a pace that for African natives was amazing.

Omar spoke little. He was always pre-occupied and thoughtful. He had told me that he now regretted having brought me with him from England, but I assured him that our misfortunes were not of our own seeking, and urged him to be of good cheer.

Truth to tell, my heart was full of dark forebodings. I saw in the ugly countenance of Kouaga expressions of deadly hatred, and I knew that they were of ill-portent. Yet to escape in that deadly bush, extending for hundreds and hundreds of miles, dark, monotonous and impenetrable, meant certain death even if we eluded the watchful vigilance of this muscular negro.

One day, when passing through a forest village, a half-naked savage rushed towards us brandishing his spear and uttering a loud yell, but whether expressive of hatred or joy I knew not. Suddenly, as he approached the hammock in which Omar was lying, my friend addressed him in some tongue that was strange to me, but to which the native answered readily.

"As I thought, Scars!" Omar shouted to me in English a moment later. "We have travelled away from Mo, crossed Tieba's territory, and have now entered the country of the great Mohammedan chief Samory, my nation's bitterest enemy. It was he who seized my father by a ruse and sent his head back to my mother as a hideous souvenir."

"But what object has Kouaga in bringing us here?" I asked.

"I cannot imagine," he answered. "Unless he travelled to England, for the sole purpose of delivering me into the hands of our enemies. Three times within the last five years has Samory attempted to invade our country, but each time has been repulsed with a loss that has partially paralysed his power. All along the right bank of the Upper Niger his bands of hirelings and mercenaries, whom we call Sofas, are constantly raiding for slaves. Indeed Samory's troops are the fiercest and most merciless in this country. They are the riff-raff of the West Soudan and are a terror to friend and foe, a bar to the peaceful settlement of all lands within the range of their devastating expeditions."

"Do they make raids towards your country?" I inquired, for I had heard long ago of this notorious slave-dealing chief.

"Yes, constantly. They are pitiless marauders who lay waste whole kingdoms and transform populous districts into gloomy solitudes. While on my way from Mo to England we passed through Sati, a large market town at the convergence of several caravan routes, which was only three months before a prosperous and wealthy place situated fifty miles south of our border. We found everything had been raided by the Sofas, who had sacked, burned or destroyed what they were unable to take away. Heaps of cinders marked the sites of former homesteads, the ground was strewn with potsherds, rice and other grain trodden under foot, while our horses moved forward knee deep in ashes. The whole land, lately very rich, prosperous and thickly peopled, was a melancholy picture of utter desolation."

"Do you think we have actually fallen into Samory's hands?" I asked.

"I fear so."

"But is not Kouaga Grand Vizier of Mo? Surely he would not dare to take us through the enemy's land," I said.

"Do you not remember that when he met us at Eastbourne he forbade us to inform Makhana of our intended departure?" he answered. "He had some object in securing our silence and getting us away from England secretly. It now appears more than probable that my mother has dismissed and banished him, and he has gone over to our enemy, Samory, who desires to seize our country."

"In that case our position is indeed serious," I observed. "We must do something to escape."

"No," he said. "We cannot escape. Let's put on a bold front, and if we find ourselves prisoners of the slave-raiding chief, I, at least, will show him that I am heir to the Emerald Throne of Mo."

As each day dawned we still held upon our way, until at length, under a broiling noon-day sun, we crossed a wide stretch of fertile grass-land where cattle were grazing, and there rose high before us the white fortified walls of a large town of flat-roofed Moorish-looking houses. It was, we afterwards learnt, called Koussan, one of Samory's principal strongholds.

As we approached the open gate, flanked on either side by watch-towers and guarded by soldiers wearing Arab fezes and loose white garments, a great rabble came forth to meet us. We heard the din of tom-toms beaten within the city, joyous shouts, and loud ear-piercing blasts upon those great horns formed out of elephant tusks.

Thus, in triumph, amid the howls and execrations of the mob, Omar, son of Sanom, and myself, were marched onward through the gate and up a steep narrow winding street, where the solidly-built houses were set close together to obtain the shade, to the market-place. Here, amid the promiscuous firing of long flint-lock guns and quaint ancient pistols, such as one sees in curiosity shops at home, a further demonstration was held, our carriers themselves infected by the popular enthusiasm, seeming also to lose their senses. They heaped upon Omar every indignity, scoffed and spat at him, while my own pale face arousing the ire of the fanatical Mohammedan populace, they denounced me as an infidel accursed of Allah, and urged my captors to kill me and give my flesh to the dogs.

Truly we were in pitiable plight.

I looked at Omar, but heedless of all their threats and jeers, he walked with princely gait. His hands were tied behind his back, his head erect, and his eyes flashed with scorn upon those who sought his death. Presently, turning sharply to the left, we found ourselves in another square which we crossed, entering a great gateway guarded by soldiers, and as soon as we were inside the heavy iron-studded doors closed with an ominous clang. I glanced round at the thick impregnable walls and knew that we were in the Kasbah, or citadel. Gaily-dressed soldiers were leaning or squatting everywhere as we crossed the several court-yards, one after the other, until, by the direction of one of the officials who had joined us on entering, we were led through a low arched door, and thence a dozen soldiers who had come forward hurried us down a flight of dark damp steps into a foul noisome chamber below.

Struggles and protestations were useless. We were pushed forward into a deep narrow cell lit only by a tiny crack in the paving of the court above and the door quickly bolted upon us.

"Well, this is certainly a dire misfortune," I said, when we had both walked round inspecting the black dank walls of our prison. "I wonder what fate is in store for us?"

"Though they destroyed my jujus, they cannot invoke the curses of Zomara upon me," he said. "The Crocodile-god will not hear any enemies of the Naya."

"But have you no idea whatever of the motive Kouaga has had in bringing you hither?" I asked.

"Not the slightest," he answered, seating himself at last on the stone bench to rest. "It is evident, however, that he is a traitor in the pay of Samory. On each occasion when the Moslem chief endeavoured to conquer our country, it was Kouaga who assumed the generalship of our troops; it was Kouaga who fought valiantly for his queen with his own keen sword; it was Kouaga who drove back the enemy and urged our hosts to slaughter them without mercy; and it was Kouaga who, with fiendish hatred, put the prisoners to the torture. In him my mother had a most trusted servant."

"He doesn't seem very trustworthy now," I observed. "It seems to me we are caught like rats in a trap."

"True," he said. "We are beset by dangers, but may the blessings of their Allah turn to curses upon their heads. It may be that our ignominious situation will not satisfy the malice that Samory has conceived against me, but if a single hair of the head of either of us is injured, Zomara, the Crocodile-god, will punish those who seek our discomfiture."

It occurred to me that it was all very well to speak in this strain, but as no man is a prince except in his own country, it seemed idle to expect mercy or pity. Omar was in prison for some unknown offence, and I was held captive with a well-remembered threat from Kouaga that my life should be sacrificed.

For six hours we remained without food, but when the light above had quite faded, three soldiers with clanging swords unbarred the door and pushed through some water in an earthen vessel and some *fufu*, a kind of dumpling made of mashed African potato. During the night, disturbed by vermin of all sorts, including some horrible little snakes, we slept little, and at dawn we were again visited by our captors. The next day and the next passed uneventfully. For exercise we paced our cell times without number, and when tired would seat ourselves on the rough stone bench and calmly discuss the situation.

The Naya, the mysterious Great White Queen, had ordered Omar to return with all haste, yet already two moons had run their course since we had landed in Africa. This troubled my companion even more than the fact of being betrayed into the hands of his enemies.

WILLIAM LE QUEUX

The tiny streak of light that showed high above our heads grew brighter towards noon, then began slowly to decline. Before the shadows had lengthened in the court above, however, the sound of our door being unbarred aroused us from our lethargy, and a moment later, three soldiers entered and told us to prepare to go before the great ruler Samory. Omar, attired only in a small garment of bark-cloth, took no heed of his toilet, therefore we at once announced our readiness to leave the loathsome place with its myriad creeping things, and it was with a feeling of intense relief that a few minutes later we ascended to the blessed light of day.

Marched between a small posse of soldiers, we crossed the court to a larger and more handsome square, decorated in Arab style with horseshoe arches and wide colonnades, until at the further end a great curtain of crimson velvet was drawn aside and we found ourselves in a spacious hall, wherein many gorgeously attired persons had assembled and in the centre of which was erected a great canopy of amaranth-coloured silk supported by pillars of gold surmounted by the crescent. Beneath, reclining on a divan, slowly fanned by a dozen gaudily-attired negroes, was a dark-faced, full-bearded man of middle age, whose black eyes regarded us keenly as we entered. He was dressed in a robe of bright yellow silk, and in his turban there glittered a single diamond that sparkled and gleamed with a thousand iridescent rays. His fat brown hand was loaded with rings, and jewels glittered everywhere upon his belt, his sword, and his slippers of bright green.

It was the notorious and dreaded chieftain, Samory.

VIII

The Secret of the Queen

As we were led forward to the space in front of the divan all eyes were directed towards us. The glitter and pomp of the merciless slave-raider's court was dazzling. Before their ruler all men salaamed. His officers surrounding him, watched every movement of his face, and the four-score slaves behind him stood mute and motionless, ready to do his bidding at any instant.

When our feet touched the great carpet spread before him, and we halted, he raised himself to a sitting posture, fixing his dark, gleaming eyes upon us. At sight of Omar a sudden frown of displeasure crossed his features, but an instant later a grim smile of triumph lit his sinister face.

Apparently he was waiting for us to bow before him, but Omar had forbidden me to do so.

"And who, pray, art thou, that thou deignest not to bend the knee before me?" he cried, in anger that his people should witness a slur thus cast upon his power.

"I am Omar, son of the Naya of Mo," my companion answered, folding his arms resolutely, and regarding the potentate with supreme disdain. "Princes do not make obeisance to any but their equals."

"Am I not thine equal, then, thou son of offal?" cried Samory.

"In strength thou art, possibly, but not by birth. In order to protect thy country against the white men thou hast sought to make palaver with Prempeh of Ashanti, but I would remind thee that the rulers of Mo have never besought any aid of their neighbours."

"Thou speakest well, lad," he said thoughtfully. "Thine is a mighty kingdom, but by peace or war I will rule over it."

"Never, while I live," answered Omar with pride.

"But thou art the last of thy race. If thou diest—what then?"

"If I die, then every man in Mo will seek blood revenge upon thee, and Zomara will guide them into this, thy land, and arm them with spears of fire."

"I care nought for thy Naya nor thy pagan Crocodile-god," exclaimed the Mohammedan chief impatiently. "Bow unto my divan, or of a verity my slaves shall compel thee."

"I refuse."

"May thine entrails be burned," cried Samory in anger, and raising his hand he ordered the guards of the divan to cast us both to earth before him.

They threw us down, and their ruler, rising, placed his foot firmly on the neck of the heir to the throne of Mo, saying in a loud voice:

"As I hold thee thus within my power, so also will I, ere many moons have run, hold thy country. Cursed by the Prophet may be thy detested race. There is neither peace nor friendship, there is neither gratitude nor love in the people of Samory, and they shall be the first to curse thee. When I enter Mo every day shall the knife of the executioner be fed with blood; thy cities shall mourn the loss of their sages, husbands their wives, wives their children, and children their fathers. The country shall be devastated to its most northerly limits and it shall be rendered a wilderness of silence and sorrow."

Then withdrawing his foot, amid the plaudits of his crowd of fierce-looking courtiers, Omar sprang to his feet in rage, and facing him, cried:

"The men of Mo are forewarned already against thy designs, notwithstanding that our ex-Grand Vizier Kouaga, the son of a dungheap who betrayed us hither, hath joined thine accursed ranks. The soldiers of the Naya are still anxious for the fourth time to try conclusions with thy white-cloaked rabble. Come, march forward into Mo—thou wilt never return."

"Thou defiest me, even as thy mother hath done," he roared, his hand upon the bejewelled hilt of his curved blade. "Were it not for one fact I would smite thee dead."

"I fear thee not," Omar answered with a calmness that astounded me. "Sooner or later thou wilt, I suppose, order my death, therefore the sooner the better."

"Why insultest thou our race by bringing hither with thee this dog of a Christian?" the chief enquired, looking at me with a terrible expression of hatred.

"He cometh as my companion," replied Omar briefly.

"As thy companion he shall accompany thee to the grave," Samory cried fiercely, his eyes swimming in malice.

"So be it," answered Omar, with a smile of contempt. "May Zomara curse thy work."

"Speak, infidel!" Samory said, fixing his fiery glance upon me. "Whence comest thou?"

"From England," I answered briefly, in fear.

"From that country where dwell the accursed of Allah," he said, as if to himself. "They are pig-eaters who despise the Book of Everlasting Will and declare our great Prophet—on whom may be everlasting peace—to be a false one. Accursed be thy country, infidel! May thy people suffer every torment of Al-Hâwiyat; may their food be offal, and may they slake their thirst with boiling pitch. The white men have sent their messengers to me time after time to urge me to ally myself with them, but it shall never be recorded that Samory besought the assistance of infidels to extend his kingdom. We fight beneath the green banner of Al-Islâm, and will continue to do so until we die. Ere long, the day of the Jehad will dawn; then the forces of Al-Islâm will unite to sweep from the face of the earth those white parasites who seek the overthrow of the Faithful. Allah is merciful, and his servant is patient," added the old scoundrel piously.

There arose, as if with one voice from those assembled, the words: "Samory hath spoken! Allah send him blessings abundant!" and as they did so each fingered his amulets, little scraps of parchment whereon verses from the Korân were written in sprawly Arabic. At that moment, too, I noticed, for the first time, that right opposite us was the grinning, evil face of the black giant, Kouaga, the man who had so foully betrayed us.

We exchanged glances, and he laughed at us in triumph.

"Dost thou intend to keep me as hostage?" Omar asked his mother's enemy boldly.

"Until thou hast performed the service for which I caused thee to journey hither with our good Kouaga."

"The traitor's head shall fall," Omar blurted out with pardonable passion. Then he asked, "Thou desirest a service of me. Well, what is it?"

There was a silence so deep that a feather if dropped upon the cool floor of polished marble would have made audible sound, and Samory slowly seated himself.

"Give ear unto my words," he said a few moments later, in a clear voice, as he stroked his beard with his fat hand. "I know that within thine impenetrable kingdom many undreamed-of mysteries and wealth untold lie concealed. This is common report. Thine ancestors in their treasure-house, the whereabouts of which is known only to the Naya and to thyself, have deposited heaps of jewels and great quantities of gold, the spoils of war through many generations. I desire to ascertain, and I will ascertain from thine own lips, the exact spot where we may seek that treasure."

A look of abject bewilderment crossed Omar's features, and he turned to me, saying in English:

"All is now plain, Scars. Because only the Naya herself is aware of the spot where the treasure of the Sanoms is deposited, my mother, on the eve of my departure for England, divulged to me the secret, fearing lest she should die before my return. Kouaga was the only person who knew that my mother had thus spoken to me, and he has informed Samory and joined him for the purpose of obtaining the treasure."

"Is not Kouaga aware of the spot where the treasure is hidden?" I asked hurriedly.

"No. He came to England at Samory's suggestion to convey me hither so that they could get the secret from me. On gaining the information it is apparently their intention to make a raid, with Kouaga leading, in order to secure our wealth."

But Samory himself interrupted our consultation.

"Speak not with thine infidel companion," he roared. "Answer me. Tell me where this treasure of the Sanoms lieth."

"The son of the Naya is no traitor," he answered with hauteur.

"If thou speakest thou shalt have thy liberty. Indeed, if thou deemest fit thou shalt join the expedition into Mo, and share with us the loot," the chief urged.

"Thy words insult me," cried Omar, full of wrath. "I will never share with thee, who murdered my father, that which is my birthright."

"Very well," answered Samory indifferently. "Thou needest not. We will take it, kill thy mother and annex thy country. Already the whole kingdom is ripe for revolt, and we shall quickly accomplish the rest. I had thee brought hither because thou alone holdest a secret I desire to know—the secret of the royal Treasure-house, and—"

"And I refuse to disclose it," my companion said, interrupting the gaudily-attired potentate.

"If thou wilt not speak willingly, then my executioners shall force thee to loosen thine obstinate tongue's strings," Samory cried, frowning, while the hideous face of the black traitor grinned horribly.

"The secret of the queen is inviolable. My lips are sealed," answered Omar with resolution.

"Then my executioners shall unseal them."

"If I cannot save my country from desolation at the hands of thy lawless bands," exclaimed my friend, "I can at least preserve from thee the treasure accumulated by my ancestors to be used only for the emancipation of our country should evil befall it. Until the present, Mo hath been held against all invaders by the hosts ready at the hands of my mother and her predecessors, and even now if thou marchest over my dead body thy path will not be clear of those who will oppose thee. Remember," he added, "the army of the Naya possesses many pom-poms* of the English, each of which is equal in power to the fire of one of thy battalions. With them our people will sweep away thine hosts like grains of sand before the sirocco."

"Darest thou oppose my will?" cried Samory, rising in a sudden ebullition of wrath.

"Thy will ruleth me not," Omar answered, his face pale and calm. "A Sanom never betrayed his trust, even though he suffered death."

"Very well, offspring of sebel," he hissed between his white teeth. "We will test thy resolution, and cause thee to eat thy brave words. Thy body shall be racked by the torture, and thy flesh given unto the ants to eat." Then, turning to the executioner, a big negro with face hideously scarred by many cuts, who stood at his side leaning upon his razor-edged *doka*, he added:

"You know my will. Loosen the lad's tongue. Let it be done here, so that we may watch the effect of thy persuasion."

And all laughed loudly at their ruler's grim humour, while twenty slaves of the executioner rushed away in obedience to their master's command to bring in the instruments of torture.

I turned to Omar. He still stood erect, with arms folded. But his face was pale as death.

---

* Maxim guns. They are called "pom-poms" by the African natives on account of the noise they cause when fired.

IX

CONDEMNED TO THE TORTURE

E ager to witness the agony of the son of the powerful Naya of Mo, the crowd of evil-faced men in silken robes who surrounded their brutal chief watched with lively anticipation the preparations that were in a few moments in active progress. The black slaves of the weirdly-dressed executioner first carried in a large blazing brazier, and rolling away the thick crimson carpet placed it upon the floor of polished marble in front of Samory's divan.

A slave boy had, in response to a sign from the great chief, lit his long pipe with its bejewelled mouthpiece, and as he half reclined on the couch he smoked on calmly, regarding the execution of his orders with undisguised satisfaction.

The slaves, each wearing black loin-cloths with bunches of sable ostrich feathers on their heads that waved like funeral-plumes as they walked, brought in grim-looking instruments of iron like blacksmiths' tools, strange spiked chains, fetters with sharp spikes on the inside, and many curiously-contrived irons, each devised to cause some horrible torture, each red with rust, the rust of blood.

As my eyes fell upon them I involuntarily shuddered. Omar, my loyal friend, was about to be murdered by these inhuman brutes, and I knew that I was powerless to defend him from their fiendish wrath. Already he was standing in the grip of two black-plumed slaves, while no attempt had been made to secure me. I stood near him, breathlessly anxious, wondering what the end would be.

Presently, when all was ready, a silence fell. Then, the deep voice of Samory was heard, asking the final question:

"Speak, son of a dog," he cried, addressing my unhappy friend. "Wilt thou tell us where the secret Treasure-house of the Sanoms is situated?"

"No," Omar answered, flashing at his enemy a look of defiance. "I will not betray my mother's secret to my father's murderer."

"Then use thy powers of persuasion," he said, lifting his hand towards the executioner. "Unseal his lips, and that quickly."

"Chief of our race, whose praises rise earliest and most frequent in the presence of Allah, I am ready to obey thee," answered the hideous functionary. So saying, he took up a long iron instrument, fashioned like a pair of pincers and thrust it into the burning coals.

"Vain, O persecutor," cried Omar in a loud voice. "Vain are thy tortures against the will power of the son of the Great White Queen, whose veins are filled with royal blood. Tremble at thy doom, a myriad of my race are determined against thee, and thy throne noddeth over thine head. The fiend of darkness is let loose, and the powers of evil shall prevail."

"Hold thy peace," shouted the Moslem chieftain, enraged. "Thine own blood shall make satisfaction for those of my race slain by thy warriors when last we marched upon thy kingdom."

"The curses of Takhar, of Tuirakh, and of Zomara, dreaded by all men, be upon thee," my companion cried, lifting his voice until it sounded loud and clear through the vaulted hall, and pointing to the slave-raiding king whose power no European influence could break. "May the vengeance of my injured blood fasten upon thy life."

Those around Samory looked aghast as Omar uttered these ominous predictions in the spirit of prophecy, for they perceived he spoke as he was moved, and the whole council seemed dismayed. Silence and amazement for a few moments prevailed. Omar alone appeared unconcerned at his fate.

Quickly, however, the executioner bent over his fire, and as the wretched victim of the potentate's hatred was dragged to a kind of square iron frame that lay upon the floor, thrown down, and fastened thereto by his wrists and ankles, the fiendish-looking hireling took the long pincers, now red hot, and tore from Omar's shoulder a great piece of flesh.

A piercing scream of agony rent the air, mingled with the triumphant jeers of the excited councillors, but my friend's teeth were tightly clenched and his face blanched to the lips. Again and again cries of agony escaped him as the red-hot iron touched him, although he exerted every nerve to maintain a dogged silence. From his back, shoulders, and chest the brutal negro ruthlessly tore pieces, holding them up to the assembled court in triumph, while the air was filled with the nauseating odour of burning flesh.

The sight was so sickening that I turned faint, and with difficulty prevented myself from falling.

"Wilt thou now impart to us the knowledge that we seek?" asked Samory in ringing tones that sounded above the whispered exultations of his courtiers.

"Never," gasped Omar in a weak voice, his eyes starting from his head. "Life cannot be unchequered by the frowns of fate, but death must bring dumbness to my lips. Caution, when besmeared in blood, is no longer virtue, or wisdom, but wretched and degenerate cowardice; no, never let him that was born to execute judgment secure his honours by cruelty and oppression. Hath not thy Korân told thee that fear and submission is a subject's tribute, yet mercy is the attribute of Allah, and the most pleasing endowment of the vicegerents of earth."

"From the lips of a fool there sometimes falleth wisdom," Samory said impatiently. "Thou hast deemed it wise to thwart the will of one whose wish is law, therefore ere the bud of thy youth unfolds in the fulness of manhood, thou shalt be cut off as the husbandman destroyeth the deadly serpent in the field."

"Is there no way to build up the seat of justice and mercy but in murder?" cried Omar. At a signal from the slave-raider, however, the scarred-face brute again withdrew the pincers from the fiery brazier, and applied them once more to the wretched prince's back.

He winced and turned with such strength that his limbs, fettered as they were in bonds of blood-smeared iron, cracked, while the muscles and veins stood out knotted like cords. The spotless marble of the floor was stained by a dark red pool, becoming larger every moment as the life-blood dripped slowly from beneath.

The scene was revolting. I placed my hands over my eyes to shut out from my gaze the horrible contortions of the victim's face.

Yet those assembled were gleeful and excited. Omar was the son of their unconquerable enemy, and they delighted in witnessing his humiliation and agony. Times without number the negro with the strangely-marked visage seared the flesh of my helpless companion; then in response to his orders his black-plumed slaves drew tighter the bonds that confined his ankles and wrists until the sound of the crushing of bones and sinews reached our ears.

Again a loud shriek echoed along the high-roofed hall. Omar was no longer able to bear the excruciating pain in silence.

"Courage," I cried in English, heedless of the consequences. "Courage. Let this fiend see that he cannot rule us as he does his cringing slaves."

"Think! think of yourself, Scars!" he gasped with extreme difficulty. "If they kill me, forgive me for bringing you from England. I—I did not know that this trap had been prepared for me."

"I forgive you everything," I answered, glancing for a moment at his white, blood-smeared countenance. "Bear up. You must—you shall not die."

But even as I spoke, the executioner, who had been bending over the fire, withdrew with his tongs a band of iron with long sharp spikes on the inside now red with heat, and as the slaves released the pressure upon his wrists and ankles the sinister-faced negro placed the terrible band around the victim's waist and by means of a screw quickly drew it so tight that the red-hot spikes ran into the flesh, causing it to smoke and emit a hissing noise that was horrible.

Again poor Omar squirmed in pain and gave vent to a shrill, agonised cry. But it was not repeated.

Everyone stood eager and open-mouthed, and even the villainous Samory rose from his divan to more closely watch the effect of the fearful torture now being applied.

The victim's upturned face was white as the marble pavement. From the corners of the mouth a thin red stream oozed, and the closed eyes and imperceptible breathing showed plainly that no torture, however inhuman, could cause him further agony. He had lapsed into unconsciousness.

"Hold!" cried Samory at last, seeing the executioner about to prepare yet another torture. "Take the pagan author of malice from my sight, let his wounds be dressed, and apply thy persuasion unto him again to-morrow at sundown. He shall speak, I vow before the great Allah and Mahomet, the Prophet of the Just. He shall tell us where the treasure lieth hidden."

"O, light of the earth," cried one of the councillors, a white-bearded sage who wore a robe of crimson silk beautifully embroidered. "Though the hand of time hath not yet spread the fruits of manhood upon this youth's cheeks, yet neither the splendour of thy court nor the words from thy lips could steal from the young prince the knowledge of himself. He hath cursed thee with the three curses of the pagans Takhar, Tuirakh, and Zomara, the Crocodile-god, held in awe by all."

"Well, thinkest thou that I fear the empty threats of a youth whose hostility towards me arises from the fact that I captured his father on the Great Salt Road, and smiting off his head, sent it as a present to the Naya?" asked Samory in indignation.

But as the black-plumed slaves removed the inanimate form of Omar, the aged councillor stepped forward boldly, saying:

"I perceive, O source of light, that the dark clouds of evil are gathering to disturb the hours of futurity; the spirits of the wicked are preparing the storm and the tempest against thee; but—the volumes of Fate are torn from my sight, and the end of thy troubles is unknown."

The councillors exchanged glances and stood aghast, but Samory, livid with rage, sprang from his divan and commenced to upbraid the aged seer for his words of warning. I was not, however, allowed to listen to the further discussion of the old man's prophecy, being hurried by two of the torturer's slaves back to my underground cell, where I remained alone for many hours awaiting Omar, who, I presumed, was being brought back to consciousness in another part of the great impregnable fortress, the mazes of which were bewildering.

X

ZOMARA

In darkness and anxiety I remained alone for many days in the foul subterranean prison. Had the fiendish tortures been repeated upon my hapless friend, I wondered; or had he succumbed to the injuries already inflicted? Hour by hour I waited, listening to the shuffling footsteps of my gaolers, but only once a day there came a black slave to hand me my meagre ration of food and depart without deigning to give answer to any of my questions.

I became sick with anxiety, and at last felt that I must abandon all hope of again seeing him. I was alone in the midst of the fiercest and most fanatical people of the whole of Africa, a people whose supreme delight it was to torture the whites that fell into their hands as vengeance for the many expeditions sent against them. Through those dismal days when silence and the want of air oppressed me, I remembered the old adage that when Hope goes out Death smiles and stalks in, but fortunately, although wearied and dejected, I did not quite abandon all thought of ever again meeting my companion. The hope of seeing him, of being able to escape and get into the land of Mo, was now the sole anchor of my life, yet as the monotonous hours passed, the light in the chink above grew brighter and time after time gradually faded into pitch darkness, I felt compelled to admit that my anticipations were without foundation, and that Omar, the courageous descendant of a truly kingly race, was dead.

In the dull dispiriting gloom I sat hour after hour on the stone bench encrusted with the dirt of years, calmly reflecting upon the bright, happy life I had been, alas! too eager to renounce, and told myself with sorrow that, after all, old Trigger's school, or even the existence of a London clerk, was preferable to imprisonment in Samory's stronghold. Many were the means by which I sought to make time pass more rapidly, but the hours had leaden feet, and while the tiny ray struggled through above, my mind was constantly racked by bitter thoughts of the past, and a despairing dread of the hopeless future.

One morning, however, when I had lost all count of the days of my solitary confinement, my heart was suddenly caused to leap by hearing the unusual sound of footsteps, and a few moments later my door was thrown open and I was ordered by my captors to come forth.

I rose, and following them unwillingly, wondering what fate had been decided for me, ascended the steep flight of steps to the courtyard above, wherein I found a crowd of Arab nomads in their white haicks and burnouses. Samory was also there, and before him, still defiant and apparently almost recovered from his wounds, stood my friend Omar.

I sprang towards him with a loud cry of joy, and our recognition was mutually enthusiastic, as neither of us had known what fate had overtaken the other; but ere he could relate how he had fared, the Mohammedan chief lifted his hand, and a dead silence fell on those assembled.

"Omar, son of the accursed Naya whom may Eblis smite with the fiery sword, give ear unto my words," he said, in a loud, harsh voice. "Thou hast defied me, and will not impart to me the secret of the Treasure-house, even though I offer thee thy freedom. I have spared thee the second torture in order that a fate more degrading and more terrible shall be thine. Hearken! Thou and thy friend are sold to these Arab slavers for this single copper coin."

For an instant he showed us the coin in the palm of his brown hand, then tossed it far away from him with a gesture of disgust.

"Ye are both sold," he continued, "sold for the smallest coin, to be taken to Kumassi as slaves for their pagan sacrifice."

At his words we both started. It was indeed a terrible doom to which this villainous brute had consigned us. We were to be butchered with awful rites for the edification of Prempeh and his wild hordes of fanatics!

"Rather kill us outright," Omar said boldly, his hands trembling nevertheless.

"Death will seize thee quite soon enough," laughed the chief derisively. "Mine ally Prempeh will have the satisfaction of offering a queen's son to the fetish."

"Rest assured that the god Zomara will reward thee for this day's evil work," Omar cried, with a fierce look in his eyes. "Thou hast spent fiercest hatred upon me, but even if I die, word will sooner or later be carried into Mo that thou wert the cause of the death of the last of my race. Then every man capable of bearing arms will rise against thee. Standing here, I make prophecy that this thy kingdom shall be uprooted as a weed in the garden of peace, and that thine own blood shall make satisfaction for thy cruelty."

"Begone!" cried Samory, in a tumult of wrath. And turning to the Arabs he cried in a commanding tone: "Take the dog to the slaughterers. Let me never look again upon his face."

But ere they could seize him, he had lifted his hand, invoking the curse of Zomara, saying:

"Omar, Prince of Mo, has spoken. This kingdom of Samory shall, ere many moons, be shaken to its foundations."

But the fierce Arabs quickly dragged us forth, bound us when out of sight of the great chief, and led us beyond the gates of the Kasbah to where we found a great slave caravan assembled in readiness to depart. Fully one hundred black slaves, each fastened in a long chain, were lying huddled up in the shadow, seeking a brief rest after a long and tedious march. Most of them were terrible objects, mere skin and bone, and all showed signs of brutal ill-treatment, their backs bearing great festering sores caused by the lashes of their pitiless captors. The majority of them had, I ascertained, been captured in the forest wilds beyond the Niger, and all preserved a stolid indifference, for they knew their terrible doom. They were being hurried on to Kumassi to be sold to King Prempeh for sacrificial purposes.

To this wretched perspiring crowd of hopeless humanity we were bound, and amid the jeers of a number of Samory's officials who had crowded to the gate to see us depart, we moved onward, our steps hastened by the heavy whips of our masters who, mounted on wiry little ponies and heavily armed, galloped up and down the line administering blows to the laggards or the sick.

From the city away across the open grass-lands we wended our way, a dismal, sorrowful procession, but Omar, now beside me again, briefly related how, after being removed from the torture-frame, his wounds had been dressed and he had been tenderly nursed by an old female slave who had taken compassion upon him. A dozen times messengers from Samory had come to offer him his liberty in exchange for the secret of the Treasure-house, but he had steadfastly refused. Twice the scoundrel Kouaga had visited him and made merry over his discomfiture.

"But," said my friend, "the boastings of the traitor are empty words. When we laugh it shall be at his vain implorings for a speedy death."

"To him we owe all these misfortunes," I said.

"Yes, everything. But if only we get into Mo he shall render an account of his misdeeds to my mother. No mercy will be shown him, for before the Naya's wrath the nation trembles."

"But our position at the present moment is one of extreme gravity," I observed. "We are actually on our way to another of your mother's enemies, whose relentless cruelty is common talk throughout the world."

"True," he answered. "If we find the slightest loop-hole for escape we must embrace it. But if not—" and he paused. "If not, then we must meet our deaths with the calm indifference alike traditional of the Sanoms and of Englishmen."

Whenever misfortune seemed to threaten he appeared only the more composed. Each day showed me that, even though an African and a semi-savage, yet his bearing in moments when others would have been melancholy, was dignified and truly regal. Even though his only covering was a loin-cloth and a piece of a white cotton garment wrapped about his shoulders, Omar Sanom was every inch a prince.

"If we made a dash for liberty we should, I fear, be shot down like dogs," I said.

"Yes," he answered. "The country we shall now traverse will not facilitate our flight, but the reverse. From the edge of the Great Forest to Buna, beyond the Kong mountains, it is mostly marshy hollows and pestilential swamps, while the lands beyond Buna away to Koranza, in Ashanti, are flat and open like your English pastures. We will, if opportunity offers, endeavour to escape, but even if we succeeded in eluding their vigilance death lurks everywhere in a hundred different forms."

"Well, at present we are slaves hounded on towards the dreaded Golgotha of the Ashantis," I said. "We have escaped one fate only to be threatened by one more terrible."

"True," he answered. "But down on the Coast they have an old proverb in the Negro-English jargon which says, 'Softly, softly catchee monkey.' Let us proceed cautiously, bear our trials with patience, seek not to incense these brutal Arabs against us, and we may yet tread the path that leads into my mother's kingdom. Then, within a week, the war-drums will sound and we will accompany our hosts against Samory and his hordes."

"I shall act as you direct," I replied. "If you think that by patience all may come right no complaint shall pass my lips. We are companions in misfortune, therefore let us arm ourselves against despair."

The compact thus made, we endured the toil and hardships of travel without murmur. At first our bearded masters heaped upon the queen's son every indignity they could devise, but finding they could not incense him, nor cause him to utter complaint, ceased their taunts and cuts from their loaded whips, and soon began to treat us with less severity.

Yet the fatigues of that march were terrible. The suffering I witnessed in that slave gang is still as vivid in my memory as if it were only yesterday. Ere we had passed through the great forest and gained the Kong mountains, a dozen of our unfortunate companions who had fallen sick had been left in the narrow path to be eaten alive by the driver-ants and other insects in which the gloomy depths abound, while during the twenty days which the march to the Ashanti border occupied many others succumbed to fever. Over all the marshes there hung a thick white mist deadly to all, but the more so to the starving wretches who came from the high lands far north beyond the Niger. Scarcely a day broke without one or more of the lean, weak negroes being attacked, and as a sick slave is only an incumbrance, they were left to die while we were marched onward. Whose turn it might next be to be left behind to be devoured alive none knew, and in this agony of fear and suspense we pushed forward from day to day until we at last reached the undulating grass-land that Omar told me was within a few days' march of Kumassi.

Here, even if the sun blazed down upon us like a ball of fire, it was far healthier than in the misty regions of King Fever, and at the summit of a low grass-covered hill our captors halted for two days to allow us to recuperate, fearing, we supposed, that our starved and weak condition might be made an excuse for low prices.

Soon, however, we were goaded forward again, and ere long, having traversed Mampon's country, entered the capital of King Prempeh, slaves to be sacrificed at the great annual custom.

No chance of escape had been afforded us. We were driven forward to the doom to which the inhuman enemy of the Naya of Mo had so ruthlessly consigned us.

XI

The Human Sacrifice

K umassi, the capital of the Ashanti kingdom, was, we found, full of curious contrasts. We approached it through dense high elephant grass, along a little beaten foot-path strewn with fetish dolls. It was evening when we entered it, and drums could be heard rumbling and booming far and near. Presently we passed a cluster of the usual mud huts, then another; several other clusters were in sight with patches of high jungle grass between. Then in a bare open space some two hundred yards across, were huts, and more thatched roofs in the hollow beyond. This was Kumassi.

During that day three of our fellow-sufferers, knowing the horrible fate in store for them, managed to snatch knives from the belts of our captors and commit suicide before our eyes, preferring death by their own hands to decapitation by the executioners of Prempeh, that bloodthirsty monarch who has now happily been deposed by the British Government, but who at that time was sacrificing thousands of human lives annually, defiant and heedless of the remonstrances of civilized nations.

In size Kumassi came up to the standard I had formed of it. The streets were numerous, some half-dozen were broad and uniform, the main avenue being some seventy yards wide, and here and there along its length a great patriarchal tree spread its branches. The houses were wattled structures with alcoves and stuccoed façades, embellished with Moorish designs and coloured with red ochre. Red seemed the prevailing colour. Indeed it is stated on good authority that on one occasion Prempeh desired to stain the walls of his palace a darker red, and used the blood of a thousand victims for that purpose. Behind each of the pretentious buildings which fronted the streets were grouped the huts of the domestics, inclosing small courtyards.

Passing down this main avenue, where many people watched our dismal procession, we came to the grove whence issued the terrible smell which caused travellers to describe Kumassi as a vast charnel-house; we, however, did not halt there, but passed onward to the palace of Prempeh, situated about three hundred yards away and occupying a level area in the valley dividing the two eminences on which the town is situated. The first view of what was designated as the palace was a number of houses with steep thatched roofs clustered together and fenced around with split bamboo stakes, while at one corner rose a square two-storeyed stone building. The lower part of the lofty walls of stucco was stained deep red, probably by blood, and the upper part whitewashed.

Presumably our captors had received a commission from Prempeh to supply him with slaves for the sacrifice, for we were marched into a small courtyard of the palace itself and there allowed to rest until next day, being given a plentiful supply of well-cooked *cankie*, or maize pudding wrapped in plantain leaves. Our position was, we knew, extremely critical. Attired in the merest remnant of a waist cloth, with a thick noose of grass-rope securely knotted around our necks, we lay in the open court with the stars shining brilliantly above us, unable to sleep from the intensity of our feelings. In the next court there were more than a hundred unfortunates like ourselves huddled together, ready to be sacrificed on the morrow.

Soon after sunrise, while moodily awaiting our fate, we were made to stand up for inspection by one of the King's Ocras. These men were of three classes; the first being relatives of the King and entrusted with State secrets, were never sacrificed, the second were certain soldiers appointed by the king, and the third slaves. All, on account of their distinguished services, were exempt from taxes, palavers and military services, and were kept in splendid style by the Royal exchequer, those of the inferior classes being expected to sacrifice themselves upon the tomb of the king when he died.

The tall, rather handsome, man who inspected us was an Ocra of the first class, for he wore a massive gold circle like a quoit suspended around his neck by golden chains, and, walking beneath an enormous, gaudily-coloured silken umbrella bearing the crude device of a crouching leopard, was attended by a numerous retinue, who paid him the greatest respect.

The Arabs who had brought us there made him profound obeisance, while some members of the retinue snapped fingers with several of the Arabs, and the usual teetotal ceremony of drinking water to "cool the heads" was gone through. The inspection was a keen one, each of us being passed in review before the Ocra, who made brief comments to the Arabs at his side. As Omar passed the dark-faced official scrutinised him carefully and seemed interested to learn what the leader of the slave caravan told him in a tongue unknown to me regarding us both, for his gaze wandered from my companion to myself, and I was at once called out to pass before his keen glance. We were both kept there several minutes while the Arab presumably explained how we had been entrapped at the court of Samory. At last, however, we were allowed to retire, and very soon afterwards the great Ocra moved forward into the next court, followed by a couple of youths bearing long knives and a thin, lean-looking wretch with a stool curiously carved from a solid block of cotton wood, richly embellished with gold ornaments.

When he had gone I cast myself upon the ground in the shadow beside Omar, saying:

"After all, it would have been better if we had died in the woods than to endure this torture of waiting for execution."

"Yes," he answered, gloomily. "That Ocra who has just inspected us was Betea, a bitter enemy of my mother. He is certain to revenge himself upon us."

But even as he spoke we heard the adulatory shouts of the royal crier somewhere in our vicinity. They were more than sufficient to transform any man, white or black, into a vain despot, and as translated by Omar were in the strain of:

"O, King, thou art the king above all kings! Thou art great! Thou art mighty! Thou art strong! Thou hast done enough! The princes of the earth bow down to thee, and humble themselves in the dust before thy stool. Who is like unto the King of all the Ashantis?"

It was the preliminary of the great sacrifice!

King Prempeh, though arrogant, vain and cruel beyond measure, had, we afterwards saw, the eye of a king, which means that it was the eye of one possessing unlimited power over life and death. It was the custom for the king to be placed on the stool by the united voice of the chiefs; but immediately he was seated in him became vested the supreme power.

Soon the firing of guns and the loud beating of the great *kinkassis*, or drums ornamented with human skulls, sounded outside the walls wherein we were confined, while the air was rent by the wild yells of the excited populace. For nearly an hour this continued, and we thus remained in terrible suspense until at last the gate opened, and with the grass ropes still around our neck we were marched out of the palace under an escort of the king's slaves.

Turning to the left along the broad avenue we saw upon a long pole a human head grinning at us, two vultures perched upon it eagerly stripping it. It was, Omar told me, the head of a thief. The street was crowded with people, who shouted to their gods as we passed in procession, and presently we came to a great fetish-gallows, from the cross beams of which hung the decomposing body of a ram. Some of the men forming our escort were a strangely-dressed set, their uniform consisting of striped tunics reaching to the knee, confined round the waist by belts profusely decorated with strips of leopard skin and tiny brass bells which tinkled musically as they moved. In their belts they carried several knives, while the musket and the little round cap of pangolin skin completed their equipment.

At last we reached the grove at Bantama on the out-skirts of the town, one of the three execution places. Several thousand people had assembled around a great tree where a number of gorgeous umbrellas of every hue and material had been erected. Many were ornamented with curious devices, and the tops of some bore little images of men and animals in gold and silver. Under the centre umbrella, upon a brass-nailed chair close to the tree, sat King Prempeh in regal splendour, surrounded by a crowd of chiefs, whose golden accoutrements glittered in the sun. Three scarlet-clad dwarfs were dancing before him amid the dense crowd of sword-bearers, fly-whiskers, court criers and minor officials. As he sat there, his thin flabby yellow face glistening with oil, he looked a truly regal figure, wearing upon his head a high black and gold crown, and on his neck and arms great golden beads and nuggets. His habit was to suck a large nut that looked like a big cigar, and as he sat there with it in his mouth it gave his face a strangely idiotic expression.

The whole Ashanti court had assembled at the theatre of human sacrifice.

As we approached the drumming grew louder, the roar of voices filled the air, and the great coloured umbrellas were seen whirling and bobbing above the heads of the surging crowd of natives. The great barrel-like drums, with their grim ornamentations, boomed forth, and bands of elephant-tusk horns added to the deafening din.

In the distance could be seen the great fetish-house, with its enormous high thatched roof wherein was supposed to be hidden Prempeh's great treasures of gold-dust and jewels. The ground whereon the glittering court had assembled was covered with the skulls and bones of thousands of former victims, and as we advanced slowly through the turbulent crowd we saw a sight that froze our blood. At the foot of the fetish tree was placed a great brass execution-bowl, about five feet in diameter. It was ornamented with four small lions and a number of knobs all around its rim, except at one part where there was a space for the victim's neck to rest upon the edge. The blood of those sacrificed to the gods was allowed to putrefy in this great bowl—which has recently passed into the hands of the English, and is now in London—and leaves of certain herbs being added it was considered valuable as a fetish medicine.

As we entered the cleared space between the chiefs and caboocers surrounding the King and the thousands of warriors and spectators, salvo after salvo of musketry was fired, until the smoke obscured all objects in our immediate vicinity. Around the sacrificial bowl were grouped a dozen or more royal executioners with their faces whitewashed and hideously decorated. Some upon their heads wore caps of monkey skin with the face in front, while others had high head-dresses of eagles' feathers, their tunics of long grasses being covered with magical charms tied in little bunches. All were copiously smeared with blood, while each wore a necklace of human teeth, and carried a heavy broad-bladed sword rusted by the blood of former victims. Behind them were twenty or thirty Ashantis, each with a knife stuck through both cheeks, to prevent the unhappy victims from asking the King to spare their lives, which, according to national law, must be granted, while a broad-bladed dagger was in many cases run under the shoulder-blades. They were prisoners who had tried to stir revolt, and were, we understood, to be sacrificed first. Our turn would come later.

The scene was horrible; we were appalled. At a signal from the King the first unfortunate wretch was instantly seized by two executioners and held over the bowl, while a third lifted his keen sword, and with a dull, sickening thud brought it down upon the poor fellow's neck, hacking into his spine until the head was severed. Then there arose a loud shout of triumph. The offering to the fetish was the signal for the most enthusiastic rejoicing, and the shouts of adulation were deafening. The people, ground down by a crafty priesthood, and steeped in the most degrading superstitions, looked upon the wholesale butchery that followed without a shudder. King, courtiers and slaves seemed seized with an insatiable desire for blood, and as one head fell after another, the cries of the victims drowned by the vociferous shouts of the onlookers, Omar and I stood shackled and trembling.

One after another the victims were thrown across the bowl and their life-blood gushed into it as the cruel swords descended, while the King gloated over the sight with an expression of pleasure upon his oily sinister face, until the heap of headless trunks grew large, and the number sacrificed must have been over a hundred.

Suddenly the chief executioner took one of his knives which had a human skull upon the hilt, and holding it up, commanded silence.

Then spoke the Ocra Betea, who, rising from his stool, waved his hand across the veritable Golgotha, crying:

"Behold! Tremble! The King makes the great yam custom. The death-drum beats, and to the fetish we offer sacrifice. Who is so great as the King of all the Ashantis, and who is so powerful as the fetish? Yonder are the graves of the great kings, and the marks on yonder walls show the number of men who were sacrificed when their graves were watered. Listen! The mighty King Prempeh is about to sacrifice. To-day he sends five hundred men to the dark world as a thank offering for the harvest, and as an offering to the fetish to enable us to eat up our enemies, the whites. When our mighty King says war, we will arm against them, and their heads shall fill many baskets. Of a truth our lord Prempeh is the greatest monarch who has ever sat upon the stool. The earth quakes when he speaks, and his enemies are paralysed by fear. Betea has spoken."

Then the crowd set up a series of wild shrieks and yells, they gesticulated, fired guns indiscriminately, and danced wildly, while some of the enthusiasts pressing forward, dipped their hands into the blood already in the bowl, and besmeared themselves with it; and others, turning upon myself and my companion as we stood silent and trembling, heaped every insult upon us.

In a few moments, however, the crowd was driven back, and at a signal from the King the executions recommenced, until the smell of blood grew sickening, and the awful scene caused me to shake like an aspen.

I knew that nothing could save me from the hands of these demoniacal whitewashed executioners, and in a few moments I, a slave purchased like an ox for the slaughter, would be borne down over the bowl and decapitated.

I looked at Omar. His face was pale, but his lips were tightly set, although there was an expression of utter hopelessness upon his countenance.

The horror of that moment held me breathless.

XII

In the Sacred Grove

One by one the slaves of the gang in which we had travelled were dragged forward, held over the execution bowl and sent as messengers to spirit-land, until it came to Omar's turn. In a second two white-faced demons with keen swords seized him, and despite the cry for mercy that escaped his lips, he was rushed forward, the frenzied executioners flinging him down unceremoniously, and bending his head over the warm blood with which the basin was now filled to overflowing.

At that instant, as the chief executioner strode forward and held his dripping blade uplifted, ready to strike, the King raised his hand to command silence, and the hideously-dressed official paused in wonder, his sword poised in air.

Betea, the Ocra, bending low, was whispering to the King, when the latter suddenly took the nut from his mouth and said:

"So it is upon Omar, son of my enemy the Naya of Mo, that my eyes rest! Let him stand forth with his white companion."

Obedient to the command of the King, the executioners allowed Omar to rise, and in a few moments we both stood before the royal stool.

"How came you here?" asked Prempeh, scowling.

"I was captured and sold as slave to the Arab dealers," he answered, drawing himself up with that princely air he always assumed in moments of danger.

"And your white companion? How is it he is in our capital?"

"I have been to the land of the white men across the sea, and he returned as my friend," Omar replied. "We were travelling homeward to Mo when by treachery I was entrapped."

"By whom?"

"By Samory."

Across Prempeh's evil face there spread a sickly smile. He was an ally of the great Mohammedan chief, and saw at once that Samory had sold the son of their mutual enemy into slavery.

"Your queen-mother," he said, "has times without number sent her armed hordes over the border to raid our villages, and it is the fetish that has delivered you, her son, into our hands. The fetish has not sent you hither as a sacrifice, but as a hostage. Therefore your life shall be spared together with that of your white friend, but you shall both be given as slaves to our trusted Ocra Betea. Let the sacrifice proceed. Prempeh, King of all the Ashantis, has spoken."

Next second a poor black wretch was dragged along in Omar's place and the sword fell heavily upon him, while we were both hurried away in charge of a caboocer to the residence of the man who was, according to Omar, one of his mother's bitterest foes. Glad were we to escape with our lives from that awful scene of inhuman butchery, but it seemed that as slaves of this court favourite to whom we had been given, there would be but little brightness in our lives.

As day succeeded day our gloomy forebodings were only too truly realized. Betea, the most powerful of the King's Ocras, seemed to delight in making our lives a burden to us, for amid luxurious surroundings we were beaten, starved, and ill-treated, until even death under the executioner's knife seemed a preferable fate.

Six months passed; six weary months of slavery and wretchedness. Our position seemed absolutely hopeless, and I began to fear that we should never escape from the City of Blood. The scenes we witnessed there were so revolting, that I cannot now reflect upon them without a shudder. The ghastly "customs," the absence of all protection for life and property, the grinding oppression, the nameless horrors of all kinds, were terrible. Blood was continually flowing, for every anniversary demanded fresh holocausts, and the "Golgotha" presented a sight of indescribable horror. The unwritten code of laws were of such a sanguinary nature, that the public executioners formed a numerous section of the community and were constantly employed collecting their victims, leading them for exhibition through the capital and then hacking them to pieces in presence of the king. Soldiers, slaves, retainers of the nobles and conquered tribes possessed no defined rights, and their lives and property were practically in the hands of the royal and governing classes.

Close to the house of our inhuman master was the fetish grove, a horrible place, surrounded by rank grass, dirt, and reeking with odours pestilential. Once or twice I wandered in that grove, treading upon human bones at every step—the heaped-up remains of thousands of miserable creatures slaughtered to please the Ashanti ruler's lust for blood. Poor crumbling bones, mouldy and sodden as the rotten wood of older trees, yet once clothed with form and vigour, lay everywhere,

WILLIAM LE QUEUX

while under the cotton wood trees skulls were heaped and vultures hovered about in hundreds.

One evening we attended our master on one of his official visits to Bantama, the fetish priest's village where we so narrowly escaped execution, and were able to thoroughly inspect the gruesome place. The most horrible blood-orgies known to superstition and fetish-worship were almost daily practised there, and in nearly every abode there were stools and chairs smeared with human blood, drinking bowls were stained with it, and some vessels were half-filled with black clotted blood. In the priests' inner chambers, dark dens filled with foul odours, to which we entered with Betea, we found not only the whole apartment smeared with blood, but bones and portions of human remains lying about openly, or wrapped in rags to serve as charms. One building, probably the residence of one of the chief priests, was embellished with mud-moulded panels and scroll work, and the columns facing the principal quadrangle were fluted. The colours were the prevailing white clay, and red ochre plastered upon the wattle and mud pillars.

Suddenly, as in the dusk we left this house, a loud horrible shriek sounded. At first we thought some poor wretch was being sacrificed, but again and again it sounded, and all turned pale, even the royal Ocra himself.

"What's that, I wonder?" I asked Omar, who, bearing our master's sword, was walking at my side.

"The gree-gree!" he gasped, looking round in fear, while at that moment there sounded two ear-piercing blasts upon a horn.

"Hark!" cried Betea himself, trembling. "The gree-gree is out to-night!"

I remembered that I had been told by one of our fellow-slaves that the gree-gree was a great fetish who appeared horned like a demon, and killed all persons he came across. None dare lock their doors when the gree-gree walked, and only the King himself was invulnerable. This no doubt was another trick of the priests to frighten the superstitious natives, and at the same time wreak vengeance upon those who had offended them. Once again the notes of the horn rose weird and shrill, and died away. Then Betea, himself affrighted, turned to us saying:

"Fly! fly for your lives. If the gree-gree catches you you will be struck upon the brow. His arm deals death everywhere."

In a moment all took to their heels, including the royal Ocra, but Omar, grasping my arm, whispered excitedly:

"Stay. We may now escape."

As the words left his lips we caught sight of a weird black figure dressed in long coarse grass, with rams' horns upon his head, his face whitened and a second pair of eyes painted over his own. In his hand gleamed a long bright knife, while at his side was suspended a freshly-severed human arm and hand. Yelling and leaping like a veritable demon, he suddenly noticed the flying figures of our fellow-slaves, and halting a moment, dashed after them, leaving us alone.

"He will return here, so we must hide," Omar said quickly, and glancing round, we both saw at the end of the dark ghostly avenue of fetish-trees an oblong windowless mud building with a high-pitched triple grass thatched roof. Running towards it we managed to wrench off the padlock from the door and enter. It was, we discovered, the reputed sepulchre of the Ashanti kings. Without, it was guarded by all sorts of fetish-charms, extraordinary odds and ends, animals' claws, broken pottery, scraps of tin, bits of wood, stones and human bones. Within, by the aid of a lamp we found burning were revealed several great coffers clamped with copper and iron, each resting upon two big stools of carved cotton-wood. Jars and vases filled with water and wine, braziers full of sweet-smelling leaves, and plates of food were placed beside each, offerings for the use of the dead.

Omar told me that when an Ashanti king died, he was buried in an ordinary coffin for a time, but afterwards the body was invariably disinterred, and the joints of the skeleton articulated with gold bands and wire. It was then placed, doubled up, in one of these spacious coffers—fully four feet long by two feet wide and deep—and the other skeletons were attendants, slaughtered and sent to the land of Shades to wait on the monarch's ghost.

"Possibly," I said, "much of the ghostly grimness and worked-up horrors about this place are cunningly devised, not only to protect the Royal tombs from being plundered by the superstitious natives, but to help to safeguard the State treasures concealed in yonder coffins."

"Yes," he said. "In this priest-ridden country all the superstition is heaped up for their benefit and profit. But we must get out of here before dawn, run past the gree-gree if he is about, and make a dash for the open forest. It is our only chance of escape, for at dawn the priests will come again to watch beside the tombs, and if discovered we are certain to be skewered through the mouth, dragged before Prempeh and hacked to pieces by the criminal executioner."

"Well, any fate is better than that," I observed. "Let us wait an hour or so, and then make a rush for it."

"Very well," he answered, and together we resumed the work of exploring the strange place.

Soon, however, our lamp burned dim, flickered, and went out; then, after waiting in silence for half an hour in the pitch darkness, we softly opened the door, and, holding our breaths, crept out. With noiseless tread we stole along the sacred grove and were nearly at the end when, without warning, the hideous gree-gree, with a fiendish yell of triumph, sprang out of some bushes upon us.

Involuntarily, I put up my fist to ward off attack, and in doing so gave him a well-directed blow full in the face, sending him down flat on his back.

"Hurrah!" cried Omar in delight. "Floored him! Let's run for our lives."

Ere the midnight murderer could spring to his feet, we had dashed away as fast as our legs could carry us, running along the fetish-grove, past the cluster of executioners' houses, across the open space where in the centre stood the great tree under which Prempeh had sat to witness the wholesale sacrifice, and continuing until we came to a path through the high elephant-grass, we soon left the city far behind us, and plunged into the dark, dismal forest by the narrow winding way that led to the unexplored regions of the north.

When at length we paused to take breath Omar, panting, said:

"At last we are free again. Betea will not seek us, for he naturally believes we were killed by the gree-gree. If Zomara favours us we shall yet live to enter Mo and lead our hosts into the country of Samory."

Then, taking from his neck a little bag of some strange powder, he took therefrom a pinch, and with fervent words scattered it to the four quarters of the wind, thus making a thank-offering to the Crocodile-god.

XIII

The Way of the Thousand Steps

To describe in detail our long toilsome journey and the terrible hardships we suffered during the next two months is unnecessary. Suffice it to say that without means of barter, unarmed, and living upon fruit and roots, we tramped along that narrow path through the pestilential marshes and the great forests where no light penetrated through the thick foliage of the giant trees for several weeks, always due north and passing villages sometimes, until we crossed the Sene river, ascended the mountains beyond, and found ourselves upon a great level grass-covered plateau, which occupied us several days in traversing. At last we came to the border of Prempeh's kingdom, crossed the Volta river that wound in the brilliant sunlight for many miles like a golden thread among the trees, and soon entered the fertile country of the Dagombas, a wild-looking tribe who were allies of the great Naya. At Yendi, seven days' march through the bush from the Volta, we interviewed the Dagomba king and received a most enthusiastic welcome. Presents of food and slaves were given us, as well as a musket each, with some curious ivory-hilted knives, and we were treated as honoured guests of his sable majesty, who, Omar informed me, was indebted to the Naya for his royal position.

This welcome was therefore only what we expected, nevertheless, our life during the few days at Yendi was of a very different character to the miserable existence we had experienced during our long march to the confines of Ashanti. But Omar was impatient to fulfil the commands of his mother, and we did not remain longer than was absolutely necessary, in order not to give offence to the king; however, one morning we snapped fingers with him and, with two hundred decidedly savage-looking men as escort, we moved away still due north on our journey to the mysterious land of the Great White Queen.

The King of Dagomba had told me, in answer to my enquiries, that neither himself nor any of his men had ever entered Mo. The inhabitants were a very powerful and fearless people, he knew, and their soldiers were as numerous as an army of locusts. The men of Mo were an admirable race, he added, and although no stranger had ever been admitted to the mysterious realm, yet its power was feared by every West African ruler without exception.

It gratified me to think that I should be the first to set foot within a land forbidden to any who had not been born there, and I grew extremely impatient to set eyes upon the country to the throne of which my light-hearted friend Omar was heir. Travelling quickly, with but few delays, we crossed the Busanga country, mainly covered by dense, dark forest and unhealthy marshes, where the odour of decayed vegetable matter was sickening, until we came to a great mountain rearing its snowy crest into the clouds, which Omar told me was called the Nauri. Hence, when we had rested two days to recruit in the sunlight after the dispiriting gloom of the primeval forest, we held on our way, passing many native villages, the inhabitants of each showing marked friendliness towards our Dagombas.

Kona, our headman, was a tall, pleasant-faced negro, raw-boned and awkward, with huge hands and splay feet, but his muscles were hard as iron and his strength astounding. He treated Omar as a prince, always deferential to his wishes, and regarded me as an honoured visitor to the unknown but powerful protector of his sovereign. Though fraught with many dangers on account of the wild beasts lurking in the forests and the snakes on the plains, our journey nevertheless proved extremely pleasant, for in Kona we found a true and sympathetic friend.

Once he spoke to me of Queen Victoria, and his words amused me. He said with impressive earnestness:

"Ah! The Queen of the English is, next to the Great White Queen, the mightiest and cleverest woman in the world. She sees the treasures in the interior of the earth, and has them lifted. She spans the world with iron threads, and when she touches them they carry her words into the world. She has steamers running on dry land. If a mountain is in her way she has a hole made through it. If a river interferes, she builds a road across in the air. And the Queen of the English and the Great White Queen of Mo are richer than all other women together. They are the most beautiful women in the world, and their husbands paid nothing for them."

When at night around our camp fire we would relate to him the treachery of Kouaga, and our adventures in the hands of Samory and Prempeh, he would stir the embers viciously and call down the curse of Zomara upon them all.

"When the son of the great Naya of Mo punishes his enemies, Kona will go and assist in their destruction," he said one night. "Kona's knife shall seek their hearts."

"So it shall," Omar had replied, assured of the loyalty of this negro ally. "You are our guide and friend; rest assured that when we enter Mo you shall not be forgotten."

And we went forward next day all in excellent spirits, all eager to enter the unknown land.

A few days' march from the mystic mountain of Nauri we approached a little town called Imigu, but found it had been sacked and burned, evidently by Arab slave-raiders, who, Omar said, were constantly descending upon the towns and villages on the border of his land. At evening we went over the ruins of what not long ago must have been a populous trading town, saw how wanton had been the destruction, and judged from the heaps of bleaching bones how terrible had been the butchery of its inhabitants.

At dawn, however, we moved forward again, but at noon, while we were descending a beautiful fertile valley Kona stopped suddenly, gazed around wonderingly, and then halting his men addressed them, telling them that they were about to enter a country wherein no stranger had ever before set foot, and urging them to patiently face any difficulty they found in their path, and to offer sacrifices of food to the fetish to give them strength to surmount all obstacles.

Omar, with folded arms, stood by and listened. When Kona had finished he raised his hand, saying:

"Men of the Dagomba. You have guided us to the furthermost limit of the earth as known to you; in fact to the point where your knowledge of this land ends and mine commences. For this service you deserve reward, and I, Omar, Prince of Mo, promise that none who have accompanied me hither shall leave the palace of the Great White Queen without his just reward."

Two hundred black faces thereupon glistened with delight. All were eager to see the wonders of this much-talked-of country, but the promise of a reward at the hands of the great queen was a pleasant surprise that evoked the wildest enthusiasm. They yelled with pleasure, bestowed upon us all the terms of adulation until they exhausted their vocabulary, and blew their elephants' tusks until I confess I was compelled to stuff my fingers into my ears, fearing deafness.

"Lead us on, O our lord the prince!" they cried. "Let us go forward.

We will follow thee if thou wilt point out the right path leading unto Mo, and appease thy land's jealous guardians who smite back all would-be intruders with swords of fire."

This latter was a tradition. I had heard it many times during my journey with Omar. The natives of Ashanti, of Kong, of Gurunsi, and of Dagomba, had all told me that the country of Mo, wherever it might be situated, was surrounded by a great cordon of guards—demons they believed them to be—who had never allowed a stranger to enter, for they simply lifted their deadly swords that blazed like fire-brands, and slew the offending wanderer.

"The guardians of Mo shall be appeased," Omar assured them. "Not a hair on the head of any of our party shall be injured, although the way is still long and full of terrors and pitfalls. But I will lead, and those who obey will enter Mo. Those who depart from my words will assuredly perish. Omar, Prince of Mo, has spoken."

"May the fetish be good," they all cried aloud. "We will follow and attend to each word that falleth from thy lips."

Then in a few minutes we moved on again down the long beautiful valley through which a clear river wound among green swards and clumps of trees, forming a park-like scene such as might have been witnessed in England. Presently, however, the character of the country suddenly changed, and we were passing through a rocky defile, arid and waterless, while at the end could be seen a wide open country without rock or tree stretching away as far as the eye could reach to the misty horizon.

It appeared like a great limitless wilderness, and those in front quickened their pace in order to fully view the character of the land we were approaching.

For their haste, however, they received an unpleasant reward.

When those who ran forward emerged into the open plain, they suddenly found the soft earth give way beneath their feet without warning, and ere they realized their danger a dozen of them were struggling up to their arm-pits in the sea of fine ever-shifting sand that seemed kept in constant motion by some unknown natural cause. With each movement they sank deeper, until, fearing that the sandy quagmire would envelop and suffocate them, they cried aloud for assistance. Help was ready at hand, for the remainder of our followers ran forward, and stretching forth ropes of monkey-creeper were enabled to drag out their intrepid companions, much to Omar's amusement.

"Those who deviate from the course that I myself take will assuredly perish," he exclaimed a moment later. Then, turning to me, he added: "This desert you see before you is one of the barriers dividing my land from those of our enemies. To those who know not the secret it is impassable."

"Yes," I answered, surprised at the strange treacherous character of the sand. "Those who ventured upon it had narrow escapes."

"Exactly. Any weight upon its surface will sink to the depth of many feet, sucked down as swiftly and surely as a piece of wood is drawn down by a whirlpool. In an attempt to cross this unsafe region many men have lost their lives, for once upon its surface escape is impossible. See!" And he cast his staff away upon the sand. In an instant it had sunk out of sight.

"Then how shall we gain the land beyond?" I asked in fear at the soft nature of the earth's surface.

"There is but one way. It is known only to the Naya and to myself, and is called the Way of the Thousand Steps. Its existence is preserved as a royal secret in case my family are compelled at any time to fly from our country, in which case they could escape safely, while all their pursuers would assuredly be overwhelmed and perish. For that reason the knowledge has been for centuries solely in the keeping of the reigning Naya or Naba. It was by this secret path that I left Mo and came to you in England; by the same path I return."

"Lead the way. We will follow," I said.

"Come, men," he exclaimed, lifting his hand as he addressed them. "Fear not, but follow so closely in my footprints that your feet obliterate them, and I will bridge the great gulf that lieth between Mo and the outer world."

The mishap to the advance guard had evoked the wildest speculations among the natives, and all were eagerly pressing forward, when, in a few moments, Omar took up his position before them, and urging the utmost caution held up the staff he took from my hand, taking what appeared to be the bearings between his own eye and the summit of a low mound far away on the horizon. The preparations did not take long, and very soon, with his staff held in the same position before him, he began to venture forward upon the unsafe sand.

Carefully he trod the great treeless plain, being followed by all in single file. With such caution did we tread, and so excited were we all, that at first scarcely was a word spoken. Very soon, however, with confidence in Omar's leadership the natives grew hilarious again, and keeping straight behind the young prince they found the way, about a foot in width, hard, although dry, and extremely unpleasant to tread. Nevertheless we all were ready to encounter and overcome every obstacle providing that we could enter the forbidden land, and thus we went forward. Now and then one of the natives, in speaking to the man next behind him, would turn and thus deviate from the path over which Omar had passed, and he would quickly pay for this carelessness, suddenly finding himself floundering helplessly up to the ears in the deadly quicksands. Then the whole of our party would halt and, amid broad laughter and much ridicule, the unfortunate one would be dragged forth from a certain and terrible doom.

But the path was not straight. Heedless of the chatter and excitement behind him Omar walked on before, his staff raised on a level with his eye, counting aloud each step he took, measuring the distance, until when he had taken a thousand paces he suddenly stopped, examined the ground well, and then turning at exact right angles, took bearings by another mound that I had noticed far in the distant haze.

Again and again we faced always at exact angles after pacing a thousand steps, so that our path became a zig-zag one, long and toilsome, with many halts, yet without rest and without seeing anything beyond the wondrous expanse of burning sky and the loose sand that swallowed all things dead or living.

Everything thrown upon it sank and disappeared almost as quickly as iron cast into water.

XIV

Foes

W hen we had been several hours upon our hot, tedious journey there arose a quarrel out of a practical joke played by one native upon the man walking before him. Quick, hasty words led to blows being exchanged.

Both men were walking immediately in front of me, and I did my best to quell the disturbance, but either they did not understand me or affected ignorance of my words, for suddenly one of them raising his spear leapt forward upon the other. The man attacked sprang aside and in so doing left the narrow path, at that spot not more than twelve inches in width, followed by the would-be assassin.

Next second they sank into the sand, and although loud cries of horror escaped them, both disappeared into the terrible gulf ere a hand could be outstretched to save them. Hearing their cries I leant forward, but before I could grasp either of them the fine sand had closed over their heads like the waters of the sea, leaving a deep round depression in the surface. They had disappeared for ever.

The instant death of the two combatants before my gaze caused me to shudder, and I confess that from that moment I kept my eyes rivetted upon the strange narrow path by which we were crossing the impassable barrier.

Through three whole days we continued along the Way of the Thousand Steps, resting at night and journeying while the light lasted. To halt was even more perilous than to progress, for when we encamped we simply sat down upon the spot where our footsteps had been arrested, and food was passed from hand to hand along the line. This latter was somewhat unsatisfactory, at least as far as I was concerned, for the eatables that reached me were not improved by passing through the hands of thirty or forty malodorous negroes. But the fatality that had at first appalled us had now been forgotten, and everyone kept a good heart. Led by Omar we were approaching a land hitherto unknown; a country reputed to be full of hidden wonders and strange marvels, and all were, hour by hour, eagerly scanning the mysterious horizon.

Across the level sand, swept by winds that parched the lips and filled the eyes with fine dust, causing us infinite misery, our gaze was ever turned northward where Omar told us lay our land of promise. The very last hesitations on the part of our followers had long been overcome. The African savage is not given to roaming far from his own tract, fearing capture or assassination at the hands of neighbouring tribes, but such confidence had the men of Dagomba that if Omar had plunged into the quicksands they would have followed without comment.

When at Trigger's I had often read stories of African adventure. I used to fancy myself buried in forest wilds, or eating luncheon upon the grass, on the edge of a tumbling brook in the shadow of great outlandish trees; I could feel the juice of luscious fruits—mangroves and bananas—trickle between my teeth. I had once read in one of the boys' papers about the daughter of an African colonist abducted by the son of a West African king who had fallen in love with her; and the ups and downs and ins and outs of this love drama had opened a boundless vista to my imagination. But life in Africa contained far more excitement than I had ever imagined. Death threatened everywhere, and I received constant warnings from Omar, who gave me good advice how to avoid sunstroke or ward off the effects of the chill wind that blew nightly across this wonderful limitless plain.

One evening, when the horizon northward looked grey and mysterious, and to our left the fiery sun's last dying ray still lingered in the sky, there was a sudden halt, the cause of which was I afterwards found due to the sudden stoppage of our leader, Omar. All were eager to know the cause, until in a few moments an amazing announcement spread from mouth to mouth along the line.

There were strangers on ahead of us! They were actually traversing the Way of the Thousand Steps!

Shading my eyes with my hands I eagerly scanned the horizon in the direction indicated, and there, to my astonishment, saw a long thin black line. At first I could not distinguish whether it was a file of men or some inanimate object, but the keen eyes of the savages before and behind me soon detected its presence, and dozens of voices were in accord that it was a line of armed men, and that they were moving in our direction.

Instantly it flashed across my mind that whoever they were, friends or foes, there was not sufficient room for them to pass us upon that narrow path, and knowing the determination of our followers I wondered what the result would be when we met. Unable to approach Omar sufficiently near to converse with him, I watched his face. By the heavy look upon his brow I knew that trouble was brewing. It was the same look his face wore when we had been held captive at Kumassi, an expression of resolution and fierce combativeness.

Soon, however, we moved along again, eager to ascertain who were the strangers who knew the secret supposed to have been jealously guarded by the great Naya and her son, and for over an hour pressed forward at a quicker pace than usual. Fortunately for us the sunset lingered long away to our left, for by its light we were enabled to see the men approaching, and before it died out to distinguish, to our amazement, that they all wore white Arab burnouses and were armed to the teeth. In point of numbers they were quite double the strength of our little force, but we knew not whether they were friendly or antagonistic.

This point, however, was at last cleared up by Omar himself, who, just as it was growing dusk halted, and, turning towards me, shouted in English:

"Scars, are you there?"

"Yes," I answered. "What's up?"

"Those devils in front! Can't you see their banner?"

"No," I answered. Then remembering that he had always possessed a keen vision, I added: "Who are they?"

"Some of Samory's men, evidently in flight," he answered. "On seeing us they raised their banner, and are, it seems, determined to cut their way past us."

"But where have they been that they should know the secret of the Thousand Steps?" I inquired astounded.

"I'm quite at a loss to understand," he replied puzzled. "The only solution of the mystery seems to be that Kouaga has, by some means, obtained knowledge of the secret way, and has directed a marauding force thither. Evidently they have been defeated by the guardians of Mo, and the remnant of the force—a strong one, too—are retreating, flying for their lives."

"How do you know there has been fighting?" I enquired.

"Because I can just detect near the banner two wounded men are being carried."

"Then we must fight and wipe them out," I said.

"Easier said than done," he answered. "But it means life or death to us."

On they came in single file, nearer every moment, and soon I also could see the dreaded banner of the Mohammedan sheikh Samory. Near the flag-bearer were several wounded men being carried in litters, while the white-robed soldiers carried long rifles and in their sashes were pistols, and those keen carved knives called *jambiyahs*. At first our natives, believing that they were friendlies, went forward enthusiastically, determined to drive them back with banter, there not being room to pass, but very soon Omar ordered another halt, and turning towards us, cried in a loud voice in his native tongue:

"Behold, O men of the Dagomba! Yonder are the fighting men of Samory, who times without number have raided your country, killed your fathers and sons, and sold your wives and sisters into slavery in Ashanti. They have endeavoured to enter Mo by the Way of the Thousand Steps, but being defeated by the guardians of our border are flying towards their own land. We too must fight them, or we must perish."

The air was immediately filled with fierce howls and yells. The announcement that these men were the hated slave-raiders of Samory caused an instant rush to arms. Loud cries of revenge sounded on every side, spears were flourished, knives gripped in fierce determination, and those who had muskets made certain that their weapons were loaded. The air was rent by shrill war shouts, and the great drum with its hideous decorations was thumped loudly by two perspiring negroes who grinned hideously as they watched the steadily marching force approaching.

"Courage, men of the Dagomba," sounded Kona's voice above the din. "Sweep these vermin from our path. Let not a single man escape; but let them all be swallowed by the Sand-God."

"We will eat them up," cried half-a-dozen voices in response. "Our spears shall seek their vitals."

"Guard against their onward rush," cried Omar. "They will seek to throw us off the path by a dash forward. Thwart them, and victory is ours."

Ere these words had left our leader's lips, the air was again filled by the wild clamours of my dark companions, and as we had halted just at a point where we would be compelled to turn at right angles, we remained there in order to attack the Arabs as they advanced.

The sun's glow had faded, dark clouds had come up on the mystic line where sand and sky united, and dusk was creeping on apace when the enemy, sweeping forward, shouting and gesticulating, came within gunshot. From their van a single flash showed for an instant, followed by the sharp crack of a musket, and a bullet whizzed past Omar, striking one of the natives a few yards away, passing through his brain and killing him instantly.

A silence, deep and complete, fell for an instant upon us. In that exciting moment we knew that the fight must be fiercely contested, and that, unable to move scarcely an inch from the spot where we were standing, the struggle must be long and sanguinary.

XV

A Natural Grave

The single shot from our opponents was quickly replied to by myself and my companions, and we had the satisfaction of seeing half-a-dozen Arabs fall backward from the path and disappear in the soft sand. Instantly the rattle of musketry was deafening, and over my head bullets whistled unpleasantly close. The weapon with which I was armed was old-fashioned, and as I fired it time after time it grew hot, and the smoke became so thick that everything was obscured.

Meanwhile fierce hand-to-hand fighting was taking place between the vanguard of the Arabs and a dozen of our men led by Omar. Fiendish yells and shouts sounded on every side as they hacked at each other with their long curved knives, each fearing to step aside lest he should be swallowed by the sand. Once or twice, as the chill night wind parted the smoke, I saw Omar and our Dagombas struggling bravely against fearful odds. Omar had cast aside his gun and, armed with a keen *jambiyah*, had engaged two tall, muscular Arabs, both of whom he succeeded in hurling from the path, gashed and bleeding, to instant death.

Those behind him, armed with long spears with flat double-edged points similar to the assegais of the Zulus, were enabled to reach and dispatch several of the Arabs who had lost their guns or discarded their pistols for their knives. Situated as we were on the angle of the secret path the enemy were to our right. Their fire upon us was very hot and effective. Their aim was so true and their bullets so deadly, that very soon fully a dozen of our brave escort had sunk wounded, disappearing in the terrible sea of sand.

Suddenly a noise sounded about me like the swish of the sea, startling me for a second, but instantly I saw what had caused it. The Dagombas had let loose a flight of poisoned arrows upon our opponents.

From that moment their fire became weaker, and time after time my companions, kneeling upon the ground, drew their bows and released those terrible darts, the slightest scratch from which produced tetanus and almost instant death. Each arrow was smeared with a dark red substance, and their deadly effect was sufficiently proved by the manner in which the ranks of Samory's men were soon decimated. Dozens of Arabs, touched by the poisonous darts, staggered unevenly, and falling to earth sank into the unstable sand, while the red flash of their line of muskets visibly decreased.

Around Omar our men pressed valiantly, and several with bows discharged their missiles with fatal effect, sweeping away the Arabs one by one and apparently striking terror into the hearts of the others. Arabs are not so vulnerable by arrows as other people on account of their voluminous robes, which savage weapons seldom penetrate, it being only head, legs and hands that arrows can reach. Nevertheless so full were the quivers of our sable escort, that the flights were of sufficient magnitude to reach the unprotected parts of the Arabs and lay dozens of them low.

One native next me, whose bow had constantly been bent, suddenly received a bullet full in the breast and was knocked backward off his feet by the concussion. So swiftly was he swallowed by the shifting sand, that ere I could glance behind he had already been buried. Of all who fell, not a single body remained, for if they dropped dead upon the path they were pushed aside in the *mêlée* and instantly disappeared. Again and again our companions sent up their shrill yells and the war-drum was thumped with ear-piercing effect, while opposition shouts rose from our Arab enemies. Still the fight continued as stubborn as it had begun. Omar, with loud shouts of encouragement, fought on with unerring hand, cutting, thrusting and hacking at his opponents until they stumbled to their doom, while across our line of vision where the fire of Arab musketry blazed in the choking smoke, the thin deadly arrows sped, striking our enemies and sweeping them into a natural grave.

Fearing to tread lest I should fall into the terrible quicksand, I knelt and kept up a continuous fire with my musket, shooting into the dense smoke whenever I saw the flash of an Arab gun. It was exciting work, not knowing from one second to another whether the ping of a bullet would bring death. Still I knew that to save our own lives we must sweep away the host of invaders, and, reassured by the knowledge that Omar had met with no mishap, I kept on, heedless of all dangers, thinking only of the ultimate rout of our enemy.

How long the terrible fight lasted I know not. We stood our ground, the majority of us kneeling, engaging the Arabs in mortal combat for, I believe, considerably over an hour. Several times the firing seemed so strong that I feared we should be vanquished, nevertheless the Dagombas proved themselves a valiant, stubborn race, well versed in savage warfare, for the manner in which they shot their arrows was admirable, and even at the decisive moment when all seemed against us they never wavered, but kept on, fierce and revengeful as in the first moments of the fight.

Gradually, when Omar's voice had been heard a dozen times urging us on to sweep every invader from our path and not to let a single man escape, we found our enemy's fire slackening. The smoke, moved by the sand-laden wind that swept across the plain each night after sundown, became less dense, and at last we realized that the tide of battle had turned in our favour, and that we were conquerors.

Then, loud fierce yells rose from the Dagombas and with one accord we struggled to our feet. Each with his hand upon the shoulder of his companion in front we moved cautiously forward, shooting now and then as we went. But the reply to our fire was now spasmodic, and we were convinced that only a few of the Arabs survived.

For some minutes we ceased the struggle and moved forward, but suddenly, to our amazement, a long line of muskets again blazed forth upon us, committing serious havoc in our ranks. We were victims of a ruse!

This aroused the anger of the Dagombas, who recommenced the fight with almost demoniacal fierceness, and as the van of both forces struggled hand-to-hand, we found ourselves slowly but surely gaining ground until half an hour later we were standing upon the path where our enemies had stood when they had attacked us, and of that long line of Samory's picked fighting-men not a single survivor remained.

We had given no quarter. All had been swallowed in that awful gulf of ever-shifting sand. When we had thoroughly convinced ourselves of this we threw ourselves down upon the narrow pathway, and slept heavily till dawn.

When I awoke and gazed eagerly around, I saw that although a number of our men were wounded, their limbs being hastily bandaged, yet few were missing. Of our enemies, however, all had either fallen wounded, or had been hurled from the secret path and overwhelmed by the sand.

A high wind constantly blew, and I noticed that this kept the grains of sand always in motion, thus preventing the surface from solidifying. Waves appeared every moment, ever changing and disappearing in a manner amazing. At one moment a high ridge would be seen before us, appearing as a formidable obstacle to our progress, yet a moment later it would be swept away by an invisible force.

The rosy flush of dawn had been superseded by the saffron tints that are precursory of the sun's appearance when we moved forward again on our cautious march. Our companions, though far from fresh and many of them seriously wounded, were all in highest spirits and full of their brilliant victory. It had indeed been a gratifying achievement, and now, feeling that at least their gods were favourable to their journey, they pushed forward with eyes scanning the far-off horizon where lay the mysterious realm.

During our march that day, Kona, the headman of the Dagombas, on account of three men behind me having fallen in the fight, occupied a place immediately at my rear, and thus I was enabled to hold conversation with him.

"It was a near thing, that fight last night," he exclaimed in the language that Omar had taught me. "But our arrows wrought surer execution than the Arab bullets. The desert-dwellers are no match for the forest-people."

"No," I answered. "Your men are indeed brave fellows, and are entitled to substantial reward."

"I have no fear of that," he said. "The great Naya is always just. She stretches forth her powerful hand to protect the weaker tribes, and smites the raiders with sword and pestilence. What her son promises is her promise. Her word is never broken."

"Have you ever seen her?" I inquired.

"Never. Our king once saw one of her messengers who brought the royal staff and made palaver. To us, as to all other men outside her country, she is known as the Great White Queen."

"Tell me what more you know of her?" I urged.

"Very little," he answered. "In every part of the land, from the great black waters to the Niger and far beyond, even to the sun-scorched country of the Maghrib, her fame is known to all men. She is rich, mighty and mysterious. Her power is dreaded throughout the forests and the grass-plains, and it is said that in her wrath her voice is so terrible that even the mountains quake with fear."

"By what means do her fighting-men come forth from her unapproachable land?" I inquired, remembering that we were travelling by the secret way known only to herself and Omar.

"I know not," he replied. "The manner in which the hosts of Mo appear and disappear have, from time immemorial, formed a subject of speculation among our people. That they have appeared on the Ashanti border and sacked and burned many towns in retaliation for some outrages committed by the Ashantis upon our people is well-known, but by what route they came or returned is a mystery. Some say they came like flocks of birds through the air; others declare that they can transfer themselves from one place to another and become invisible at will. Neither of these theories I myself believe, for I am convinced that between the land of Mo and the Great Salt Road there exists a secret means of communication, so that the armies of the Naya can appear so suddenly and unexpectedly as to escape the vigilance of their enemy's scouts. Many are the battles they have fought and great the slaughter. In the slave-land of Samory they engaged twelve moons ago the pick of the Arab army, and defeated them with appalling loss. It is said, too, that they carry some of the strange guns made by your people, the white men."

"You mean Maxims," I said.

"I know not their name, nor have I ever seen one," he answered. "I have heard, however, from a Sofa who fought against the English in the last war, that the weapons are so light that a man can easily carry one, and that when fired they shed streams of bullets like water from a spout. A single gun is equal to the fire of two hundred men. Truly you white men possess many marvels."

"Yes," I said, smiling at his unbounded admiration for the weapon. "But is it not strange that the Naya should also possess similar marvels?"

"No. Everything is strange in the land of the Great White Queen. It is said to be a country full of amazing mysteries. Many are the extraordinary stories related by my people of the wonders of Mo; wonders that we shall ere long witness with our own eyes."

"What are the stories?" I asked, keenly interested. "Tell me one."

"There are so many," he answered, "I do not know which one to tell. One, however, will illustrate the awe with which the Naya is regarded, even by the powerful Prempeh, King of Ashanti. A story is current that one day, many moons ago, the King had ordered a great 'custom' to take place in Kumassi. War had been declared against the Queen of the English, and in order to obtain the good graces of the fetish a thousand slaves were ordered to be sacrificed. All was ready and the king sat upon his stool awaiting the decapitation of the first victim, when suddenly there swept down from above a large white dove, which, after circling for a moment above the monarch's umbrella, perched upon the edge of the execution bowl. The executioner swept it aside with his ready sword, but in an instant, by some invisible power, the broad-bladed weapon fused and melted as if in a furnace, while the executioner himself, struck down as if by lightning, fell upon his face stone dead. Still the dove remained where it had perched with its head turned towards the ruler of the Ashantis. A second executioner, ere it was discovered that the first was dead, struck at the bird with his hand, and he too, as well as a third and fourth, were similarly smitten with death. 'It is an evil omen!' the people cried, and Prempeh, his eyes rivetted upon the white, innocent-looking bird, trembled. Suddenly, one of the sages at the king's right hand cried: 'See, O Master! It is the Great White Queen, the ruler of Mo! She taketh the form of a dove when she seeketh the destruction of her enemies!' Then spake the dove, saying: 'Yea, O hated king who sheddeth the blood of the innocent and exalteth the guilty. The sacrifice of victims to the fetish shall not avail thee, for I, Naya of Mo, tell thee that thy downfall is at hand, and thine enemies the English will press their way from the great sea, bridge the Prah, and cut a road across the great forest to this thy capital, where thou shalt make abject submission to their head-man and shall be carried into degrading captivity by them. Thy treasures shall be seized, the tombs of thy fathers shall be opened and desecrated, thy fetish-trees shall be cut down and thy slaves shall revel in thy palace. And it is I, in my present form, who shall guide the white men unto their victory.' The king, dumbfounded at these ominous words proceeding from the beak of a bird, rose to retort, but ere a word left his mouth the dove spread its wings and flew away northward in the direction of the land we are now approaching."

"That's merely a tale," I observed, laughing at this latest illustration of the African's belief in the impossible.

"Of course. You asked me for one of the stories told by our people," Kona said. "I have told you one."

"Do you believe that this Great White Queen is invested with such extraordinary power that she can cause herself to be invisible, and while bringing destruction to her enemies, assist her friends?" I asked.

"I know not what to believe," he replied in honest bewilderment. "So many are the tales I have heard that I find it impossible to believe all, and have ended by disbelieving most. Many of the men with us firmly believe at this moment that the Naya, invisible, is at our head guiding her son across the Way of the Thousand Steps, and that to her our victory last night was due. Our fate lies in her hands."

"Well," I answered, amused, "it matters not who leads us so long as we enter the promised land. At any rate we could have no better nor more trustworthy guide than he who is at our head."

Next second, a loud cry from Omar attracted our attention.

XVI

Words of Fire

Raising our eyes from the straight narrow path whereon we set our feet in the footprints of those before us, we halted and looked eagerly ahead.

We had come to the edge of what seemed a shallow depression, and already Omar had disappeared from view, followed cautiously by those immediately behind him. Owing to the cries of warning and astonishment from each man who reached the edge, I advanced, carefully following my black companion in front until I at length gained the spot where the path ended.

Involuntarily a cry of amazement escaped me. I looked over into a fearful abyss. Below was a fertile valley, but so deep was it that the river looked only like a silver thread, and the trees but an inch in height. I was standing on the edge of a huge granite cliff that went down sheer into the valley, its face almost as flat as the side of a house.

The descent appeared terrible. I shuddered as I looked over, and Kona, who came behind me, also peeped down and cried:

"See! It is the Great Gulf about which we have heard. Into this the Naya hurls her enemies."

On the opposite side, about a quarter of a mile distant, gigantic overhanging crags rose from the valley to a height greater than the rock whereon we were kneeling. At a glance we could both see that to scale the wall of rock opposite would be impossible owing to its overhanging nature, therefore, we concluded that our way lay along the fertile valley where the cool welcome green refreshed our eyes.

Already Omar and a couple of dozen of our black followers were carefully swarming down the face of the rock. Now and then warning shouts arose from them, and ever and anon Omar's voice could be heard giving directions, or urging caution. The latter was certainly necessary, for a single false step would mean a terrible death.

As I gazed down into the deep abyss I felt my head reeling. There is a fascination in great heights that impels one to thoughts of self-destruction. A sudden dizziness seized me as I placed my foot over the edge of the fearful precipice, and were it not for Kona, who, noticing my condition, gripped me by the arm, I should have certainly missed my footing and been dashed to pieces on the needle-like crags at the base.

The sudden knowledge that I had been within an ace of death caused me to hold my breath; then I crept cautiously over the edge. For a moment, with my hands clutching frantically upon a jutting piece of rock, my legs swung in mid air, failing to find a foothold, and I cried out, fearing lest I should again fall. But at last my feet struck against a projection, and upon it I carefully lowered myself, while Kona also swung himself over, taking the perilous position I had a moment before occupied. Again and again I lowered myself, gripping on to the successive projections, and lowering myself until my feet touched the one below, thus descending as Omar had done.

"Be careful, Scars," he presently cried from far below. "Drop straight, and look to your footing."

His words caused me to reflect upon the strange fact that each of these projections, almost like natural steps, were placed immediately below one another. Whether they were actually natural formations, or whether they were the work of man I could not determine. Yet they seemed interminable, and sometimes so far apart that I remained stationary, fearing to let myself go until, urged downward by Kona, I held my breath, and, steadying myself, dropped upon the narrow ledge below. Dreading a recurrence of giddiness I dared not to look down at my companions. My bare feet and hands were blistered and cut by the sharp edges of the rocks, and my movements were seriously hampered by the musket slung at my back.

The descent was terribly fatiguing. The way across the quicksands had been so level that we had walked, counting our paces mechanically, but now in every movement there was danger, and terror gripped my heart with a gauntlet of steel. From every pore there broke from me a cold perspiration, as from each tiny projection I lowered myself, not knowing whether my feet would find another resting-place. For my black companions, who were taller and more muscular, the way was not nearly so difficult, and Kona, aware of this, assisted me whenever possible.

Once, when I found myself progressing well, and apparently having successfully negotiated the more dangerous of these natural steps, I paused for a few moments to breathe, and, summoning courage, looked down to where the others were scrambling below. I was then amazed to discover that, notwithstanding all the fatigue, the distance I had covered was scarcely perceptible. I still seemed almost as far from the base of the rock as I was when first I had peered over into the abyss. Suddenly, without warning, I felt the rock give way beneath my feet, and the next instant the whole projection, loosened by the weight of Omar and his followers who had preceded me, fell away beneath me, and crashed straight down into the valley.

My presence of mind caused me just at that instant to grip the ledge above, otherwise I, too, must have gone with my unstable resting-place. It was indeed a narrow escape, and as clinging on with my hands, my legs again swinging in mid air, I heard the heavy rock, weighing perhaps a ton, strike a projection under me and then crash down, carrying all before it.

There was an appalling shriek from below, and I dreaded to turn my gaze downward, fearing that my companions had been swept away by the great mass of stone. At last, however, I looked in trepidation and was gratified to notice that the projection struck by the rock had been left by the man preceding me, and that the course of the descending stone had been altered so that all had escaped.

"Careful up there!" shouted Omar angrily. "Don't spring upon the steps, or they will become loosened like that one. It might have swept the whole lot of us into the valley if its course had not been turned. Lower yourselves slowly—very slowly—take plenty of time."

"I did it, Omar," I cried breathlessly. "It was an accident. I could not avoid it, and nearly fell, too."

But it was apparent that my voice did not reach him, for he slowly lowered himself over the next projection, and continued giving directions to the men who followed, while I, with the next ledge fallen away, was compelled to let myself drop a distance of about nine feet on to one that seemed far below.

From that point the descent became much easier, although during the two hours it occupied I stumbled and nearly lost my foothold many times. My feet and hands were covered with blood, my elbows were severely grazed, and from my knees the skin was torn by the constant scrambling over the edges of the ledges.

Truly the approach to the Land of the Great White Queen was fraught with a myriad dangers.

When about half-way down the steep rock another piercing shriek broke forth immediately below me, and glancing down I saw one of our black companions who had dropped from one ledge to the next lose his footing, stumble, and fall headlong into the great chasm. Cries of horror escaped us as we saw him strike a rugged ledge of rock far below, rebound, and then fall head foremost to the rock's base, his skull already battered to a pulp.

This terrible lesson was heeded by everyone, and for fully half an hour the silence was almost complete, save for the gasps and hard breathing of our followers as they toiled onward down the steep face of the gigantic rock.

Someone cried out that here, as across the quicksands, there were a thousand steps. If this were true, as I believe it was, then the average distance between the ledges being about five feet, the height of the rock was somewhere about five thousand feet. When progress at last became easier, I tried to attract Omar's attention, and inquire whether we should have to scale the rock opposite, but I could not project my voice far enough below to reach him. When he shouted I could hear, as his voice ascended, but he apparently could not distinguish what I said in reply.

Kona, his bow and empty quiver slung behind him, scrambled down after me ever nimble as a cat. His black skin shone like ebony, but here and there were cuts from which blood freely flowed, showing that he too, although inured to a savage life, had not altogether escaped in this struggle to enter the land unknown.

As we approached the base the ledges became more frequent, and hastening in my downward climb I at last experienced gratification at finding the peril past, and myself standing at the foot of the great precipice.

"Well?" asked Omar, approaching me quickly. "How did you fare?"

"Badly," I answered with a smile. "A dozen times I gave myself up for lost."

"Care and courage may accomplish everything," he said, laughing. "Few, however, would care to risk the perils of the Thousand Steps without a guide, or even if they did, and succeeded in accomplishing the journey to this point, they could not enter our land."

"Why?"

He turned towards the flat, bare face of overhanging rock opposite, and gazing up to its towering summit, answered:

"Because our land lies yonder. We must, after resting, ascend."

"How?" I inquired, noticing that the wall of the great cliff was perfectly smooth.

He smiled.

"Be patient, and you shall see. Only friends can enter Mo; an enemy never."

At that moment Kona desired to consult him regarding our camping arrangements, and turning I left them and wandered a little way along the valley. Presently, although its fertility was pleasant, I noticed that the air had a strange foetid odour, and, shortly afterwards, while walking in the long rank grass my feet struck against something, which, on examination, I found to be the decomposing body of a man. He wore a burnouse, and from the long-barrelled musket that lay by his side I concluded it was an Arab. As I went forward I discovered bodies scattered in twos and threes over the grass-plain. Great grey vultures were tearing the rotting flesh from the bones, feasting upon the carrion. Broken guns, bent swords and blunted daggers lay about in profusion, while the further I went, the more numerous became the hideous bodies which the long grass seemed to be striving to hide. This was assuredly the battle-field whereon the army of the Great White Queen had defeated the expedition sent by Samory. Truly the slaughter must have been appalling, and little wonder was it that the survivors whom we had met and annihilated should have fought so desperately for their lives.

Judging from the great pile of corpses, the stand made by Samory's Arabs must have been a dogged and stubborn one, for traces of a most desperate battle were everywhere apparent, yet their defeat must have been crushing and complete, for hundreds of the invaders had apparently been mowed down where they had stood. Others had fallen in hand-to-hand encounters, their limbs slashed and disabled by keener swords than their own, while many seemed literally riddled by bullets which could never have been fired by ordinary guns, or if so, at such close quarters that in nearly every case the balls had passed clean through their bodies.

The number of corpses lying in the grass were too numerous to count, but at a rough estimate there must have been several thousands. The air of that beautiful valley was suffocating on account of the stench they emitted, and the river was poisoned by the heaps of bodies that had been hurled into it.

This valley, that had appeared a veritable paradise from the summit of the rock, was in reality a Valley of Death.

So nauseating was the smell that Omar decided upon pitching the camp at a point lower down, for so exhausted were we all and so dark was it growing that it became imperative we should remain there for the night. So we bivouacked half a mile away from the spot where the Thousand Steps descended, our fire was lit, and after a little food had been served out, we threw ourselves upon the grass, and, worn out by fatigue, slept heavily and well.

The valley was filled with a thick mist that rose from the river, overspreading everything and saturating our scanty clothing with moisture, causing us to be chilly and uncomfortable. It was this fact, perhaps, that awakened me during the night, when all my companions lying around were snoring soundly, dreaming most probably, of their triumphant entry into the land of the great Naya. Becoming fully awake, I heard the swish of a footstep through the grass, and, raising my head, saw at a little distance from me Omar, standing alone. With his back turned to me he was gazing up at the summit of the rock we had yet to gain, bearing in his hand a fire-brand that had apparently been lit at the dying embers of our fire. The brand, blazing and crackling, threw his lithe figure into relief, and I saw that his face wore an eager, anxious look. His gaze seemed rivetted upon the highest pinnacle of the great rock, as if he had noticed some unusual aspect.

During several minutes he remained motionless, his eyes fixed in that direction. At first I was impelled to rise and join him, but not knowing why, I remained there motionless watching. Presently I heard a loud cry of joy escape his lips, and with frantic gesture he waved the fire-brand quickly from left to right, sometimes with a sharp motion, and at others slowly.

He was signalling to someone on the brow of the precipice!

Open-mouthed I watched the result. The glare of his torch prevented me from distinguishing the crest of the rock distinctly, yet as I looked in the direction he was gazing I presently saw far away on the summit, glittering like a brilliant star, a bright light that seemed in answer to Omar's signals to appear and disappear rapidly, evidently flashing back a reply from the mysterious realm above.

Suddenly the distant light became totally obscured, and from Omar's lips there fell an expression of disappointment. His own fire-brand was burning but dimly, therefore, rushing to the embers, he drew another from the fire, blew upon it violently until it flamed, and then recommenced the puzzling signals, the system of which seemed very similar to those used in the British Army.

Again and again he repeated the long and short waves of the flaming torch, but no answering light appeared. All was dark upon the towering summit, that loomed up black and lonely against the deep vault of dark, star-lit blue. His was a weird figure, standing in the centre of the circle of uncertain light shed by the flambeau, watching eagerly, and waving his signals with untiring energy.

"Fools!" he cried aloud to himself. "They are so fearful of treachery that they feign not to be able to distinguish the name of their ruler."

But ere the words had fallen from his lips the star-like light again shone forth white, with intense brilliancy, but in a different position. It seemed to have moved along the brink of the precipice, nearer to us, and its whiteness had been somehow intensified. In appearance it was very similar to an electric search-light, and so powerful were its rays that they streamed forth in a long line of brilliancy that slowly swept the valley where the corpses of the Arabs lay piled until it reached us, illuminating our camp with a light almost bright as day.

Several minutes elapsed, and Omar, standing in the centre of the light, casting a long grotesque shadow behind, continued waving the word he was so desirous of signalling. In the meantime those who were working the light had undoubtedly ascertained the extent of our numbers, for very soon the light slowly travelled over the adjoining rocks, and even searched the further end of the valley; then suddenly it shed upon us again, and instantly became obscured.

Nothing daunted, Omar continued his signals until at last they were evidently noticed and read, for suddenly the light streamed forth again and commenced a series of vivid flashes that lit up the valley like shafts of lightning.

Thus came the answer, for next second Omar, overjoyed, and unable to contain himself, again cried aloud:

"Seen! Hurrah! At last!"

The signals exchanged between those on the lofty summit of the insurmountable barrier, and my friend Omar were long, and, to me tedious. I could make nothing of them, although it was apparent that my old chum was carrying on an interesting conversation with some person unseen. Once again the light swept across the silent battle-field, showing, as if with justifiable pride, the wholesale slaughter that had been there committed by the defenders, and again fell full upon the son of the dreaded Naya. Then it flashed quickly many times and suddenly disappeared.

Omar seemed at last satisfied, for, holding the brand before him, he took from the tiny bag around his neck a pinch of the magic powder that was included in his jujus, and pronouncing words that conveyed some mystical meaning, slowly let the powder fall into the flickering flame, causing it to hiss and splutter.

He was sacrificing to the fetish for our deliverance from the perils of the Way of the Thousand Steps. Even as he stood performing this pagan rite, there sounded afar off a dull, low boom like the distant report of heavy cannon. It echoed weirdly along the valley where all was quiet and at rest, and was three times repeated, like some ominous voice of warning.

Omar heard it. Surely the noise was an unexpected one, for it instantly filled him with apprehension, and he listened attentively, little dreaming that I also was his companion upon this strange midnight vigil.

XVII

A Salute of Bullets

The low booming was, however, not repeated, and by this my companion apparently became reassured, for shortly afterwards he threw himself down near me to snatch a few hours' repose before dawn. I suppose I, too, must have slept for some time, until suddenly a noise like thunder that seemed to cause the earth to tremble awakened me, and together with the rest of our party I sprang to my feet, fancying that some terrible earthquake had occurred.

It was still dark, and as each asked breathlessly of his neighbour the cause of the deafening noise a sudden red flash showed for an instant on the summit of the rock near where I had seen the light, and a second report thundered forth, making the valley echo and startling the birds in thousands from their roosting-places.

"We are attacked!" the natives cried. "It is a gun!"

It was a gun undoubtedly. Again it belched forth, its fire causing the earth to tremble, sending some small shots unpleasantly close, and striking terror into the hearts of our companions, who started to fly for safety, expecting each moment that a shower of lead would sweep upon them.

"Stay, cowards!" Omar cried. "Yonder gun fires not with anger, but with joy. It is my welcome home; its fire is but powder play!"

Then a loud, joyous laugh arose, and the black faces broadened into great grins, displaying red lips and white teeth.

"Truly the land of the great Naya is a land of wonders!" cried Kona, in astonishment. "Here they welcome the queen's son by shooting at him. Surely those shots a moment ago were more than powder play!"

"A mistake no doubt," Omar answered laughing. "Already it is known in Mo that we are here in the Grave of Enemies, and the guns are being fired as welcome, while steps are being taken to convey us into yonder land."

"How shall we be conveyed thither?" the headman asked, looking up puzzled at the bare face of the rock, the summit of which was now obscured by a bank of cloud.

"Wait until sun-rise. Then you will see," answered my friend mysteriously, and as he spoke the blood-red flash showed again and the great gun thundered forth its salute.

While the dawn was spreading we ate our morning meal with eyes fixed upon the great high crag whence the gun belched forth with monotonous regularity; then Omar and I strolled away together further up the valley to occupy our time until the sun-rise. Here I saw for the first time that natural curiosity, the honey-bird. Omar pointed it out to me. It was a little grey common-looking bird about the size of a thrush. It first forced itself upon our notice by flying across our path, uttering a shrill, unlovely cry. It then sat on a neighbouring tree still calling and waiting for us to follow. By short rapid flights the bird led us on and on till we noticed that it stopped its onward course and was hanging about among a certain half-dozen trees. These we visited one after another and carefully examined them, our search being rewarded by finding a nest of bees in each of them. It is a matter of honour with the natives to set aside a good portion of the honey for the bird. Although this action of the honey-bird is an established fact in natural history, it would be interesting to know whether he ever tries to entice quadrupeds also in assisting him in obtaining his much-loved honey.

As we walked back to the camp the sun suddenly broke forth, the clouds rolled away, and on looking up at the point where the guns had been fired we saw on the summit a number of moving figures, looking like black specks against the morning sky. Everyone stood watching the far-off inhabitants of the mysterious realm, wondering how we were to gain the high overhanging rock that descended sheer to where we stood. Presently the excitement reached fever-heat when we saw the small black figures grouping themselves into a mass, and then we noticed that one man was being slowly lowered by a rope over the precipice. The rope was apparently passed under his arms, and as he swung out into mid-air his companions began to let him down rapidly to where we stood. Owing to the overhanging nature of the rock the wind caused the man to swing backwards and forwards as a pendulum, and by reason of hitches that seemed to occur in the arrangements above he was several times stopped in his descent.

At last, however, his feet touched the ground and headed by Omar, we all rushed towards him. He was a very tall, loosely-built man, his complexion almost white with just a yellowish tinge, colourless lips, colourless drab hair; vague irregular features, with an entire absence of expression. He wore an Arab haick upon his head bound with many yards of brown camel's hair, a long white garment, something like a burnouse, only embroidered at the edge with crimson thread and confined at the waist by a girdle containing quite a small arsenal of weapons, while at his back he carried a rifle of European manufacture, and around his neck was the invariable string of amulets.

"I seek Omar, son of the Naya, the Great Queen," he cried with a loud voice, as his feet touched the grass and he disengaged himself from the swaying rope, which still continued to descend.

"I am Omar, Prince of Mo," answered my friend, stepping forward quickly.

The messenger from the mysterious realm above regarded him keenly from head to foot, not without suspicion. Then looking him straight in the face, he said with a puzzled expression upon his countenance:

"Thou hast altered since thou hast dwelt among the English. Thy face is not that of Omar who left many moons ago with our Naya's trusted servant Makhana."

"Yet I am still Omar," he exclaimed, laughing. "Thy caution is commendable, Babila, son of Safad, but as the moon groweth old so does the boy turn youth, and the youth man."

"Thou knowest my name, 'tis true," observed the messenger gravely. "But where are thy royal jujus; those placed upon thy neck by the great Naya in the presence of the people?"

"I fell among enemies who burned them."

"The curse of Zomara be upon them," Babila said. "Who were they?"

"The hirelings of our enemy, Samory."

"Then some have already met with their deserts, for three thousand of them lie here in this valley," and he pointed to the gruesome corpses scattered upon the grass. "But hast thou no possession to assure me that thou art actually the long-absent son of our Naya?" he inquired.

"Thou carriest thy caution a little too far in this affair, Babila," Omar answered smiling. "True, I have lost my jujus, nevertheless I can answer thee what questions thou puttest to me regarding my youth and my life in Mo. I know that thou art determined to satisfy thyself that I am actually the Prince, ere thou admittest us to our kingdom."

"The caution I exercise is my duty to the great Naya and my country," Babila answered. "No invader nor intruder hath ever entered Mo, and none shall while I am chief custodian of its Gate. The bones of many adventurers lie here in this valley."

"Yes, I know that well," Omar answered good-humouredly. "But what must I do to satisfy thee?" Then turning to me, he exclaimed in English, "This is amusing, Scars. I am actually prevented from entering my own country because I have grown a trifle taller!"

"What sayest thou in a foreign tongue?" Babila inquired, with a quick look of suspicion.

"I commented upon the absurdity of my situation to my companion, Scarsmere, who has accompanied me from England," Omar answered frankly.

"Scarsmere," repeated the man from the unknown region. "Scarsmere. And is he your friend?"

"Yea, my best friend."

"If thou art actually Omar then his friend will assuredly find welcome in Mo," the man said with courtesy. "But answer the questions I put to thee. Canst thou tell me anything regarding myself?"

"Well, I think I can," answered my friend with a laugh. "When I was quite a young lad thou wert one of the guardians of the outer gate of our palace. Once I was threatened by a ruffianly soldier as I passed, and thou didst strike him dead with one blow of thy sword. For thy prompt punishment of the fellow thou wert exalted by the Naya and given command over her body-guard. It was because thou didst unearth the dastardly conspiracy against her life that thou wert given the custodianship of the Gate of Mo."

"True," the man answered with a smile of satisfaction. "In one of my age loss of memory is excusable, yet now on looking closely at thee, I see the resemblance—yea, I welcome thee home, my lord the prince."

In an instant his manner had changed, and he became the most obedient of slaves.

"Very well," Omar said. "Now thou art satisfied that I am what I said we will lose no time in passing the last barrier."

"But these?" Babila inquired, glancing suspiciously at the black rabble forming our Dagomba following.

"They are my escort," Omar answered. "Every man, from Kona, the head-man, to the meanest slave, is my trusted servant, and they all deserve reward. Each shall enter Mo and receive it at the hands of the Naya herself. This I have already promised."

"The servants of the lord prince are welcome. The people shall *fête* them, and make their days pass as quickly as seconds fly. If thou art desirous they shall enter and be presented to the great Naya before whose eyes all men quail," Babila said, bowing humbly before his royal master.

"Then let us not pause. We desire to enter Mo without an instant's further delay. The way has been long and the obstacles great, but we have successfully accomplished all, and seek now to enter the palace of my queen-mother."

"Thy commands shall be obeyed," the man replied, again salaaming, and, walking to the rope, he placed the loops under his arm-pits, and a few minutes later was on his way back to the mysterious land, waving his hand to us and promising that ere an hour passed we should enter the realm of the Great White Queen.

With eager upturned faces we watched the cautious custodian of the mystic kingdom dangling at the end of the rope, gradually leaving us, until at length he was hauled up upon the far-off summit of the rock and disappeared among the small crowd collected at the brow. The men were evidently soldiers, and the eager manner in which they grouped themselves about Babila when he stepped into their midst, showed what intense excitement our arrival had caused.

As we watched we soon afterwards saw lowered from the towering height what appeared at first to be a thin black cord, but which, when the end fell at our feet, we found to be a ladder of curiously-knotted ropes about as thick as packing twine, so flimsy in construction that it seemed as though the weight of a single man would break it.

"Are we to climb to the top?" I asked Omar, who passed me by quickly in order to examine the ladder.

"Of course," he said.

"But surely these ropes will not bear our weight!" I observed. "They are only like string."

"Yes, but the core of each is of steel wire of such strength that it would bear our whole party all together," he answered. "Nevertheless, it is perhaps best to avoid running risks, so only a dozen shall ascend at a time."

I looked up at the swaying ladder with distrust. I had heard many stories of ropes chafing on the edges of rocks and being cut through, and my awful experience in descending the face of the precipice opposite had been sufficiently terrifying.

"The land of the Great White Queen is, indeed, unapproachable," I said. "Surely no enemy could invade you?"

"We fear no outside enemy," Omar answered with sudden seriousness. "It is internal dissensions that may cause trouble. Every precaution is taken here, at the gate of our land, to prevent an enemy from gaining

WILLIAM LE QUEUX

Mo. The valley is commanded by guns in such a manner that it can be swept from end to end, so that even if a foe were to succeed in treading the Way of the Thousand Steps he must descend here and remain under the fire of the guns."

"I noticed that last night you signalled with a torch," I said.

"Ah! you were awake and did not speak," he laughed. "Yes, I flashed my name, with a message to the Naya. This was conveyed to her by a system of signals flashed from one point to another across the country in similar manner to those of European armies. At night the signals are constantly at work and take the place of your telegraphs. When the message reached the Naya she sent me a word in return, but even then Babila was far too cautious to afford us means to enter the country without first inspecting us himself."

"You've grown a bit, and become more Anglicized since you left," I said, smiling.

"Yes, possibly," he answered, adding, "I was, however, going to explain that so elaborate are the precautions against invasion that even now the ladder has been lowered, nay, even if we were at the top, the custodians of the Gate could, by simply pressing a button, send a current of electricity through the wires that form the cores of the ropes of such a strength, that the ropes and ourselves would almost instantly be fused into a shapeless mass. See! the ropes are wet, so that the full strength of the current could, if desired, be turned upon us." And he pulled forward the ladder and placed it in my hand.

Instinctively I shrank away, saying:

"I have no desire to be electrocuted just yet."

"Well, it's merely one of the many devices we have here for the warm reception of any enemy," he answered. "The number of bodies yonder are sufficient proof that any expedition against us must be ill-fated."

But just at that moment a rapid signal was flashed by the sun's rays upon a mirror, and reading it, he exclaimed in English:

"All is fast above. Come, Scars, old chap, follow me and let me hear your opinion of my country. Keep your chin raised and don't look down, or you may turn giddy."

Then, giving directions to Kona to allow only twelve men to swarm the flimsy ladder at one time, he placed his foot upon the first rung and commenced the long straight ascent.

As soon as he had climbed a dozen feet I glanced up at the towering crag, then followed his example.

XVIII

THE MYSTERIOUS REALM

So unsteady was the ladder, straining and springing at every step I took, that I was compelled to grip its wet cords with all the strength of which I was capable. It swayed to and fro fearfully, and more than once I dreaded that I should lose my hold and fall backwards to earth.

Omar above me, lithe and active as a cat, climbed on, chaffing me for my tardy progress, and now and then halting and mischievously shaking the ladder to increase my fear. The higher I ascended the more strongly blew the wind, until it whistled in the thin ropes and blew through my scanty clothing, chilling my bones. My hands and feet were bruised and sore from the previous day's descent, nevertheless I thought not of pain, only of peril. The climb was long and tedious. Even Omar, who had commenced by running up like a squirrel in his eagerness to gain the land from which he had so long been absent, was soon compelled to pause and steady himself, or he would assuredly have been jerked from his insecure position.

The ten men plodding up after us seemed to be keeping step, causing the ladder to spring fearfully each time they ascended the next rung. Omar, himself fearing disaster, at last called to them, but jabbering among themselves in the highest spirits, each eager to set foot in the land of mystery, they took no heed of their guide's instructions.

"You fools!" he cried angrily. "Climb slowly and with care. Don't jump so. We're not on a spring-board."

Useless. We still went up and down like a ball at the end of a piece of elastic.

"Do you hear?" he shrieked in the Dagomba tongue, halting and looking down at the string of grinning blacks. "Halt!"

This sudden stoppage attracted their attention, and in mid-air he soundly rated them for their folly, instructing them how to ascend, and declaring that if they continued their hilarious progress a fearful disaster must ensue. These words immediately had the desired effect, for which I confess I was very thankful, as I had feared every moment that we should be dashed into the valley, and now as we went forward again the ladder was much steadier.

From far below we could hear the distant shouts of Kona and our excited companions encouraging us and urging us on, for they were all impatience to follow us. Now and then the great grey vultures, having gorged themselves to their full upon the corpses in the valley, circled around us as if ready to tear us from our perilous position, and more than once I saw Omar raise his arm to beat them off. We were, I suppose, passing near their nests and thus aroused their ire.

Looking up, I saw that we were slowly approaching the beetling portion of the enormous rock, but had yet a long distance to climb. Steadily, however, we all ascended, each grasping the wet slippery cords tightly to prevent being blown off by the high gusty wind, and even when we gained the jutting rock believing we had attained the summit, we found ourselves still fully two hundred feet from where Babila could be seen peering over awaiting us.

The ladder laying upon the face of the cliff at this point was much easier of ascent, for the weight of the portion below me prevented it from swaying, and by scrambling up with increased haste I soon found myself immediately behind Omar.

Then continuing steadily, now and then being compelled to bend backwards in a most perilous position in order to negotiate a projecting piece of rock, we together climbed up to the edge of the fearful precipice, each being lent a willing hand by Babila as we swarmed upon our knees to where he stood.

"Welcome, O Prince," the old man exclaimed, salaaming when Omar stood before him. "Welcome to thy white friend from beyond the great black water."

In an instant from a thousand throats rose cries of adulation, and looking around I saw that drawn up before us was a great concourse of fighting-men. Some were mounted on magnificent chargers, others were on foot, and among them were many silken banners each bearing the same device, a black vampire bat with wings outspread upon a crimson ground. Each soldier was similarly attired to Babila, with white embroidered robe and girdle, and each carried a rifle and a long curved sword.

Babila was evidently a great man in the estimation of all others, for whatever he did the soldiers imitated. In appearance they had the advantage of all coloured and most white races. As a rule they seemed very tall, well set up, with well-formed limbs covered with an almost white skin, the texture of which would excite envy in the heart of many a European beauty. The features had nothing in common with the coarse negro type which prevailed in the forest and over the grasslands, but rather inclined towards a Semitic type. Thick lips were the exception, not the rule, and a broad flat nose was also a rarity. The only sign of barbarity was in the hair which, when the head was not clean shaven, was allowed to grow straight out in every direction, giving a very wild appearance to its owner. The hair of some, however, seemed to be softer, for it hung down to the nape of the neck in long, closely-curled ringlets. The women, a few of whom were watching us curiously, were all comely, and, attired in long white robes of a more elaborate pattern than the men, had their hair enclosed in a dark blue fillet, a difference in the disposition of the latter distinguishing between a married and an unmarried woman.

A great tent of yellow silk had been erected near, presumably for our accommodation. Over it waved the hideous-looking vampire bat, and as led by Babila with frequent prostrations we entered it, I asked Omar the meaning of the sable device.

"It is the royal mark of the Sanoms, the same as the lion and the unicorn is the crest of your great Queen. The black vampire is the guardian fetish of our throne."

On entering, Omar walked to a raised daïs whereon two stools were placed, and taking one invited me to the other. Then, while awaiting the arrival of our companions, food was brought to us, and we ate and drank to our full, Babila himself attending to our wants personally. Neither were our companions forgotten, for they were arranged around the tent, and squatting upon their haunches ate and jabbered to their hearts' content.

It was highly amusing to watch the interest with which the natives regarded the stolid soldiers of Mo, who stood in long lines, motionless as statues. They went close up to them, examined them from head to foot, drew the sword from its sheath, handled it and tried its edge with a grunt of satisfaction. Then they would replace it, finger the accoutrements, examine carefully what they thought might be gold, and at last, folding their arms, would stand silent, awe-stricken at the whole effect of the unknown race.

The denizens of this mysterious country, however, seemed to regard our natives with supercilious disdain. Probably their contempt had been engendered by the fact that certain tribes had on several occasions attempted an invasion, and they had from their formidable heights simply swept them out of existence as easily as a fly may be crushed with the finger. When looking at the handsome women, the enormous mouths of the Dagombas would widen into broad grins which, intended to convey an expression of delight, in reality rendered them hideous.

For three hours we remained in the tent, sheltered from the sun's glaring heat, while parties of a dozen of our followers continued to arrive. It was Omar's intention to enter the capital with the whole of our faithful band, otherwise he would have started immediately we had gained the summit. Babila urged him to do so, but he expressed a desire that Kona and his heroic blacks should accompany us.

At last the whole of the party had gained the top of the rock and had refreshed themselves after their toil and peril; the rope ladder with its hidden electric wires had been hauled up, and, headed by men blowing loud blasts upon great horns of ivory and gold, we all moved forward, a most imposing and magnificent cavalcade.

Both Omar and myself had been mounted on fine milk-white horses with gay trappings of silver and royal blue, while behind us came Kona with a very unsteady seat upon a long raw-boned stallion. He was evidently not used to horses, and the way he clutched at the mane each time his animal trotted convulsed both his men and the soldiers in the vicinity with laughter.

A shady march of two days in a north-westerly direction up the bank of a babbling stream brought us to higher land. The journey was uneventful, the country being devoid of both game and people. We saw old traces of habitation, it is true, but the people seemed to have been driven away or killed, leaving only the empty stone-built houses. From the hill on the side of which we pitched our camp a marvellous view was obtainable. To the north a black forest extended as far as the eye could reach, broken only by three small hills that served as landmarks. To the west rolled some giant snow-capped mountains, while the range whereon we stood was a low, stone-covered stretch of round-topped hills, flanked by thick mimosa jungle and filled with rhinoceros. Wherever we went, we found traces of them, their feeding ground being apparently restricted to a very small area. Never having been hunted, they probably found no reason to leave such excellent pasture, and it was little wonder that Kona and his men were anxious to remain behind and commit havoc amongst them.

On the third day we encamped near a most extraordinary place. It was a small valley about thirty-five feet below the surrounding ground, looking like the dry bed of a stream, and was about a mile in circumference.

"Come, I want to show you Zomara's Wrath," Omar said, and dismounting we went together towards it, notwithstanding the loud cries of warning that arose on every side. A dog—a lean, hungry, strange-looking brute, who accompanied the troops—bounded after us, and as we approached the place I noticed a suffocating smell, and was attacked by nausea and giddiness. A belt of this foetid atmosphere surrounded the valley. We, however, passed through it, and in purer air, with hands still over my nose and mouth, was permitted to view the awful spectacle—for it was awful.

The entire bed of the valley seemed like one solid rock, but scattered over the barren floor were skeletons of men, wild hogs, deer, rhinoceros, lions, and all kinds of birds and smaller animals. I could discover no hole or crevice in any place whence the poisonous fumes were emitted. I was anxious to reach the bottom of the valley, if possible, but my suggestion was at once negatived by my companion, who said:

"To go further is certain death. Come, let us return quickly, or we may be overpowered. This is one of the natural wonders of our land."

I determined, however, to see what the fumes smelled like, and, greatly to Omar's horror, started to descend. The dog was with me, and as soon as he saw me step over the side of the bank he rushed down ahead of me.

I endeavoured to call him back, but too late. As soon as the animal reached the rocky bed below he fell upon his side.

He continued to breathe a few moments only, then expired.

XIX

The City in the Clouds

"There is a strange story connected with this place known to us as Zomara's Wrath," Omar said, when together we turned away and mounted our horses to ride back to the camp.

"Relate it to me," I urged eagerly.

"To-night. After we have eaten at sundown I will tell you about it," he answered, and spurring our horses we galloped quickly forward.

When we had eaten that evening and were seated aside together, I reminded him of his promise.

"It is a story of my ancestors, and it occurred more than a thousand years ago," he said. "Ruler of the great kingdom of Mo, King Lobenba had no children. The three queens observed fasts, kept vows, made offerings to the fetish, all to no effect. By a lucky chance a great hermit made his appearance in our capital. The King and queens received the visitor at the palace, and treated him with the most generous and sincere hospitality. The guest was very pleased; by a prompting of the fetish he knew what they wanted, and gave them three peppercorns, one for each queen. In due time three sons were born, Karmos, Matrugna, and Fausalya, who when they reached a suitable age married by the ceremony of 'choice,' daughters of a branch of the royal family. When the brides arrived at their husbands' family and were disciplined in their wifely duties, King Lobenba, who was growing old, thought the time had arrived for him to make over the royal burden to younger shoulders, and to adopt a hermit's life preliminary to death. So in consultation with the royal fetish-man, a day was appointed for the coronation of Prince Karmos, who had married a beautiful girl named Naya. But the fates had willed it otherwise. Long before the children were born, when King Lobenba, in his younger days, was subduing a revolt in this region where we now are he once fell from his chariot while aiming an arrow, and got his arm crushed under the wheel. The three queens had accompanied their royal husband to the battlefield to soften for him the hardships of his camp life, and during the long illness that followed the wound, Queen Zulnam, who afterwards became mother of Fausalya, nursed him with all the devotion of a wife's first young love.

'Ask me anything and thou shalt have it,' said the monarch during his convalescence. 'I have to ask only two favours, my lord,' she answered. 'I grant them beforehand. Name them,' he cried. But she said she wished for nothing at that time, but would make her request in due course. She waited twenty years. Then she repaired to her husband on the morning of Karmos' coronation and boldly requested that the prince should absent himself for fourteen years, and that her son Fausalya should be crowned instead."

"She was artful," I observed, laughing.

"Yes," he went on. "The words fell like a thunder-bolt upon the king, the light faded from his eyes and he fainted. Nevertheless, Zulnam's wish was granted, and Karmos' departure was heartrending. To soften the austerities of forest life, Prince Matrugna tore himself from his newly-married bride to accompany Karmos. But the hardest was to be the latter's wrench from his devoted Naya. The change from a most exuberant girlish gaiety to quivering grief, and the offer of the delicately-nurtured wife to share with her lord the severities of an exile's life are often told by every wise man in Mo. Fourteen long years Karmos spent in exile with his beautiful wife as companion, until at last they were free to return. The home-coming was one long triumph. The people were mad with delight to welcome their hero Karmos and their beloved Naya. Karmos was crowned, and then began that government whose morality and justice and love and purity have passed into the proverbs of my race. There was, however, one blemish upon it. Poor Naya's evil genius had not yet exhausted his malevolence. A rumour was spread by evil tongues that she was plotting to possess the crown, and Karmos, sacrificing the husband's love, the father's joy, to his kingly duty, while standing on that spot we have visited to-day—then his summer palace surrounded by lovely gardens—pronounced sentence of exile upon her. But in an instant, swift as the lightning from above, the terrible curse of Zomara fell upon him, striking him dead, his magnificent palace was swept away and swallowed up by a mighty earthquake, and from the barren hole, once the fairest spot in the land, there have ever since belched forth fumes that poison every living thing. It is Zomara's Wrath."

"And what became of Naya, the queen?" I asked, struck with the remarkable story that seemed more than a mere legend.

"She reigned in his stead," he answered. "Whenever we speak of the Nayas we sum up all that is noble and mighty and queenly in government, its tact, its talent, its love and its beneficence, for every queen who has since sat on the Great Emerald Throne of Mo has been named after her, and I am her lineal descendant, the last of her line."

That night we rested on soft cushions spread for us in our tent, and marching again early next morning, spent the two following days in crossing a great swamp, which, rather than a miasmatic death-hole, was a naturalist's paradise. As our horses trod the soft, spongy ground, a majestic canopy of stately cypress, mangrove and maple trees protected us from the burning sun, and the sweet-scented flowers of the magnolias, azaleas and wild grapes added fragrance and beauty to the scene. Flies, snakes and frogs were very numerous, but gave us little trouble, nevertheless, I was not sorry when at dawn on the third day after passing the strange natural phenomenon we saw across the level pasture-like plain, high up, spectral and half hidden in the grey haze, the gigantic walls and high embattlements of the mysterious city.

"Lo!" cried Omar, who was riding at my side. "See! At last we are within sight of the goal towards which we have so long striven. Yonder is Mo, sometimes called the City in the Clouds!"

"But for your courage we must have failed long ago," I observed, my eyes turned to where the horizon closed the long perspective of the sky. Away there was the sweetest light. Elsewhere colour marred the simplicity of light; but there colour was effaced, not as men efface it, by a blur or darkness, but by mere light. And against it rose, high and faintly outlined, the defences of the great unknown city standing on the summit of what appeared to be a gigantic rock. "Magnificent!" I exclaimed, entranced by the view. "Superb!"

"It is, as you see, built high upon the rock known as the Throne of the Naya," Omar explained. "Although founded a thousand years ago by the good queen about whom I told you, no stranger has ever yet set foot within its gates. From time to time our monarchs have sent their trusty agents among civilized nations, gathered from them their inventions, and introduced to us the results of their progress. Isolated as we are from the world, we are nevertheless enlightened, as you will shortly see."

I was prompted to make some observation regarding his paganism, but held my peace, knowing that any reference to it wounded his susceptibilities. In everything except his belief in the fetish and his trust in the justice of the Crocodile-god, he was my equal; and I knew that, on more than one occasion, he had been ashamed to practise his savage rites in my presence. Therefore I hesitated, and, as we rode along, the outline of the great city, perched high upon the rock, growing every moment more formidable and distinct, I listened to the many interesting facts he related.

Kona, who followed us, listened with strained ears, and our Dagombas were one and all laughing and keeping up a Babel-like chatter that showed the intense excitement caused among them by the sight of the mysterious capital of the Great White Queen.

We had struck a broad well-made road, and now, as with hastening steps we approached it, we could distinguish quite plainly the inaccessible character of the high rock that rose abruptly a thousand feet above the plain crowned by the frowning walls of immense thickness that enclosed the place. Beyond, rose many lofty towers and several gilded domes which, Omar told me, were the audience-halls of the great palace, and immediately before us we could see in the walls, flanked on either side by great strong watch-towers, a closed gate.

From where we stood we could distinguish no means of approach to the impregnable fortress, but on coming at last to the base of the rock we found a long flight of narrow steps mounting zig-zag up its dark, moss-grown face. When the cavalcade halted before them our trumpeters blew thrice shrill blasts upon their big ivory horns, and like magic the ponderous iron gate far above instantly swung open, and the walls literally swarmed with men, whose bright arms glittered in the sun. Above, where all had been silent a moment before, everything was now bustle and excitement as Babila sprang from his horse and commenced to mount the long flight of steps, followed by myself and my companion.

So steep were these stairs cut in the rock that an iron chain had been placed beside them by which to steady one's-self.

"Are there again a thousand steps?" I asked Omar.

"Yes," he said. "Naya, wife of Karmos, had them cut under her personal supervision. There are exactly a thousand—the number of generations which, she declared, should flourish and die ere Mo be conquered."

Then without further words we eagerly continued our upward climb to the mystic City in the Clouds.

XX

THE GREAT WHITE QUEEN

Gaining the summit and entering the ponderous gate closely behind old Babila, I was amazed at the bewildering aspect of the gigantic city. As Omar placed his foot upon the top step, great drums, ornamented by golden bats with outspread wings, were thumped by a perspiring line of drummers, horns were blown with ear-piercing vehemence, and the huge guns mounted on the walls thundered forth a deafening salute.

Then, as we walked forward along the way kept clear for us through the enormous crowd of curious citizens, Babila at last met the tall, patriarchal-looking man in command of the city-gate.

"Lo!" he cried. "With our Prince Omar there returneth a retinue of strangers. This one," indicating myself, "is from the land of the white men that lieth beyond the great black water. The others are from the borders of Prempeh's kingdom."

"Art thou certain there are no spies among them?" asked the man, glancing at me keenly in suspicion.

"I, Omar, Prince of Mo, vouch for each man's honesty," exclaimed my friend, interrupting. At these words the chief guardian of the gate bowed until his long white beard swept the ground, and we passed on, followed by Kona and our black companions, in whom the denizens of the mysterious place seemed highly interested, never before having seen negro savages.

Now and then as we passed along voices raised in dissension that strangers should be admitted to the inaccessible kingdom reached our ears, but these were drowned by the wild plaudits of the crowd. On every hand Omar was greeted with an enthusiasm befitting the heir to the Emerald Throne, and he, in response, bowed his head from side to side, as with royal gait he strode down the broad handsome thoroughfare. The buildings on either hand were magnificent in their proportions, built of enormous blocks of grey stone finely sculptured, with square ornamented windows. Apparently the manufacture of glass was unknown, for all the windows were uniformly latticed. Here and there through the open doors we caught sight of cool courtyards, with trees and plashing fountains beyond, while from the flat roofs that here seemed to be the principal promenade of the ladies, as in Eastern lands, white hands and bejewelled arms waved us dainty welcome.

Across a great market square, where slaves were being bought and sold, and business was proceeding uninterruptedly, we passed, and as we glanced at the unfortunate ones huddled up in the scanty shadow, we remembered the day when we, too, had been sold by our bitter and well-hated enemy, Samory. I smiled as I reflected what terrible revenge this great army of the Naya could wreak upon the Arab chief, and found myself anticipating the day when the soldiery of Mo should gather before the old villain's stronghold.

Kona, who had come up beside me, walked on in silent amazement. He knew nothing of civilization, and the sights he now witnessed held him dumb. The African mind is slow to understand the benefits of civilization and modern progress, unless it be the substitution of guns for bows and bullets for arrows. At last we turned a corner suddenly, and saw before us, rising against the intensely blue sky and flashing in the brilliant sunlight, the three great gilded domes of the royal palace.

"Gold!" cried Kona, in an awed tone. "See!" and he turned to several of his sable brethren. "See! they build their great huts of solid gold! What treasure they must have!"

As we advanced in imposing procession, the great gate of this royal residence, grim and frowning as a fortress, over which a large flag was floating, bearing the sign of the vampire bat, opened wide, and, unchallenged by the crowds of gaily-dressed soldiers drawn up in line and saluting, we went forward amid vociferous cheering.

Ours was indeed a progress full of triumph and enthusiasm. The heir to the throne, long since mourned for as lost, had returned, and the loyal people were filled with great rejoicing. Through one spacious courtyard after another we passed, always between long lines of stalwart men-at-arms, bearing good English rifles and well-made accoutrements, until, ascending a short flight of wide steps of polished black stone, we found ourselves in a great hall beneath one of the gilded domes that had so impressed our head-man. Before us was a huge curtain of purple velvet that screened from view the further end of the hall, but when all had assembled and stood grouped together, this drapery was suddenly lifted, disclosing to our gaze a sight that filled us with greatest wonder and amazement.

The central object was the historic Emerald Throne, a wonderful golden seat so thickly encrusted with beautiful green gems as to appear entirely constructed of them. Some of the stones were of enormous size, beautifully cut, of amazing brilliance and fabulous value. Above, was suspended a golden representation of a crocodile—the god Zomara. Lolling lazily among the pink silk cushions was a woman, tall, thin-faced and ascetic, with a complexion white as my own, high cheek bones, small black, brilliant eyes, and hair plentifully tinged with grey. Her personality was altogether a striking one, for her brow was low, her face hawk-like, and her long, bony hands resting on the arms of the seat of royalty seemed like the talons of the bird to which her face bore resemblance.

It was the Naya, the dreaded Great White Queen!

Her robes of rich brocaded silk were of a brilliant golden yellow, heavily embroidered with gold thread, and thickly studded with various jewels. In the bright flood of sunlight that struck full upon her from the painted dome above, the diamonds and rubies enriching her handsome corsage gleamed and flashed white, green and blood-red. Indeed, so covered was her breast by the fiery gems that as it heaved and fell their flashing dazzled us; yet in her eyes was a cruel, crafty gleam that from the first moment I saw her roused instinctively within me fear and suspicion.

No smile of welcome crossed her cold, implacable features as her gaze met that of her son Omar; no enthusiastic or maternal greeting passed her lips. Her maids of honour and courtiers grouped about her murmured approbation and welcome as the heavy curtains fell aside, but frowning slightly she raised her bejewelled claw-like hand impatiently with a gesture commanding silence, darting hasty glances of displeasure upon those who had, by applauding, lowered her regal dignity. On either side black female slaves in garments of crimson silk and wearing golden girdles, massive earrings and neck chains, slowly fanned the ruler of Mo with large circular fans of ostrich feathers, and from a pedestal near her a tiny fountain of some fragrant perfume shot up and fell with faint plashing into its basin of marvellously-cut crystal. The splendour was barbaric yet refined, illustrative everywhere of the tastes of these denizens of the unknown kingdom. The walls of the great hall were strangely sculptured with colossal monstrosities, mostly hideous designs, apparently intended to depict the awful wrath of the deity Zomara, while here and there were curious frescoes of almost photographic finish, the execution of which had been accomplished by some art quite unknown to European civilization. The paving whereon we stood was of jasper, highly polished, with here and there strange outlines inlaid with gold. These outlines, a little crude and unfinished, were mostly illustrative of the power of the Nayas, depicting scenes of battle, justice and execution.

"Let our son Omar stand forth and approach our Emerald Throne," exclaimed the Naya at last, in a thin, rasping voice, moving slightly as she bent forward, fixing her shining eyes upon us. They glittered with evil.

At the royal command all bowed low in submission, it being etiquette to do this whenever the Naya expressed command or wish, and Omar, leaving my side, strode forward with becoming hauteur, and, crossing the floor as highly polished as glass, advanced to his royal mother, and, bending upon his knee, pressed her thin, bony hand to his lips.

But even then no expression of pleasure crossed her stony features. I had expected to witness an affectionate meeting between mother and son, and was extremely surprised at the coldness of my friend's reception, having regard to his long absence and the many perils we had together faced on our entry into Mo.

"News was flashed unto me last night that thou hadst crossed the Thousand Steps," the Queen said, slowly withdrawing her bony hand. "Why hast thou returned from the land of the white men, and why, pray, hast thou brought hither strangers with thee?"

"These strangers are heroes, each one of them," Omar answered, rising, and standing before the throne. "Every man has already fought for thee, and for Mo."

"For me? How?"

Then briefly he related how we had met the remnant of Samory's invading force and defeated them, so that not a single fugitive remained.

"These savages fought merely for their own lives, not for me," she said with a supercilious sneer, regarding the half-clad natives with disdain. "We in Mo desire not the introduction of such creatures as these."

"Are not my friends welcome?" Omar asked, pale with anger. "A Sanom hath never yet turned from his palace those who have proved themselves his friends."

"Neither hath a Sanom sought the aid of savages," answered the Great White Queen, with a glance of withering scorn.

"Adversity sometimes causeth us to seek strange alliances," my friend argued. "These men of the Dagomba, Kona, their head man, and Scarsmere, my friend from the land of the white men, have given me aid, and if thou accordest them no welcome, then I, Omar, in the name of my ancestors, the Nabas and the Nayas, will give them greeting, and provide them with befitting entertainment while they are within our walls."

His words caused instant consternation. The will of the Naya was not to be thwarted. Her every wish was law; a single word from her meant life or death. This openly-expressed opposition was, to the court, a most terrible offence, punishable by death to all others save the heir.

The Naya, her thin lips tightly set and cruelty lurking in the corners of her mouth, rose slowly with an air of terrible anger.

"Does our son Omar thus defy us?" she asked with grim harshness.

"I defy thee not O queen-mother," answered my friend, clasping his hands resolutely behind his back, and standing with his legs slightly apart. "I bring unto thee those who have fought for me, and have been my companions through many perils, expecting welcome. Were it not for them I, the last of our regal line, would be no longer living, and at thy death our kingdom would have been without a ruler."

"Son, the claim of these, thy friends, to my protection is admitted; nevertheless, the stranger, whoever he may be, is by the law of our kingdom that hath been rigorously observed for a thousand years, debarred from traversing the Thousand Steps."

As the queen spoke I noticed two gorgeously-attired men behind her, probably her chief advisers, exchange whispers with smiles of evident satisfaction.

"Then I am to understand that the Naya of Mo absolutely refuseth to sanction these my friends to dwell within our walls?" Omar said.

"We forbid these strangers to remain," answered the Queen, crimsoning with anger that her son should have thus argued with her. "They are granted until noon to-morrow to quit our city. Those found within our land after three suns have set will be held as slaves. I, the Naya, have spoken."

"As thou willest it, so it will be," answered her son, bowing very stiffly. Then, turning to us, he said:

"Friends, the people give you cordial welcome, even though the Naya may refuse to grant you peace. You shall remain—"

"Thou insultest us publicly," cried the Great White Queen, still standing erect, her black eyes flashing beneath the wisp of scanty grey hair, and her talon-like hand uplifted. "To utter such words hast thou returned from the land beyond the black seas? True, thou art my son, and some day will sit upon this my stool, but for thus opposing my will thou shalt be banished from Mo until such time as I am carried to the tombs of my fathers. Then, when thou returnest hither, thy reign shall be one of tumults and evil-doing. The people who now shout themselves hoarse because their idol Omar hath returned to them, shall, in that day, curse thee, and heap upon thee every indignity. May the Great Darkness encompass thee, may thine enemies break and crush thee, and may Zomara, the One of Power, smite and devour thee," and as she uttered these words she held up her long skinny arms to the hideous golden crocodile suspended over her, muttering some mystic sentences the while.

Her slaves and courtiers held their breath. The Great White Queen was cursing her only son. The Dagombas understood this action and stood aghast, while across the faces of the court dignitaries a few moments later there flitted faint sickly smiles. The scene was impressive, more so perhaps than any I had before witnessed. In her sudden ebullition of anger the Naya was indeed terrible.

From her thin blue lips curses most fearful rolled until even her courtiers shuddered. As she stood, her bony arms uplifted to the image of what was to her the greatest and most dreaded power on earth, she screamed herself hoarse, uttering imprecations until about her mouth there hung a blood-flecked foam, and her long finger-nails were driven deep into the flesh of her withered palms. All quaked visibly at her wrath, for none knew who might next offend her and pay the penalty for so doing with their lives: none knew who might next fall victim to her insane passion for causing suffering to others.

Omar alone stood calmly watching her; all others remained terrified, fearing to utter a single word.

Suddenly, in her mad passion, she shrieked:

"Gankoma! Gankoma! Come hither. There is still work for thee."

In an instant the chief executioner, a man of giant stature, gaudily attired and bearing a huge curved sword that gleamed ominously in the sunlight, stood before her, and bowing, answered:

"Your majesty is obeyed."

"There is one who hath betrayed his trust," cried the angry ruler. "To Babila, guardian of the Gate, we owe this intrusion of strangers in our land and these insults from the mouth of one who is unworthy to be called son. Bring forth Babila."

The executioner, sword in hand, advanced to where the trusty old

WILLIAM LE QUEUX

custodian stood. At mention of his name a despairing cry had escaped him. He knew, alas! his fate was sealed.

Pale, trembling in the iron grip of the executioner, he was hurried forward before the dazzling Emerald Throne.

"See! he flinches, the perfidious old traitor!" the Naya cried. "His duty was to prevent any stranger from entering Mo, yet he actually assisted yonder horde of savages to gain access to our innermost courts. He—"

"Mercy, your majesty! mercy!" implored the unhappy man, falling prone at her feet. "I have guarded the Gate with my life always. I believed that thy son's friends were thine also."

"Silence!" shrieked the Naya. "Let not his voice again fall upon our ears. Let him die now, before our eyes, and let his carcase be given as offal to the dogs. Let one hundred of his guards die also. Others who would thwart us will thus be warned."

"Mercy!" screamed the wretched old fellow hoarsely, clasping his hands in fervent supplication.

"Gankoma, I have spoken," cried the Great White Queen, majestically waving her hand.

Babila, inactive by age, struggled to regain his feet, but ere he could do so, or before Omar could interfere, the executioner had lifted his sword with both hands. The sound of a dull blow was heard, and next second the head of the Queen's faithful servant rolled across the polished floor, while from the decapitated trunk the blood gushed forth and ran in an ugly serpentine stream over the jasper slabs.

A sudden thrill of horror ran through the crowd at this summary execution of one who had hitherto been implicitly trusted, but only for an instant was the ghastly body allowed to remain before the eyes of Queen and court, for half a dozen slaves had been standing in readiness with bowls of water, and some of these rushing forward carried away the head and body and flung it to the dogs, while others swiftly removed all traces of the gruesome spectacle.

Little wonder therefore that the great Naya should be held in awe by all her subjects, for in her anger she seemed capable of the most fiendish cruelty. As in Kumassi, so also in Mo, death seemed to come quickly, and for any paltry offence. Gankoma, executioner to the Great White Queen, was, I afterwards learnt, continually busy obeying the royal commands, and the rapidly increasing number of victims whose heads fell beneath his terrible knife was causing most serious discontent.

XXI

A Figure in the Shadow

An hour after sundown I was seated with Omar and Kona on a mat in the courtyard of a house not far from the gates of the palace, where hospitality had been secretly offered us. We were discussing the situation. Our black followers, on leaving the presence of the irate queen, had gone out in small groups to wander through the wonderful city, having arranged to meet again at midnight.

The man in whose house we had found shelter was named Goliba, a staunch friend of Omar's, although one of the royal councillors. As we sat together this old man with long flowing white beard, keen aquiline features and black eyes that age had not dimmed, explained facts that amazed us. He told us that Kouaga, a favourite of the Naya, had been approached secretly by her as to the advisability of Omar's assassination. The old councillor had actually overheard this dastardly plot formed by the queen against her son, for she feared that owing to the harshness of her rule popular opinion might be diverted in his favour, and that she might be overthrown, and he set upon the Emerald Throne in her stead. The Naya had regretted sending Omar away for safety, so giving Kouaga a large sum of money, she ordered him to proceed to England and assassinate the heir. He left, and apparently on his way conceived the idea that he might, with considerable advantage, play a double game. Samory, whose secret agent in Mo he was, intended, he knew, to lead a great expedition against the unapproachable country, its principal object being to secure the vast treasures known to be concealed within the City in the Clouds. As Omar alone knew its secret hiding-place it occurred to Kouaga to convey him to the stronghold of the Mohammedan chief before assassinating him, and obtain from him the whereabouts of the great collection of gold and gems. The Naya had ordered that her son should be killed secretly in England, but this cowardly crime was averted by Kouaga's cupidity, and we had therefore been enticed to the Arab sheikh's headquarters. The object of both men being thwarted by Omar's refusal to divulge the secret, we had been sold into slavery and consigned as human sacrifices before King Prempeh.

WILLIAM LE QUEUX

"We'll be even yet with that scoundrel and traitor, Kouaga," Omar said, turning to me when Goliba had finished.

"If the command be given every man in Mo would go forth against Samory's accursed hordes," Goliba declared with emphasis, removing the mouthpiece of his long pipe from his lips. "But how dost thou intend now to act?" he asked Omar. "Remember thou art banished until the Naya's death. Let us hope that Zomara will not spare her long to tyrannize over our land and to plot against thy life," he added in a half whisper.

Omar started in surprise. This man, one of the principal advisers of his royal mother, was actually expressing a wish that she might die! It occurred to me, too, that if her advisers were antagonistic towards her, might not the poor, oppressed and afflicted people also be of the same mind?

"Speak, O Goliba," Omar said. "Is the balance of popular feeling actually against the Naya?"

"Entirely. Within the past few years the loyal spirit hath, on account of the revolting cruelties practised by thy royal mother, turned utterly against her. Before thy departure to the land beyond the black water the loyal feeling was uppermost because of the efforts of Moloto to obtain the crown. Now, however, that the power of his party is broken and the Naya, feeling her position invulnerable, hath commenced a reign of terror, disgust and despair are felt on every hand."

"What must I do?" Omar asked.

"Remain here," the sage replied. "Thou art banished from the royal presence, it is true, but heed not her words, and remain with thy followers in Mo. Guard vigilantly against the attempts of secret assassins that are certain to be made when the Naya is aware of thy defiance, but remember thou art heir to the Emerald Throne, and although some of the regiments may remain loyal unto their queen, the majority of our fighting-men are thine to command."

Omar knit his brows, and thought deeply for several moments. It was apparent that this suggestion to oppose the Naya by force of arms had never before entered his mind.

"Is this really true?" he asked in a doubting tone.

"O Master, let thy servant Goliba perish rather than his word be questioned. As councillor of thy queen-mother, have I not greater facilities for testing the popular feeling than any other man in Mo? I swear by Zomara's wrath that what I have uttered is truth. If thou remainest here—in hiding for a time it may be—thou shalt either be restored to the royal favour and thy friends recognized, or thou shalt assuredly occupy the royal stool. The people, living as they do in constant dread of the Naya's cruelties, would hail with satisfaction any change of rule that would ensure safety to their persons and property. Thou art their saviour."

"Take the advice of our friend Goliba," I urged. "Let us remain and defy her."

"Yea," cried Kona, displaying his even white teeth. "The Dagombas are here and likely to remain. They will fight and die to a man in thy cause. I, their head-man, speak for them."

"Is it agreed?" asked Omar, glancing at us.

"It is," we all three answered with one voice, Kona and Goliba fingering their amulets as they spoke.

"Then if it is thy will I shall remain and defy the Naya," Omar answered, grasping the string of jujus around his neck and muttering some words I could not catch. "I, Omar, Prince of Mo, am thy leader in this struggle of my people against oppression and misrule. If they will declare in my favour I will free them. I have spoken."

"Thou hast until noon to-morrow to quit this city," Goliba said. "Hasten not thy decision, but what I will show thee secretly ere long will perhaps convince thee of the terrors of the Naya's reign. I have often counselled the queen to aspire to the virtues of truth, wisdom, justice and moderation, the great ornaments of the Emerald Throne, but my endeavours have been frustrated and the fruit of my labour blasted."

As the white-bearded sage uttered these words, I noticed that from behind one of the great marble pillars of the colonnade that surrounded the courtyard of Goliba's fine house a white robe flitted for an instant, disappearing in the fast-falling gloom. At the moment, sitting as we were smoking and chatting in the open air, the presence of an intruder did not strike me as strange, and only half an hour later did I begin to fear that our decision had been listened to by an eavesdropper, possibly a spy in the service of the terrible queen! When, after due reflection, I imparted my misgivings privately to Goliba, he, however, allayed my fears, smiling, as he said:

"Heed it not. It was but my slave Fiou. I saw her also as she passed along."

"Then thou dost not fear spies?" I said.

"Not in this mine own house," he answered proudly. "The dwelling-house of a royal councillor is exempt from any espionage in the Naya's cause."

This satisfied me, and the incident escaped my recollection entirely until long after, when I had bitter cause to remember it, as will be seen from later chapters of this record.

Soon after Omar had promised to act as our leader in his country's cause, Goliba arose, and crossing the courtyard, now lit only by the bright stars twinkling in the dark blue vault above, disappeared through a door with a fine horse-shoe arch in Moorish style. Left together, we sat cross-legged on the mat, a silent, thoughtful trio. Omar had decided to act on the sage's advice, and none of us knew what the result might be. That fierce fighting and terrible bloodshed must occur ere the struggle ended, we felt assured, but with our mere handful of Dagombas we were certainly no match for the trained hosts of the Naya.

Presently we began to discuss the matter among ourselves. Kona, enthusiastic, yet hardly sanguine, wondered whether the people were armed, and if not, where we could procure guns and ammunition. Omar, on the other hand, assured us that nearly every civilian possessed a gun, being bound by law to acquire one so that he might act his part in an immediate defence in case of invasion. He had no apprehensions regarding the materials for war; he only feared that Goliba might be mistaken in the estimate of his popularity.

"If they will only stand by me they shall have freedom," he said decisively. "If they do not, death will come to all of us."

"We are ready," Kona answered, his black face glistening in the ray of light shed by a single lamp lit by a slave on the opposite side of the court. "We will serve thy cause while we have breath."

A few minutes later footsteps sounded on the paving, and from the darkness of the colonnade Goliba, accompanied by six other younger men, all tall, erect and stately, emerged from the shadow and approached us. Addressing Omar, the sage said:

"All these men are known to thee, O Master. I need not repeat their names, but they have known thee since their birth, and are of a verity a power in our land. They have come hither to see thee."

My friend rising gave them greeting, snapped fingers with them, and answered:

"I forget no face. I remember each, and I know ye are men of might and justice. Each was ruler of a province—"

"All are still governors," interrupted the sage. "They have come hither to swear allegiance to thee."

"It is even so, O Master," exclaimed one of the men, hitching his rich cloak of gold-coloured silk more closely around his shoulders. "We have met and resolved to ask thee to defy the sentence of banishment that the Naya hath imposed upon thee."

"Already have I decided so to do," Omar answered. "Have I the support of thy people, O Niaro?"

"To a man," the Governor answered. "For the military we cannot, however, answer. They are ruled by unscrupulous place-seekers, who may defend the Naya, expecting to reap rich rewards; but such will assuredly discover that their confidence was misplaced. If the Naya seriously threateneth thee and thy friends, then assuredly she shall be overthrown and thou shalt ascend the stool in her stead."

"I thank thee for these expressions of good-will," my friend said after the remaining five had all spoken and assured us of staunch support. "I remain in Mo with my black companions, and when the time cometh I am ready to take a stand in the cause against tyranny and oppression."

"May the fetish be good," Niaro said, and as if with one voice they all cried, "We will offer daily sacrifices for the success of our arms."

Together we then went to a small apartment, well-furnished in Arab style with mats, low lounges, and tiny coffee-tables, and during the three hours that followed the more minute details of this great conspiracy against the tyrannical Naya were discussed and arranged, Goliba acting as adviser upon various points.

As I sat listening to the conversation I fully realised the seriousness of the great undertaking upon which we had embarked, and I confess my confidence in our success was by no means deep-rooted, for it was apparent that in the revolt, if revolt became necessary, the military would act on the side of the Naya and suppress it with a firm, merciless hand. What apparently was most feared by our fellow-conspirators was that in commanding the suppression of the rebellion the Naya would give orders for a general massacre of the people.

To guard against this, Niaro urged the secret assassination of the Naya immediately preceding the revolt, but Omar, rising with that regal air he now and then assumed, said:

"Give heed, O my friends, unto my words. I, Omar, Prince of Mo, will never sanction the murder of my mother. A Sanom hath never been a murderer. If this step be decided, I shall withdraw from the leadership and depart."

"But canst thou not see, O Prince, that a massacre would strike panic into the hearts of the people, and they would lay down their arms," Niaro urged.

"We must prevent all bloodshed that is unnecessary," my friend replied. "I am fully aware that in such a struggle as the coming one it must be life for life, but I will never be a party to my mother's murder. If the people of Mo desire the Naya's overthrow on account of her barbarous treatment of her subjects and the bribery and corruption of her officials, then I, to preserve the traditions of my ancestors, will lead them, and act my part in their liberation, but only on the understanding that not a hair of her head is injured."

The men grouped around nodded acquiescence, but smiled.

"When thou hast witnessed how the Naya ruleth her subjects, perhaps thou wilt not so readily defend her," one of the Governors observed. "Our ruler is not so just nor so merciful as when thou wert last in Mo. Go, let Goliba take thee in secret among the people, and only when we next meet decide the point."

"I will never allow the Naya to fall beneath the blade or poison-cup of the assassin," Omar said decisively. "A Sanom departeth not from the word he hath uttered."

After some further discussion this horrible detail of the conspiracy was dropped, and other matters arranged with a coolness that utterly astounded me.

We were plotting to obtain a kingdom!

XXII

To the Unknown

When, with elaborate genuflections and vows of allegiance, the governors of the six principal provinces of the mystic Kingdom had taken leave of Omar, we remained in consultation with the old sage for upwards of another hour. He told us many horrible stories of the Naya's fierce and unrelenting cruelty. It seemed as though during the later years of her reign she had been seized by an insane desire to cause just as much misery and suffering as her predecessors on the Emerald Throne had promoted prosperity and happiness. In every particular her temperament was exactly opposite to the first Naya, the good queen whose memory had, through a thousand years, been revered as that of a goddess.

Goliba explained how, during the past three years, the Great White Queen had suddenly become highly superstitious. This was not surprising, for as far as I could gather the people of Mo had no religion as we understand the term, but their minds were nevertheless filled with ideas relating to supernatural objects, by which they sought to explain the phenomena about them of which the causes were not immediately obvious. He told us that the Naya, preying upon the superstitions of the people, had recently introduced into the country, entirely against the advice of himself and his fellow-councillors, a number of customs, all of which were apparently devised to cause death. He told us that if a great man died his friends never now remained content with the explanation that he died from natural causes. Their minds flew at once to witchcraft. Some one had cast an evil spell upon him, and it was the duty of the friends of the dead man to discover who it was that had had dealings with the powers of darkness. Suspicion fell upon a certain member of the tribe, generally a relative of the deceased, and that suspicion could only be verified by putting the accused to the test of some dreadful ordeal. A favourite ordeal, he said, was to make the suspected person drink a large quantity—a gallon and a half, or more—of a decoction of a bitter and slightly poisonous bark. If vomiting occurred, then a verdict of guilty was passed upon the unfortunate wretch, and no protestations, or even direct proof of his innocence, could save him from the tortures in store for him. The victim was condemned to death, and death was inflicted not swiftly and mercifully, but nearly always with some accompaniment of diabolical torture.

One method was to hack the body of the wretched person to pieces with knives, the most odious mutilations being resorted to. Occasionally the unfortunate creature was tied to a stake while pepper was rubbed into his eyes until the fearful irritation so produced caused blindness. Or, again, the victim was tied hand and foot upon an ant-hill, and left to the agonies of being consumed slowly by the minute aggressors. The most satisfactory death, perhaps, was that when the condemned man was allowed to be his own executioner. He was made much of for an hour or so before the final scene, and was well fed and primed with palm wine. Under the excitement of this mild stimulant he mounted a tree, carrying in his hand a long rope formed of a kind of stringy vine of tough texture. One end of this rope he fastened to a bough, and the other he placed in a running knot over his neck. Then, quite pleased at being the centre of observation of the multitude, even on such a gruesome occasion, the criminal harangued his tribesmen in a great speech, finally declared the justice of his sentence, and leaped into space. Should the rope break, as occasionally happened, then the zeal of the executioner overcame the fear of death of the victim, for he mounted the tree nimbly once more, readjusted the knots, and did his best in the second attempt to avoid the risk of another fiasco.

"And have such pagan customs actually been introduced during my absence in England?" asked Omar astonished.

"They have, alas! O Prince," answered the sage. "The people, taught from childhood to respect every word that falleth from the lips of our Great White Queen, adopted these revolting customs, together with certain other dreadful rites, believing that only by obeying her injunctions can they escape the wrath of the Crocodile-god. As rapidly as fire spreadeth in the forest the customs were adopted in every part of the kingdom, until now the practices I have briefly enumerated are universal."

"But surely my mother could never have devised such horrible suffering out of sheer ill-will towards our people?"

"Alas! she hath," answered the old man. "If thou believest not my words, take each of you one of the cloaks hanging yonder, wrap the Arab haicks around your heads and follow me. Make no sign that ye are strangers, and ye shall witness strange sights amazing."

We all three arose, and quickly arraying ourselves in white cotton burnouses, wrapping the haicks around our heads in the manner of the Arabs—a fashion adopted by some in the City in the Clouds—and pulling them across our faces, so as to partially conceal our features, we went forth with our guide on the tiptoe of expectation.

"What sight, I wonder, are we going to witness?" I whispered in English to Omar, as we walked together along one of the narrow streets in the deep shadow so that we might not be detected.

"I know not," my friend answered, with a heavy sigh. "If what Goliba says is true, and I fear it is, then our land is doomed."

"The power of the cruel Naya must be broken, and you must reign and bring back to Mo her departing prosperity and happiness," I said.

"I'll do my best, Scarsmere," he answered. "You have been a true, fearless friend all along, and I feel that you will continue until the end."

"Till the end!" I echoed. "The end will be peace, either in life—or death."

"While I have breath I will fight to preserve the traditions of the Nabas and the Nayas who, while ruling their country, gave such satisfaction to the people that never once has there been a rebellion nor scarcely a voice raised in dissent. It has always been the policy of the Sanoms to give audience to any discontented person, listen to their grievances, and endeavour to redress them. The reign of the Naya is, according to all we hear, one of terror and oppression. The poor are ground down to swell the wealth of the rich, and no man's life is safe from one moment to another. It shall be changed, and I, Omar, will fulfil the duty expected of me."

"Well spoken, old fellow," I answered, enthusiastically. "Remember Goliba's warning regarding the attempts that may be made to assassinate you, and always carry your revolver loaded. When the Naya hears that you have defied her she will be as merciless as she was to poor old Babila."

"Ah! Babila," Omar sighed. "He was one of the best and most trusted servants Mo ever had. Having been one of my dead father's personal attendants he was faithful to our family, and altogether the last man whose head should have fallen in disgrace under Gankoma's sword."

"If the punishment she inflicted upon him was so severe for such a paltry offence, that which she will seek to bring upon you will be equally terrible," I observed. "Therefore act always with caution, and take heed never to be entrapped by her paid assassins."

"Don't fear, Scarsmere," he laughed. "I'm safe enough, and I do not anticipate that anybody will try and take my life. If they do they'll find I can shoot straighter than they imagined."

"But they might shoot first," I suggested with a smile.

"I don't intend to give them a chance," he replied. "We must not fear defeat, but anticipate success. I have made offering to the fetish, and although the struggle must be fierce and unrelenting I am determined to strike a blow for my country's freedom."

At this juncture Goliba joined us, and urging me not to speak in English lest the strange language might be overheard, we walked together for about three-quarters of an hour through thoroughfares so wide and well built that they would have been termed magnificent if constructed in any European city. Then we crossed a large square where a great fountain shooting up a hundred feet fell into its bowl, green with water-plants and white with flowers, and afterwards traversed a maze of narrower streets, now silent and deserted, where dwelt the workmen.

Suddenly Goliba halted before an arched door, and directing us to imitate him, knelt and touched the door-step with his forehead, then passed in. We followed into a place that was strange to even Omar himself, who was scarce able to suppress an exclamation of astonishment. It was a small chamber, lit by a single flickering oil lamp of similar shape to those so often found amid the traces of the Roman occupation of England, while around were stone benches built into the wall. Walking to the opposite side of the narrow, prison-like place, we saw before us an arch with an impenetrable blackness beyond. Before this arch stood a kind of frame made of iron resting on either side upon steel ropes raised slightly from the ground. Following Goliba's example, we got upon it, crouching in a kneeling position in the same manner as himself.

"Thou wilt find handles, wherewith to steady thyself," he cried to me. "Have a care that thou art not thrown off."

I groped with my companions, and we found the handles of which he had spoken. Then, when all was ready, the grave-faced sage raised some lever or another, and we shot away down, down, down into space with such fearful velocity that the wind whistled about our ears, our white robes fluttered, and our breath seemed taken away.

The sensation was awful. In utter darkness we were whirled along we knew not whither, until suddenly the car whereon we travelled gave an unexpected lurch, as a corner was turned, nearly precipitating all of us into the darkness beneath, and then continued its downward course with increased speed, until sparks flew from beneath us like flecks of fire from a blacksmith's forge, and in our breasts was a tightness that became more painful every moment.

It seemed as though we were descending to some deep, airless region, for I could not breathe; the atmosphere felt damp and warm, and the velocity with which we travelled was becoming greater the deeper into the heart of the earth we went.

"What is this place?" I heard Omar ask. "I know it not."

"Be patient, O Prince, and thou shalt witness that which must astound thee," old Goliba shouted, his squeaky voice being just audible above the loud hissing as our car flew along the twisted strands of steel.

Suddenly, above the hiss of our rapid progress, there could be heard strange noises, as if a hundred war-drums were being beaten, and at the same instant our curious conveyance gave another sudden lurch in rounding a corner. At that moment Goliba, in turning to speak with Omar, had unfortunately loosened his hold of one of the handles, and the sudden jolt at such a high speed was so violent that our faithful guide and friend was shot off backwards, and ere Omar could clutch him he had disappeared with a shriek of despair into the cavernous darkness.

A thrill of horror ran through us when we realised this terrible mishap. Yet nothing could arrest our swift headlong descent, and feeling convinced that Goliba, our host and adviser, had met with a terrible death, we sat staring, motionless, wondering whither we were bound, and how, now we had lost our guide, we should be able to reach the surface again. At the moment Goliba had been flung off we remembered that the iron frame had jolted and grated, and there seemed no room for doubt that the generous sage had been mangled into a shapeless mass. The thought was horrible.

At last, however, we felt the air becoming fresher, and the strange contraction in our breasts was gradually relieved as our pace became less rapid, and distant lights showed before us. Then suddenly we emerged from the curious shaft down which we had travelled to such enormous depth, gliding slowly out into a place of immeasurable extent, where a most extraordinary and amazing scene met our gaze.

Truly, poor Goliba had spoken the truth when he had promised that what we should witness would astound us.

XXIII

Under the Vampire's Wing

When our dazzled gaze grew accustomed to the garish blaze of lights we found ourselves standing in an enormous cavern.

Around us were glowing fires and shining torches innumerable; the smoke from them half choked us, while above there seemed an immensity of darkness, for the roof of the natural chamber was so high that it could not be discerned.

Upon one object, weird and horrible, our startled gaze became rivetted. Straight before us, at some little distance, there rose a great black rock to a height of, as far as I could judge, a thousand feet. Nearly half way up was a great wide ledge or platform larger than any of the market-places in the City in the Clouds, and upon this there had been fashioned from the solid rock a colossal representation of the vampire-bat, the device borne upon the banners of Mo. Its enormous wings, each fully five hundred feet from the body to tip, outstretched on either side and supported by gigantic pillars of rock carved to represent various grotesque and hideous figures of men and animals, formed great temples on either side of the body. The latter, however, attracted our attention more than did the wonderful wings, for as we stood aghast and amazed we discerned that the vast body of the colossus did not represent that of a bat, but the gigantic jaws were those of a crocodile.

"Zomara!" gasped Omar. "See! It is the great god with the wings of a bat and the tail of a lion!"

I looked and saw that far behind rose the tufted tail of the king of the forest. From the two great eyes of the gigantic reptile shone dazzling streams of white light, like the rays of a mariner's beacon, and everywhere twinkling yellow lights were moving about the face of the great rock, across the platform whereon the colossal figure rested, even to the distant summit.

Suddenly, as we stood gazing open-mouthed in wonder, the roar of a hundred war-drums beaten somewhere in the vicinity of the enormous representation of the terrible deity of Mo rolled and echoed to the innermost recesses of the subterranean vault, and just as they had ceased we distinctly saw the giant jaws of the crocodile slowly open.

From them belched forth great tongues of flame and thick stifling smoke that, beaten down by a draught from above, curled its poisonous fumes around us, causing us to cough violently. For fully a minute the great mouth remained open, when to our horror we saw a small knot of human figures approaching it. One loud piercing shriek reached us and at that instant we saw the figure of a man or woman—we were not close enough to discern which—flung by the others headlong into the open flaming mouth.

Again the drums rolled, and the next second the jaws of Zomara closed with a loud crash that sent a shudder through us.

"The sacrifice!" gasped Omar. "This, then, is one of the horrible customs that Goliba told us had been introduced by my mother, the Great White Queen!"

"Horrible!" I exclaimed. "That fearful cry will haunt me to my dying day."

"Let us return," said Kona. "We have witnessed enough, O Master."

"No," Omar answered. "Rather let us see for ourselves the true extent of these terrible rites. Goliba, though, alas! he is lost for ever, intended that we should."

"Very well," I said. "Lead us, and we will follow."

At that moment footsteps, pattering as those of children, reached our ears and there ran past us half a dozen hideous half-clad dwarfs. They were tiny, impish-looking creatures about three feet six high, with darker skins than the inhabitants of this mystic land, but their faces were whitewashed in manner similar to those of the royal executioners of Ashanti, and wore their crisp black hair drawn to a knot on top similar to the fashion affected by some savage tribes. As they rushed past us their little black eyes, piercing and bead-like, regarded us curiously, and with, we thought, a rather menacing glance; nevertheless they continued their way, and watching, we noticed the spot where they commenced the toilsome ascent to the platform whereon stood the colossus.

"Such a work as that must have taken years to accomplish," I observed to Omar.

"With the Sanoms of Mo everything is possible," he answered. "The ruler of our country is a monarch whose will is so absolute that he or she can compel everyone, from prince to slave, to participate in any work. Thus the Naya may have caused every male inhabitant of Mo to help in its construction."

When, however, following the dwarfs we had hurried forward to the steps cut in the black rock I bent to examine them. They were polished by the wear of ages of feet and hands passing over them, and when I pointed out this fact to Omar he agreed with me that this place must have been in existence centuries ago, and had probably been rediscovered within the last two or three years.

The dwarfs, in ascending, put their toes into holes and niches in the rocks and kept talking all the while. Every now and then they would stop, sway their heads about and sing a kind of low chant in not unmusical tones. As we crept up slowly behind, with difficulty finding the rude steps in the uncertain light, the last of the string of dwarfs kept turning to us bowing and crooning. I confess I began to be anxious, fearing that we might be going into a trap, but I noticed that my two companions were calm as iron bars. This gave me renewed courage, and we toiled up until at last we reached the great platform and stood beneath the left-hand wing of the gigantic vampire of solid rock. The pillars that had been left in the excavations to support it, were, like the steps, worn smooth where crowds of human beings had jostled against them. The manner in which they were sculptured was very remarkable, the faces of all, both men, beasts, birds and fish, bearing hideous, uncanny expressions, the fearful grimaces of those suffering the most excruciating bodily tortures. It was here apparent, as everywhere, that the gigantic figure had not been recently fashioned, but had for many centuries past been visited by vast crowds of worshippers.

Beneath the outstretched wing under which we stood a large number of people had assembled. Great blazing braziers here and there illuminated the weird place with a red uncertain glare, which falling on the faces of the crowd of devotees, showed that they had worked themselves into a frenzy of religious fervour. Some were crying aloud to the Crocodile-god, some were prostrate on their faces with their lips to the stones worn smooth by the tramp of many feet, while many were going through all sorts of ceremonies and antics.

At the end, where the colossal wing joined the body wherein burned the great fiery furnace, there stood twelve dwarfs in flowing garments of pure white. These were high-priests of Zomara. The fierce pigmies, unknown even to Omar, their prince, seemed a sacred tribe who perhaps had lived here forgotten and undiscovered for generations. In any case it was apparent that they never ascended to the land above, but devoted themselves entirely to the curious rites and ceremonies of this strange pagan religion.

In the centre of the semi-circle of tiny bead-eyed priests with whitened faces stood one of great age with flowing white beard that nearly swept the ground. His figure was exceedingly grotesque, yet he bore himself with hauteur, and as he stood before a kind of altar erected in front of a door, that seemed to lead into the body of the gigantic crocodile, he gave vent in a loud clear voice to the most earnest exhortations. Then, bathing his face and hands in a golden bowl held by the other priests, in order, so I afterwards learnt, to wash away the bad impressions of the world, he thus began an instructive lesson:

"Give ear, ye tender branches, unto the words of your parent stock; bend to the lessons of instruction and imbibe the maxims of age and experience! As the ant creepeth not to its labour till led by its elders; as the young lark soareth not to the sun, but under the shadow of its mother's wing, so neither doth the child of mortality spring forth to action unless the parent hand points out its destined labour. But no labour shall the hand of man appoint unto the people of Mo before the worship of Zomara, the sacred god of the crocodiles, and of the great Naya, his handmaiden. Mean are the pursuits of the sons of the earth; they stretch out their sinews like the patient mule, they persevere in their chase after trifles, as the camel in the desert beyond the Thousand Steps. As the leopard springeth upon his prey, so doth man rejoice over his riches, and bask in the sun of slothfulness like the lion's cub. On the stream of life float the bodies of the careless and the intemperate as the carcases of the dead on the waves of the Lake of Sacrifices. As the birds of prey destroy the carcase so is man devoured by sin. No man is master over himself, but the Naya is his ruler; and to endeavour to defeat the purpose of Zomara is madness and folly. O people! pay your vows to the King of Crocodiles alone, and not to your fetishes, which, though they be superior in your sight, are yet the work of his hands. Let virtue be the basis of knowledge, and let knowledge be as a slave before her."

The worshippers at the shrine of the dread god raising their right hands then repeated after the high priest some mystic words that, although having no meaning for me, struck terror into Omar's heart.

"Hearken!" he whispered to me in an awed tone. "Hearken! Our conspiracy against the Naya is already known! They are swearing allegiance to her, and vowing vengeance against any who thwart her will. If we are detected here as strangers it will mean certain death!"

I glanced around the strange, weird place, and could not suppress a feeling of despair that we should ever leave it again alive. The faces of

WILLIAM LE QUEUX

the worshippers, men and women, illuminated by flaming flambeaux and burning braziers, were all fierce and determined-looking, showing that the worship of the Crocodile-god was conducted in no faint spirit. Before this gigantic representation of the national deity, they became seized with a religious mania that transformed them into veritable demons.

"Lo!" cried the silver-bearded priest. "Think, O people! of all our Great White Queen hath done for you. She hath brought down the moon's rays from the realms of night to lighten our darkness, she hath marked the courses of the stars with her wand and reduced eccentric orbs to the obedience of a system. She hath caught the swift-flying light and divided its rays; she hath marshalled the emanations of the sun under their different-hued banners, given symmetry and order to the glare of day, explained the dark eternal laws of the Forest-god, and showed herself always acquainted with the dictates of Zomara."

His hearers, swaying their bodies and performing all sorts of eccentric antics, cried aloud in confirmation of the benefits bestowed upon Mo by its queen.

"The secrets, too, of chemistry have been laid open by her," continued the diminutive priest. "Inert matter is engaged in warlike commotion and she hath brought fire down from the heavens to entertain her. She hath placed our land in such a state of defence that no invader can approach it; she hath brought from over the great black water the amazing 'pom-poms' of the English, which shed a thousand bullets at one charge, and she hath caused cannon to be cast to project explosive shells beyond the reach of the eye. She hath taught you at once the beauty of nature and the folly of man. Truly she is a great queen; therefore let not her son Omar who hath returned from over the great sea, wrest from her hand the regal sceptre. Already hath our queen perceived the haughtiness and the vicious principles of her son, and maketh no doubt but that he will soon aspire to her throne. This causeth the prudent Mistress of Mo to resolve to banish him and take all power from him. Let him be ejected from our country and the queen's word be obeyed, for no beam of mercy lurketh in her eye. The Naya is determined."

"The great Naya shall be obeyed," they cried aloud. "Omar, the malicious prince, curbed by the authority of his mother, shall be banished."

"Or his life shall, like those of his followers we hold here as prisoners, pay the forfeit of presumption," added the high priest.

And as he uttered the words, those surrounding went to the door behind the fire-altar, and opening it, led forth three of our Dagombas amid the savage howls of the excited spectators.

"O, race of mortals," cried the priest, raising his hand the while, "O race of mortals, to whose care and protection the offspring of clay are committed, say what hath been the success of your labours; what vices have you punished; what virtues rewarded; what false lights have you extinguished; what sacrifices have you made to the god of Crocodiles? Helpless race of mortals, Zomara is your god and the Naya your queen. But for their protection how vain would be your toils, how endless your researches! Arm ye then and rally round the one to whom you owe all, whose power is such that this our country can never be assaulted by the tricks of fortune, or the power of man. Omar and his black swarm of intruders must be driven out or given as sacrifice to Zomara. Till this be done the curse of the god ye fear shall rest upon our land, and his presence shall nightly remind ye of your idleness. Will ye let the defiant prince overthrow your queen?"

"He shall never do so," they shouted in a tumult of enthusiasm, which, ere it died away, increased tenfold, when suddenly before us we saw a female figure in a loose yellow robe move with stately mien towards the smoking altar and kneel for an instant before it.

Then, rising, she turned towards the people with her long, bare, scraggy arms uplifted in silence.

In the red flickering light we recognized the evil bony features. It was the dreaded Naya herself!

"The vengeance of Zomara upon mine enemies," she cried in harsh, metallic tones. "I will treat each and every one who dareth to oppose me in the way I will now punish these three savages who have entered our region forbidden. Watch, and let it be a warning to those who may be tempted by bribes to entertain disloyal thoughts."

With stately stride she led the way along a dark colonnade from beneath the wing of the colossal vampire to the enormous closed mouth of the hideous crocodile, being followed by the high priest and his attendants, who dragged along the three of our unfortunate companions.

At once a headlong rush was made by the frenzied spectators to obtain a view of what was to transpire, and we followed leisurely at a respectable distance, remaining in the shadow of one of the grotesquely-carved columns of rock.

When all had taken up their places we could see the expressions of abject fear upon the glistening faces of the wretched blacks, and longed to rush forth and rescue them, but with knowledge that instant death would result from such foolhardiness we remained breathlessly silent, compelled to watch.

Again the high priest, with outstretched hands over the people, cried:

"Give heed unto me! Were Zomara, the god whom we worship, to be worshipped in perfectness, the whole length of our lives would not suffice to lie prostrate before him. But the merciful Avenger of Wrong expecteth not more from us than we are able to pay him. True it is that we should begin early, and late take rest, and daily and hourly offer up our praises and petitions to the throne of his handmaiden's grace. But better is a late repentance than none; and the eleventh hour of the day for work than perpetual idleness unto the end of our time; and this is not to be obtained for us but through our mighty Naya, the daughter of Zomara the Swallower-up of Evil."

Himself facing the hideous gigantic head with its long jaws and gleaming eyes, he flung himself suddenly upon his knees and commenced a gabbled prayer. All prostrated themselves in adoration, even to the great Naya herself, whose magnificent jewels flashed and gleamed with wondrous brilliancy each time she moved.

In order not to appear strange to this extraordinary proceeding, we, too, cast ourselves upon our knees and remained with heads bent in devotional attitude, but allowing no detail of the weird scene to escape us.

Suddenly the priest arose, and with a fire-brand ignited at the brazier near his hand, he stood before the wonderful figure of Zomara and made a mystic sign.

Instantly the ponderous jaws with their double row of iron teeth, each as long and as sharp as swords, slowly opened, and there issued forth a great roaring mass of flame that licked the upper jaw, a veritable tongue of fire.

The Naya rose, swaying her long arms wildly, but the people remained still kneeling, silent in awe.

Her voice was heard for a moment above the roaring and crackling of the furnace in the throat of the colossus, and then, at a sudden signal from the high priest, our three wretched black companions were seized by the group of dwarfs, carried up a short flight of steps by white-robed attendants, and hurled headlong into the flaming mouth of the monster.

A loud scream broke upon our ears, and for a single instant the flames belched forth with increased fury, but as the last victim of this horrible rite was consigned to his terrible doom, as sacrifice to the dreaded god, the cruel jaws closed again with a heavy clang.

The merciless barbarity of the Great White Queen horrified us. The fearful fate of those who had shared our perils during our adventurous journey to this spectral land of mystery held us dumb in terror and dismay.

Yet, ere the giant jaws of the hideous monstrosity had snapped together, the people, hilarious and excited, sprang to their feet exhorting their great deity to send his fiercest vengeance upon us, the intruders, that our sinews might be withered and that we might rot by the road-side like cattle smitten by the pest.

Then the terrible Naya, wheeling round slowly, gave her people her blessing, and they, in turn, shouted themselves hoarse in frantic adulation.

Truly, the scene was the strangest and most weird that my eyes had ever gazed upon.

XXIV

The Flaming Mouth

We stood rooted to the spot. The hideous colossus, the intensely white light streaming from its gigantic eyes, seemed to tower above us to an enormous height, its outstretched wings threatening to enclose the great swaying crowd of fanatical worshippers. With monotonous regularity the long jaws, worked by hidden levers, fell apart, disclosing the terrible pointed teeth against a roaring background of smoke and flame, and so frenzied had the people now become, that each time the mouth of the monster idol opened, numbers of wild-haired men and women rushed up the incline that led to the blazing furnace, and with loud cries of adoration of their deity, lifted their arms above their heads and cast themselves into the flames. Some fell clear of the double row of pointed teeth into the furnace, while others not leaping sufficiently far were impaled upon the great spikes of steel, and in full view of their companions writhed in frightful agonies, as slowly they were consumed by the tongue of fire lapping about them.

The scene was awful, yet the Naya, surrounded by priestly dwarfs, stood regarding it with satisfaction. Such voluntary sacrifices to Zomara, were, to them, gratifying in the highest degree.

Suddenly the light in the eyes of the giant figure changed from white to a deep blood-red, illuminating the strange place with a ruddy glow that increased its weirdness, and was a signal for a large number of sacrifices. Indeed, the worshippers now lost their self-control absolutely, and when the horrible mouth, dripping with blood, again unclosed, there was such a press of those anxious to immolate themselves, that many could not struggle forward to cast their bodies into the flames before the teeth again snapped together.

It was horrible. Nauseated by the sickening sight of men impaled and absolutely crushed to a pulp by the ascending jaw which must have weighed many tons, and the sharp teeth of which cut the unfortunate wretch to pieces, we turned away. We had emerged from the shadow that had concealed us and stood in the full white light shed by one of the monster's eyes, hesitating how to seek some means of escape, when two of the dwarfs, suddenly turning a corner, came full upon me. In an instant I remembered that on account of the suffocating atmosphere I had unwrapped my haick from about my mouth, thus allowing my features to remain uncovered. But ere this thought flashed across my mind the uncanny-looking imps had detected my features as those of a stranger.

For a second they paused, starting and glancing keenly at me, then they turned and gazed earnestly at my companions. There was, I knew, no mistaking Kona's sable yet good-humoured face.

"Lo!" they cried, shouting to the group of their priestly tribe standing rigid and silent around the bejewelled Naya. "See! There are strangers present! One is a black savage like those thou hast given unto Zomara, and the other white, like the people dwelling beyond the great black water."

Their announcement produced an effect almost electrical. In an instant a silence fell, and at the same moment the voice of the Naya was heard commanding:

"If they are strangers who have dared to descend to this our Temple of Zomara, bring them forth, and let them be given unto the great god whose maw still remaineth unsatisfied. Hasten, ye priests, do my bidding quickly; let them not escape, or the curse of the King of the Crocodiles be upon you."

The two dwarfs sprang forward to seize us, while the group of priests, fleet of foot, accompanied by the great mob of worshippers, sped in our direction. The people, having worked themselves up to such a pitch of excitement, were eager to assist in the immolation of any intruders. They were bent upon obeying the law of their queen.

But in an instant Kona felled both the dwarfs with two well-directed blows with his huge black fist, and without hesitation we all three turned and fled in the direction we had come. My companions had apparently forgotten where the steps descended, but fortunately I had fixed the spot in case any untoward incident occurred. They were over against a great pillar of rock, rudely fashioned to represent a woman with an eagle's head.

"This way," I shouted. "Follow me!" and with a bound sped in its direction as fast as my legs could carry me.

We had nearly gained the spot when to my dismay I saw a dozen of the worshippers, divining our intention, approaching from the opposite direction in order to cut off our retreat.

It was an exciting moment. Behind, was a mad, fanatical mob of five hundred men and women led by the dwarfs shrieking vengeance against us; before us were a dozen determined men ready to seize us and convey us to a horrible death in the throat of the gigantic representation of their sacred reptile. Even if we safely descended the steps, we knew not the secret means by which we might reach the earth's surface, nor did either of us remember the exact point where the long dark tunnel joined the wonderful cavern.

None, however, knew that Omar himself was one of my fellow fugitives, for the dwarfs, being consigned to a subterranean life perpetually, had never set eyes upon him, and therefore he had been unrecognized. Another moment, and I knew he must be detected by some of the devotees. If so, the hostile feeling against us would be intensified, and we should probably be torn limb from limb.

I had retained the lead in this race for life, and seeing retreat cut off by the group of men gaining the top of the steps before us I turned quickly, and, although fearing the worst, made a long detour. Determined to sell my life dearly, I drew my long knife from its velvet sheath, and gripped it, ready to strike a deadly blow in self-defence. Luckily I armed myself in time, for almost next moment a man of huge stature sprang forward from behind one of the columns of rock where he had been secreted and threw himself upon me, clutching me by the throat.

Scarce had his sinewy fingers gripped me, when, by dint of frantic effort, I freed my right arm, and with a movement quick as lightning flash, I buried my knife full in his breast. One short, despairing cry escaped him, and as he staggered back I dashed forward again, without turning to look at the result of the swift blow I had delivered. But I was desperate, and being compelled to defend my life, I do not doubt that my blow was unerring, and that my blade penetrated his heart.

Hindered thus in my flight my two companions had reached the edge of the precipice ahead of me, and were skirting it, when suddenly I saw a body of our pursuers approaching, and cried to them in warning. In dismay I noticed they took no heed of my words, but continued their swift flight right in the direction of those who sought our destruction.

"Take care, Omar!" I shouted, in English. "Can't you see those devils in front?"

But he answered not, and I was about to halt and give up all thought of escape, when I saw them both suddenly throw themselves on their knees on the edge of the abyss, and almost instantly disappear over the precipice.

They had found another flight of steps!

Eagerly I sprang forward, and in a few seconds found myself descending the rough face of the rock, scrambling desperately down into the yawning chasm with a wild horde of excited fanatics shrieking and yelling above.

Half a dozen of the more adventurous swung themselves over and commenced to follow us, but those above, determined that we should not escape, fetched huge stones and lumps of rock, which they hurled upon us. But their excess of zeal only wrought destruction upon their companions, who, being above us, received blows from the great stones which sent them flying one after another to the base of the rock, killed or stunned ere they reached it. Twice we had narrow escapes on account of the unconscious bodies of our pursuers or their companions' missiles falling against us, but while all those who had followed us, save one, fell victims to the merciless frenzy of their companions, we were fortunate enough to be enabled to descend to the base of the rock, where once again the impenetrable darkness hid, although at the same time it hampered, our movements.

For a few moments at least we were safe, and paused to recover breath. My arm was bleeding profusely where it had been severely grazed by a sharp edge of rock in our headlong flight, and the white garments of all three of us were soiled and torn. But our halt was not of long duration, for suddenly we heard whispers and the sound of stealthy footsteps in the darkness.

We listened breathlessly.

"Hark!" cried Omar. "Our pursuers are here also, and are looking for us!"

"Let us hide behind yonder rock," Kona suggested, in a half-whisper.

"No, let us creep forward," answered the son of the Great White Queen. "They will search every crevice and hiding-place now the hue-and-cry has been raised," and glancing up I saw a black stream of excited worshippers, many with torches that in the distance shone like moving stars, already pouring down over the rock in our direction like a line of ants descending a wall.

Every moment brought them nearer upon us; every instant increased our peril. Even though we were in the great chasm, the true extent of which we could not distinguish, we knew not by what means we could escape upward to the blessed light of day.

Forward we crept cautiously, in obedience to Omar's instructions, but ere a couple of minutes had elapsed it was evident that the watchful ones who had heard the shouting from above and noticed the pursuit had discovered our whereabouts, for just as we had noiselessly passed a huge boulder, a man in white robe and turban sprang upon us from behind.

"Look out, Kona!" cried Omar, his quick eyes discerning the man's cloak in the darkness ere I noticed his presence.

Next second, however, the head-man of the Dagombas and the stranger were locked in deadly embrace, notwithstanding that the man who had approached cried aloud to us for mercy.

Kona with drawn sword had gripped the man's throat with his long black fingers, when suddenly we heard a gasping cry: "Stay thine hand! Dost thou not recognize thy benefactor?"

"Hold!" shouted Omar, the words causing him to turn and run back to where the pair were struggling. "Knowest thou not the voice? Why, it is Goliba!"

And it was Goliba! Instantly the black giant released the man who he believed intended to arrest our progress, and with a word of apology we all four sped forward. How our aged host had escaped after being thrown from the frame in which we had made the descent from the city we knew not until later, when he explained that on recovering consciousness and finding himself on his back in the tunnel with a slight injury to his shoulder, he had scrambled down the perilous descent, fearing each moment that he might slip in the impenetrable darkness and be dashed to pieces ere he gained the bottom. Intensely anxious as to our fate, he had at last descended in safety, but on emerging from the tunnel found proceeding above all the commotion the discovery of our presence had caused. He watched our descent into the chasm and stood below awaiting us, but we had rushed past ere he could make himself known, and he had therefore dashed across to a corner and thus come up with us.

But our meeting, too hurried and full of peril to admit of explanation at that moment, was at any rate gratifying—for we all three had believed him dead. Our pursuers were now behind us in full cry. A number of them had gained the base of the rock and, yelling furiously, were fast gaining upon us.

"Come, let us hasten," cried the old sage, speeding along with a fleetness of foot equal to our own, skirting the base of the great rock for a short distance until we came to a portion that jutted out over the uneven ground, then suddenly turning aside, we crossed a great open space where mud and water splashed beneath our feet at every step. The further we went the deeper sank our feet into the quagmire, until our progress was so far arrested that we could not run, but only wade slowly through the chill black slime.

Even across here our progress was traced, for the lights in the eyes of the giant god were turned upon us, and our path lit by a stream of white light which guided the footsteps of those who sought our death.

At last, when we had crossed the boggy patch, the ground became quite dry again, but after running some distance further, which showed me that the natural chamber must have been of huge proportions, Goliba shouted to us to halt and remain there. We obeyed him, puzzled and wondering, but we saw him dashing hither and thither as if in search of something. At first it was apparent that he could not discover what he sought, but in a few minutes when our pursuers had crossed the quagmire and were quite close upon us he shouted to us to come forward. Together we obeyed instantly, speeding as fast as our legs could carry us to where Goliba was standing before a small fissure in the side of the cavern on a level with the ground, and so narrow that it did not appear as if Kona would be able to squeeze his big body through.

"Follow me," the old sage said in a low tone as, throwing himself down before the mysterious hole, he crept forward, being compelled to lie almost flat on his stomach, so small was the fissure.

His example we all quietly followed, finding ourselves groping forward in the darkness, but discovering to our satisfaction that the further we proceeded the wider the crack in the rock became, so that before long we were enabled to walk upright, although we deemed it best to hold our hands above our heads lest we should strike them against any projecting stones.

Without light, and in air that was decidedly close and oppressive, we proceeded. At least we were safe from the howling mob, for since leaving the great cavern all was silence, and it was now evident from the confident manner in which Goliba went forward that he was assured of the way. Soon we negotiated a steep ascent, now and then so difficult that we were compelled to clamber up on all fours, and for a long time this continued until our hands and feet were sore with scrambling upward. A spring shed its icy drippings upon us for some little distance, soaking us to the skin and rendering us chilly and uncomfortable, but

WILLIAM LE QUEUX

at length we reached what seemed to be a ponderous door that barred our passage.

Goliba groped about for a few minutes without speaking, when quickly it opened to his touch and we found ourselves in a long stone passage lit here and there by evil-smelling oil lamps that flickered in the rush of air from the great fissure through which we had ascended.

"This is amazing," cried Omar dumbfounded, as the old sage struggled to close the heavy iron door behind us. "Why, we are in the vaults beneath the palace!"

"True, O Master," Goliba answered, breathless after his exertions. "There is but one entrance and one exit to this labyrinth of vaults and foul chambers wherein the Naya confineth her prisoners. The entrance is, as thou knowest, immediately beneath the Emerald Throne; the exit is this door, which can only be opened by those possessed of the secret. Thirty years ago, when Keeper of the Prison, this door puzzled me considerably, for all attempts to open it on the part of the men I employed failed. It is of such construction and mechanism that nothing short of explosives could make it yield, and these I feared to use. But years afterwards a gaoler who had obtained the secret from his father, also a gaoler, but who was dead, imparted it to me on his death-bed in return for some good-will I had shown him. I believe therefore that I am the only person who has knowledge of the means by which to open it."

"The knowledge hath, in any case, saved our lives, Goliba," Omar answered. "But the great cavern and all those horrible rites introduced into the worship of Zomara, are not they new?"

"No," replied the sage. "They are as old as the foundation of the Kingdom of Mo. Strangely enough, however, the great cave with its colossus and its race of sacred dwarfs who live away in a small dark forest that can only be gained from the opposite side of the cave, were for centuries forgotten. The way to the Temple of Zomara was unknown and the dwarfs remained in undisputed possession of the place until three years ago, one more adventurous than the rest, succeeded in ascending to Mo, when his capture resulted in the cavern with its great wonderful image being re-discovered. Since that time the place has never been devoid of votaries, and the great fire has constantly been fed by those anxious to immolate themselves to appease the Crocodile-god."

"Ah! he is a great god," Omar observed earnestly.

"Yea, O Master, he is indeed all-powerful," answered the aged councillor. "He giveth us life, preserveth us from death, and shieldeth us from evil."

And as they uttered these words both fingered their amulets piously.

XXV

Liola

After brief consultation it was deemed insecure for us to return to Goliba's house, as search would undoubtedly be made for us there if any had detected his presence with us in the great chasm. Therefore, our guide, taking one of the lamps, led us along a number of narrow unlighted passages, threading the maze with perfect knowledge of its intricacies until, opening a door, we found ourselves in a small stone prison-chamber. Here we remained while he went to another part of the vaults and obtained for us some food, urging us to remain there until such time as we might come forth in safety.

Kona extracted from him a promise that he would place his fellow-tribesmen in a place of security, and Goliba also assured us that if we remained in that chamber and did not attempt to wander in the passages, where we must inevitably lose our way, we might ere long ascend to the city and commence the campaign against the cruel command of the merciless Naya.

Through eleven long and dreary days we remained in the narrow cell, drawing our water from a spring that gushed forth from a rock close to the door, existing on the smallest quantity of food, and scarce daring to speak aloud lest any of the gaolers should overhear. By day a faint light came through a narrow chink above, and from the fact that the steady tramp of soldiers sounded overhead at intervals we concluded that the chamber must be situated immediately below one of the courtyards of the palace. At night, however, we remained in perfect darkness, our oil having been exhausted during the first few hours. Thus we could only remain sitting on the stone bench like prisoners, inactive, discussing the probabilities of the serious movement that had been started in favour of a change of rule.

"The people apparently look to me as their rescuer from this oppression," Omar observed one day when we were laying plans for the future. "I will, if Zomara favours me, do my best."

"It is but right; nay, it is your duty towards your subjects to preserve the traditions of the Sanoms," I said. "Goliba was right when he promised he would show us the horrors introduced into Mo, or resuscitated by the present Naya. We have witnessed with our own eyes expressions of pleasure cross her countenance as each batch of her subjects cast themselves into those yawning jaws. Such a monarch, capable of any cruelty, must necessarily rule unjustly, and should be overthrown or killed."

"I do not desire her death," he said quickly. "All I intend to do is to free our people from this hateful reign of terror, and at the same time preserve my mother's life."

"But the time she gave us to quit the country has elapsed," I observed. "If we are now discovered we shall either be held as slaves, or treated without mercy—offered as sacrifices to the Crocodile-god, perhaps."

"Not while the people are in our favour," he said. "Once their adherence to my cause has been tested then we have nought further to fear, for the opinion of the populace will be found even of greater power than the military, and in the end it must prevail."

"In the fight that must ensue thou wilt find thy servant Kona at thy side," the head-man said. "Through fire or across water the Dagombas will follow thee, for their fetish is good, and they have faith in thee as leader."

"Yea, O friend," the young prince answered. "Without thee and thy followers I could never have returned hither. I owe everything to thee, and to the stout heart of our companion Scarsmere."

"No, old fellow," I protested. "It is your own dogged courage that has pulled us through so far, not mine. Up to the present all has gone well with us except the deplorable loss of some of our dark companions, therefore let us retain our light hearts and meet all obstacles with smiles."

"I am ready to lead the people against the forces of malice and oppression at any moment Goliba commands," Omar answered. "No thought of fear shall arrest my footsteps or stay my hand."

Times without number we discussed the situation in similar strain, until, on the eleventh day of our voluntary confinement we were startled by a low tapping on the door.

Each held his breath. Had it been Goliba he would have entered without any such formality. In silence, we remained listening.

Again the tapping was repeated, louder than before. Drawing our knives ready to defend ourselves, believing it to be one of the Naya's gaolers, Kona went forward, unbolted the door and opening it a few inches, weapon in hand, peered out.

Instantly an exclamation of surprise escaped him, and as he threw wide open the door, a young girl of about seventeen, with a face more beautiful than I had ever before seen, entered our cell. This vision of feminine loveliness entranced us. We all three stood staring at her open-mouthed.

Dressed in a robe of rich blue silk heavily embroidered with gold, her waist was confined by a golden girdle wherein were set some magnificent rubies, and her feet were encased in tiny slippers of pale green leather embroidered with seed pearls. Her face, slightly flushed in confusion at finding herself in the presence of the Prince, was pale of complexion as my own, her clear eyes a deep blue, her cheeks dimpled, her chin just sufficiently pointed to give a touch of piquancy to a decidedly handsome countenance. Her hair, of almost flaxen fairness, fell in profusion about her shoulders and breast, almost hiding the necklets of gold and gems encircling her slim throat.

Little wonder then was it that Kona's black visage should broaden into a wide grin in manner habitual when his eyes fell upon anything that pleased him, or that I should regard her as a most perfect type of feminine loveliness.

"I seek Omar, the Prince," she said in a silvery voice, not, however, without some trepidation.

"I am Omar," answered my friend. "Who, pray, art thou, that thou shouldst know of my hiding-place?"

"Thy servant," she said with a graceful bow, "is called Liola, daughter of Goliba, councillor of the great Naya. My father sendeth thee greeting and a message."

"Goliba's daughter!" Omar cried laughing. "And we had drawn knives upon thee!"

"Sheathe them," she answered smiling upon us. "Keep them in your belts until ye meet your enemies, for ere long ye will, of a verity, want them."

"What then hath transpired?" asked the son of the Great White Queen. "What message sendeth our friend Goliba?"

"My father directed me to come hither, for knowing the wife of the Keeper of the Prison I was enabled to pass the sentries where my father would have been remarked," she said. "He sendeth thee word to be of good courage, for all goeth well, and thy cause prospereth. The savages who accompanied thee into our land are all in safety, although the horsemen of the Naya are scouring the country in search of thee and thy companions. In secret, word of thy consent to lead the popular demonstration against oppression and ill-government hath been conveyed to the people even to our land's furthermost limits, and the reports from all sides show that thou art regarded with favour."

"And thou art also one of my partisans—eh?" asked Omar, smiling.

"I am, O Master," she answered blushing deeply. "I will make fetish for the success of thine arms."

"I thank thee, Liola," he answered. "Thou hast indeed brought us good tidings."

"But my father sendeth thee a further message," she continued. "He told me to tell thee that at sundown to-day he will come and conduct thee hence. Rest and sleep until then, for the way may be long and great vigilance may be demanded."

"Whither does he intend to take us?" our companion asked.

"I know not, O Master," she replied. "Already the people have armed, and are assembling. I heard my father, in conversation last night with one of the provincial governors who hath lately joined us, declare that the struggle could not be much longer delayed."

"Then thou meanest that a fight is imminent?" he asked.

"I fear so. Word of thine intention hath been conveyed by some spy unto the Naya, and the city now swarmeth with her soldiers and janissaries, who have orders to suppress the first sign of any insurrection. But in the fight thou shalt assuredly win, for the opinion of the people is in thy favour. May Zomara's jaws close upon thine enemies, and may they be devoured like sacrifices."

"The people are assembling, thou hast said," Omar observed. "Are they in great numbers?"

"It is impossible to tell. The news of thine opposition to the Naya spread like wildfire through the land, and secret agents soon ascertained that the balance of opinion was in thy favour. For eight days past I have been at work secretly in thy cause, and from my own observations in the city I know that among the palace officials we have many adherents, and even here and there the soldiers will turn against their own comrades. In our own house arms and ammunition are stored, and we have been fortunate enough in obtaining from the arsenal through the governor, who is on our side, ten of those wonderful guns of the English that fire bullets like streams of water."

"Maxims, I suppose," I interrupted.

"I know not their name," she replied. "I heard my father say that they are most deadly, and with them we might hold an army at bay."

"Truly thy father hath neglected nothing on my behalf," Omar said with sincerity. "Dost thou return unto him?"

"I go at once."

"Then tell him we are anxious to accompany him, and will be ready at sundown."

"Thy words will I convey to him, O Master. Liola shall make great fetish for thine ascent to the Emerald Throne."

Then, wishing us adieu, the slim handsome girl with the deep blue expressive eyes slipped out of the door, and noiselessly crept away down the long stone corridor.

"Of a truth, O Master, there can be no fairer daughter on earth than Liola," Kona observed, addressing Omar when the pretty messenger had gone.

"Yea, she is beautiful. Her face is like the lily, and her eyes as mysterious as the depths of the sea. I have never encountered one so fair," Omar answered.

"Nor I," I said. "Her beauty is incomparable."

"I had no idea old Goliba had a daughter," Omar exclaimed. "He is indeed fortunate to have one so amazingly lovely."

"She is one of your partisans," I observed smiling.

And he laughed, while Kona, grinning with glee, declared chaffingly that the Prince had fallen in love with her.

The subject, however, was not further pursued, but now and then Omar would express a hope that she had returned in safety to her father, or wonder why she had been working in his cause, his words showing plainly that his head was still filled with thoughts of our pretty visitor.

Soon after the light had faded from the tiny chink above, Goliba's voice was heard calling outside, and we at once opened the door to him.

"Let us hasten, O Master," the old sage cried breathlessly. "Every instant's delay meaneth peril, and peril is first cousin to disaster."

"Lead," I cried. "We will follow."

A moment later we all four were creeping softly along the corridor past doors of the foul reeking dungeons wherein those who for some cause or another, often the most trivial, had fallen into disfavour with the Naya and were rotting in their silent living tombs. Many were the grim and fearful stories of injustice and agony those black walls could tell; many were the victims consigned there, although innocent of any offence, never again to see the light of day. As we walked huge grey rats, some the pets of the wretched prisoners, scurried from our path, and now and then as we passed the small closed door of heavy sheet-iron the groans and lamentations of the unhappy captives reached our ears.

At last, after traversing many passages turning to right and left in such a manner that the extent of the great place amazed us, we ascended a flight of well-worn steps.

"The sentries now on guard are loyal to us," the royal councillor whispered, turning to Omar as we went up, and when we emerged into the chamber wherein stood the Emerald Throne, the three tall soldiers with drawn swords, two standing mute and motionless as statues on either side of the door, and the other pacing up and down, took no notice of our appearance, but regarded us with stolid indifference. In the rosy evening light we sped across the beautiful court to a gate opposite, and passed out by a private way of which Goliba held the key until we found ourselves beyond the frowning walls.

Kona looked around longingly as we passed through the courts and chambers. He was anticipating with eagerness the time when he and his men would re-enter the place as conquerors, and was probably reflecting upon the amount of loot his men could obtain in the event of an order being given to sack the palace of the dreaded Naya. But without pausing to glance behind, our guide hurried us forward along a number of winding back streets of the city, hot, dusty and close-smelling after the broiling day, until he stopped before the door of a fine house, the walls of which were of polished white marble, that reflected the last rays of the sun like burnished gold. Striking the door thrice, it opened, and on going in he conducted us to a spacious hall, where we found exposed to our view a great collection of arms and warlike accoutrements. All kinds of instruments of death, which the inventive malice of man had ever discovered had been collected for the use of those determined to accomplish the overthrow of the wicked rule of the Naya. First, there were sticks, staves and knotty clubs. Next to these, spears, darts, javelins, armed with brass or iron, or their points hardened with fire, and innumerable bows with quivers and arrows, which Kona examined critically, giving low grunts of approbation as he scrutinized a specimen of each.

After these, instruments of dubious use originally designed for the assistance of man, but perverted through cruelty and malice to the service of slaughter and death; such as knives, scythes, axes and hammers. On these were heaped arms, deliberately fashioned for the offence of mankind, swords, daggers, poignards, scimitars, and rapiers, while on the opposite side of the spacious place were stored the more refined and destructive instruments of European war, rifles, muskets, revolvers, bayonets, small field-pieces, machine-guns of various patterns, including four Maxims and their food, boxes of cartridges, kegs of powder, cakes of dynamite, bombs and shells.

"Behold!" exclaimed Goliba, halting before them. "Here is one of our secret stores of arms."

"One of them!" said Omar. "How many, then, have we?"

"In the city there are sixteen, all similarly filled. Away in various parts of the country there are depôts in every populous centre," he replied.

"But it must have taken a long time to obtain all these," the Prince observed, puzzled.

"The munitions of war were swiftly obtained for a popular rising," the aged sage replied. "When the word went forth in secret to the people, they responded almost to a man. Arms were actually carried from the royal arsenal in great quantities, and even the spies of the Naya found themselves thwarted and powerless. We have obtained nearly all the Maxims purchased in England, by the Naya's agent, Makhana; some are here, others at various depôts, and each will be in charge of fighting-men, who know their use. The few remaining in the arsenal and forts have all been disabled by those of our sympathisers in government employ."

"Truly," I said, turning to Omar, "the Naya who gave an order for your assassination is seated on the edge of a volcano."

"Yes," cried the white-bearded old councillor. "The country hath struggled and groaned long and in vain under the Naya's tyrannical sway; the uprising will be swift and revengeful."

"When will it occur?" I asked, with eagerness.

"To-night," answered Goliba in a quiet tone.

"To-night?" we all three cried, amazed that the preparations were already complete.

"Yes," he said, in a low tone. "As the bell on the palace-gate chimeth the midnight hour a great mine will be fired that will proclaim with the earth's sudden upheaval the rising of the people of Mo against their ruler. Then the people, ready armed with these weapons, will strike such a blow as will sweep away all oppression and tyranny from our land, and leave it free as it hath ever been, free to prosper and retain its position as the only unconquered nation on the face of earth."

XXVI

The First Blow

Leaving the store of arms we returned to Goliba's house; not by the high road, but by little winding lanes with tunnel-like passages under the overhanging eaves of houses; through a small open square or two, past a few richly-painted and carved doors of tombs, and so on once more to the residence of the old sage, with its spacious courts and beautiful gardens. We passed some handsome blue-tiled public fountains, and some fine buildings several storeys in height, open in the centre with a patio, and surrounded by galleries of carved wood, which seemed to answer to our corn exchanges. One, near Goliba's house, was especially remarkable for its architectural beauty, not only with regard to its interior, but also its magnificent gateway. There were others also of far less pretensions, which answered more to the caravanseri of Samory's country, where the weary animals who had borne their burdens from some far away corner of the mystic land were resting during their sojourn in the city.

When, in the cool dusk of evening we had eaten in the marble court, with its fountains and flowering plants, Omar being waited upon personally by our host, Liola came, and, lounging gracefully against one of the marble columns, gossipped with us. Afterwards, a professional story-teller was introduced to amuse us during the anxious time that must elapse before the fateful hour when the signal for the great uprising would be given.

He was an old man, small of stature, in fact, I believe he must have been one of the tribe of dwarf cave-dwellers. Of darker complexion than the majority of this curious people, he was dressed in a long garment of white, wearing on his head a conical head-dress, shaped somewhat like a dunce's cap, and as he took up his position, squatting on a mat before us, he made deep obeisance to the son of his ruler. While we regaled ourselves with grapes and other luscious fruits as a satisfactory conclusion to a bountiful feast, he told us a story which, as far as I could translate it, was as follows:

"Ages ago," he said, "in the days of the good king Lobenba and Prince Karmos"—here he kissed his hand as a sign of reverence, as did all his listeners—"there was a poor man, a cowherd, who lived a very righteous life, nor did he commit any sin. But he was terribly poor, starving because he had not the wherewithal to supply himself with food. One night while asleep in his lonely hut on the mountain over against the Grave of Enemies, a vision appeared to him, and he saw standing before him the god Zomara"—more hand-kissing—"in a flame of fire. And the King of Crocodiles said to him: 'Gogo, I have seen thy poverty and am come to give thee succour. I have seen how, even in the days when no food hath passed thy lips, thou hast never committed theft, nor borrowed not to return, and now thou shalt have great wealth. Speed early to-morrow to thy friend Djerad and borrow his black horse. I will put it in his mind to lend it thee; and take this horse and ride it to the Gate of Mo, and then leap on thy horse from the precipice, and assuredly thou wilt find great wealth.'

"Ere Gogo had time to thank the great god—whose name be exalted above all others—he had vanished. Early he rose, donned his ragged garments, set forth and begged the loan of the black horse of Djerad, his friend. After a ride of many hours, he came at sundown to the Gate of Mo, and gazed over the fearful precipice. Gathering the reins in his hand he rode back a little distance, then gallopped full speed to the brink. But his heart failed him, and on the edge he reined his horse for fear.

"Nine times he essayed to go, but each time his courage was insufficient. While he was sitting on his horse, preparing for the tenth time to obey the instructions, he heard a great noise behind him, and turning, saw the god Zomara with fire bursting from his mouth and streams of light in his eyes, crawling towards him.

"'Weak man,' he cried, as he passed. 'Thou fearest to obey. Follow me.'

"An instant later the great crocodile had crawled over the edge of the precipice, and a moment afterwards Gogo had followed his example. It seemed as if he were in the air an hour, but suddenly his horse's hoofs touched earth again; the animal never fell into the terrible abyss, but merely tore up a piece of the turf where he had stood. He looked around; Zomara had disappeared, but in the hole that the horse's hoof had caused he saw a large ring of iron. Dismounting, he tried to raise it, but only after two hours' work he succeeded in moving it and excavating from its hiding-place an enormous chest filled with gold pieces and costly jewels, and so he lived in affluence the remainder of his life, till Zomara took him to be one of his councillors. So are the righteous rewarded."

Then some thick-lipped musicians struck up music on quaintly-shaped stringed instruments, and the strange old man, bearing a kind of tambourine in his hand, came round to collect coins, the collection being repeated at the conclusion of each legend.

In one of his stories mention was made in the most matter-of-fact manner of a sick person being buried alive. This caused me to address some questions to Liola, who, seated near me, told me that this terrible custom was one recently introduced by the Naya.

"The ghastly practice is supposed to appease Zomara and give us victory over our enemies," she said. "As soon as any serious illness setteth in, the patient is taken from his house wrapped in his best robes, deposited in a grave and then covered with earth. No one in Mo now dieth a natural death. When the body hath been placed in the grave, the friends of the dead man set forth to kill the first living creature they can encounter, man, woman or beast, believing that through their victim their friend hath been compelled to die. When thus in search of an expiatory victim, they take the precaution of breaking off young shoots of the shrubs as they pass by, leaving the broken ends hanging in the direction they are going as a warning to people to shun that path. Even should one of their own relatives be the first to meet the avengers they dare not suffer him to escape."

"Life is not very secure in Mo when sickness rageth," I observed.

"No," she replied, sighing. "It is merely one of the many horrible practices the Naya hath introduced into our land. Whether a man is buried alive, or whether he dieth in the fight, his kinsmen at once assemble and destroy all his goods, saving only his vessels of gold which are confiscated for the Naya's use. The curse of Zomara would fall heavily upon anyone who attempteth to make use of any article once owned by a dead person. After the destruction of the property hath taken place the house is filled with the fumes of burning resin. The guests then sit in the perfumed atmosphere drinking large draughts of fiery liquids and give vent to their feelings in violent shouts."

"A strange custom, indeed," I said, astonished. "And it is only of recent introduction?"

"When, three years ago the ancient Temple of Zomara was discovered beneath the earth and all in Mo descended to witness its wonders, the Naya gave orders for the custom, as I have described, to be rigorously observed," she answered, turning her clear, trusting eyes upon Omar as she spoke.

Soon afterwards she left us in order to give some orders to the slaves, and the story-teller and musicians also departing, Goliba brought in three of the provincial governors who had visited us on the last occasion we had been the aged sage's guests, and together we discussed and criticised for the last time the arrangements made for the revolt. After an hour's consultation these men again departed, and Goliba himself having brought us our arms, consisting of an English-made magazine-rifle each, some ammunition, and a short but very keen sword manufactured in Mo, left to make a tour of his house to personally inspect the measures taken for its defence.

The next hour was so full of breathless excitement that we dared only converse in whispers. The atmosphere was hot and oppressive, the sky had grown dark and overcast, threatening ominously, while ever and anon could be heard the faint clank of arms; men, tall, dark and mysterious, passed and repassed along the dark colonnades, or stood in knots leaning on their rifles discussing the situation in undertones.

On returning to us our host told us that the store of arms we had seen, as well as others in various neighbourhoods, had all been distributed, and that the whole city was awaiting the signal.

"Roughly speaking, thou hast in the capital alone thirty thousand adherents," the councillor said to Omar. "Thou hast therefore nothing to fear. The path to victory is straight, and little danger lurketh there."

Almost ere these words had fallen from his lips, loud shouting sounded at the door that gave entrance to the patio wherein we stood, and we were startled to notice a scuffle taking place between a number of those who were about to guard the house and some would-be intruders. Yet ere we could realise the true state of affairs, we saw dozens of the royal soldiers scrambling down from the walls on every side, rifles flashed here and there, and within a few moments the place was in possession of the troops of the Naya.

"We seek Omar, the prince, and his companions," cried a man in a shining golden breastplate, evidently an officer of high rank, striding up to Goliba. "We hold orders from the Naya to capture them, and take them to the palace. We know thou hast harboured them."

Before our host could reply twenty of the fighting-men of Mo, having recognized us, dashed across, and notwithstanding our resistance, had seized us. Goliba, too, was quickly made prisoner, and above the shouting and hoarse imprecations we heard in the darkness a loud piercing woman's scream.

Liola had also fallen into their hands!

We fought our captors with all the strength of which we were capable, but were unarmed, for on receiving the rifles and swords from Goliba we had placed them together at a little distance away in a corner of the court. It took fully a dozen stalwart soldiers to hold the black giant Kona, and even then it was as much as they could do to prevent him from severely mauling them. His grip was like a vice; his fist hard as iron.

In the hands of three of these white robed soldiers, who had on our arrival in Mo cheered and belauded us, I struggled fiercely, but to no avail, for they dragged us all onward across the patio and out into the street, now crowded by those attracted by the unusual disturbance in the house of the Naya's councillor. The huge grim gateway of the royal palace stood facing the end of the long, broad thoroughfare, and from where we stood we had an uninterrupted view of it. Our arrest was indeed a disaster when we seemed within an ace of success. The people regarded us indifferently as we were hurried up the hill towards the great stone arch with its massive watch-towers, and it appeared as though the swift decisive step of securing the ringleaders of the revolt had entirely crushed it, for the people, instead of showing defiance, shrank back from the soldiers, cowed and submissive.

Suddenly, as we went forward, the great bell in one of the high turrets of the Naya's stronghold boomed forth the first stroke of the midnight hour.

Then, in an instant, a bright red flash blinded us, followed by a report so deafening, that the very rock whereon the city was built trembled, and we saw amid the dense smoke before us the great black gateway, with its watch towers where the sentries were pacing, break away, and shoot in huge masses high towards the sky.

The explosion was terrific; its effect appalling. The glare lit the whole city for a brief second with a light like a stormy sunset, then upon us showered great pieces of iron and stone with mangled human limbs, the *débris* of a gateway that for centuries had been considered absolutely impregnable.

The first blow against tyranny and oppression had been struck, terrible and decisive. It was the people's call to arms. Would they respond?

XXVII

By the Naya's Orders

A short time only did we remain in doubt as to the intention of the populace. The suppressed excitement found vent even before the clouds of choking smoke had rolled away. The signal had been given, and instantly they responded with fierce yells, throwing themselves suddenly upon the soldiers, using weapons that seemed to have been produced like magic.

Those who had effected our capture, dumbfounded, first by the appalling explosion, and then by the hostile attitude of the people, released us instantly, being compelled to fight for their lives back towards the smoking ruins of the palace-gate.

Within a few moments the great broad thoroughfare, with its handsome houses, became the scene of a most fierce and sanguinary conflict. Rifles flashed everywhere, in the street, from the windows and roofs of surrounding buildings, pouring a fire upon the soldiers so deadly that few succeeded in escaping back to the place whence they came. With startling suddenness I found myself in the midst of this stirring scene, fighting for life beside Omar. Both of us had snatched rifles and ammunition from fallen soldiers, while someone in the crowd had given me a fine sword with bejewelled hilt, which I hastily buckled on in case of emergency. Behind us a great barricade was being built of the first things that came to hand. The houses were being divested of their furniture by a hundred busy hands, and this, piled high, with spaces here and there for the guns, soon presented a barrier formidable, almost insurmountable. The erection of barricades was, we afterwards found, part of the scheme, for in all the principal thoroughfares similar piles were constructed, each being manned by a sturdy body of men, well-armed and determined to hold in check and repulse the attack which they knew would, ere long, be made upon them by the military.

The forces of Mo, feared on every hand for their daring and brilliant feats were, we knew, not to be trifled with, and as word had been secretly conveyed to Omar that the Naya, on hearing of the intention of the people, had ordered her soldiers to institute an indiscriminate massacre, we should have to fight hard to save our lives.

The barricade was soon completed, and quickly word spread from mouth to mouth to get behind it. This we all did, to the number of about three thousand; then came a period of waiting. It was not our object to renew the attack, but to await reprisals. Apparently, however, the blowing up of the palace-gate had utterly disconcerted the royal troops whose barracks were in that vicinity, and we could see by the crowd of moving torches that the soldiers were engaged in repairing the huge breach made in the walls before marching forth to quell the insurrection.

In the darkness we waited patiently. A few desultory shots, fired by some of our more adventurous partisans, who, climbing to the top of the barricade, aimed where they saw the torches moving, broke the ominous silence, but in distant parts of the city we could hear the rapid firing of musketry, with now and then a loud thundering roar when a heavy field-piece was discharged.

Each moment seemed an hour as we remained inactive behind that improvised barrier of doors, shutters, furniture, iron gates and railings. Omar and I were standing together beside one of the three Maxim guns by which our position was defended, watching the preparations being made on the top of the hill for assaulting us, when suddenly there was a bright flash, and next instant a great shell fell behind us, bursting and dealing death and destruction among our ranks. The air became rent by the shrill cries of the wounded and the hoarse agonized exclamations of the dying, for this first shot from the palace had been terribly effective, and fully fifty of those anxious to bear their part in the struggle for liberty had been killed, while many others were wounded. The shell had unfortunately fallen right in the centre of the crowd.

Again another was discharged, but it whistled over our heads and exploded far away behind us, shattering several houses, but injuring nobody. A third and a fourth were sent at us, but neither were so effective as the first. The breach in the wall where the gate had once been had now been repaired, and the adherents of the Great White Queen were at last taking the offensive.

Both Omar and myself had earlier that day, during our visit to the store of arms, been instructed in the use of that terror of modern warfare, the Maxim gun, and the one against which we stood with two men had been allotted to us.

My companion, who had been watching with the deadly weapon ready sighted to sweep the street, turned to ask news of Liola, whom we had not seen since we were dragged from her father's house, and I had taken his place, my hand ready to fire. Of Liola's fate I feared the worst. She had been taken prisoner, and had probably been killed or injured in the fierce *mêlée*.

Suddenly with wild yells, several hundred of the Naya's horsemen dashed down the hill, their swords whirling, followed by a huge force of men mounted and dismounted. I saw that at last they had come forth for the attack, and without a second's hesitation bent and commenced a fire, the terrible rattling of which held me appalled. The guns on either side followed mine in chorus, and almost momentarily we were pouring out such a hail of bullets, that amid the smoke and fire the great body of horses and troops were mowed down like grass before the scythe. The foremost in the cavalry ranks had no time to lift their carbines to reply, ere they were swept into eternity, and those coming behind, although making a desperate stand, fell riddled by bullets from our three terrible engines of destruction.

The fight with Samory's fugitives on the Way of the Thousand Steps had been exciting enough, but in extent or bloodshed was not to be compared with this. In that single onward rush of the Naya's troops hundreds were killed, for, ceasing our fire for a moment or two while the smoke cleared, we saw, lying in the street, great piles of men and horses, who had fallen upon one another in their forward dash and died under our frightful hail of lead.

A short pause, and the rifles and all the chorus of surrounding artillery took up their thunder-song with increased energy. These works of man outrivalled the natural elements by their tremendous booming and their disastrous power. Shells from the palace walls fell upon us thick and fast. No lightning's flash can accomplish such ruin as the modern ordnance projectile. A few centuries back the thought would have been incomprehensible; even so the visionary and ridiculed idea of to-day may be realised in the future. The shots descended, a veritable storm of lead, and several times the clouds of choking dust they set up enveloped us; but we were undaunted, and continued to work the Maxim, spreading its death-dealing rain up the broad thoroughfare and preventing any from reaching our barricade.

The idea of the troops was no doubt to gradually force us back from the external positions of the city into the central, and from the centre to the east in the direction of the gate that gave access to the country. By this means the fighting area would be compressed, and we should be surrounded by a large body of our enemies who had massed outside the gate to cut off our retreat. But the thundering boom of cannon and sharp rattle of musketry on our right, showed that our comrades, barricaded in a great thoroughfare running parallel with the one wherein we were, had also set to work to repel their enemy.

Barricades had sprung up in all directions like magic. The four corners of intersecting streets were the positions mostly chosen for them, and every conceivable article was used in their construction. Women and children vied with the men in activity and resourcefulness in the erection of these improvised works of defence, and the work slackened not even when shells and bullets fell about in dangerous proximity.

Our companions, the partisans of Omar to whom they looked to deliver their country from the thraldom of tyranny, were fortunately not devoid of those soldier-like qualities which in past ages had raised the military renown of Mo to the greatest altitude; what they lacked mostly outside of themselves were capable officering and generalship. There were a few officers of the royal army among them, men who had become convinced that a change of government was necessary, but the people were left to do battle mainly on the principle of individual enterprise.

Time after time attacks, each increasing in strength and proving more disastrous to us than the first, were made upon us. But our Maxims kept up their rattle, and from every part of the great wall of paving stones, furniture, trees and heaped-up miscellaneous articles, there poured out volley after volley from bristling rifles.

The troops quickly found the street absolutely untenable, for each time they made a rush to storm our position they were compelled to fall back, and few indeed reached a place of safety amid our deadly fire. When we had held the barricade for nearly an hour, Kona, Omar and myself being close together bearing our part in repulsing our opponents, a loud roar suddenly sounded before us and at the same instant a huge shell, imbedding itself in our defences, exploded with a bright light and deafening report.

The havoc caused was appalling. Half our barricade was blown completely away, and besides killing and maiming dozens of our comrades, it shattered several houses close by, and its force sent me down flat upon my back. Instantly I struggled to my feet, and finding myself uninjured save for a severe laceration of the hand, glanced round seeking my two friends. But they were not there!

The shell had set part of the barricade on fire, and already the flames were rising high, lighting up the terrible, lurid scene. Again I bent to my Maxim and recommenced firing, but as I did so another shell, only too well directed, struck the opposite end of our defences, and instantly a disaster resulted similar to the first, while a house at the same moment fell with a terrible crash, burying several unfortunate fellows beneath its *débris*.

Instantly I saw that our defences were partially demolished, and as shell after shell fell in rapid succession in our vicinity and exploded, our gallant defenders, still determined to prove victors, rushed up the hill to try conclusions with the Naya's troops. It was a wild, mad dash, and I found myself carried forward in the onrush of several thousand excited men. Meeting the remnant of the cavalry we fought with savage ferocity, alternately being beaten and beating. I had lost Omar, Kona and Goliba, half fearing that they had been blown to atoms by the shell, nevertheless the courage of my comrades never failed, although gaining the top of the hill and defeating the cavalry by sheer force of numbers, they were driven back again at the point of the bayonet, while from the ruins of the palace-gate a steady rifle fire was poured upon us at the same time.

Half-way down the hill we made a gallant stand, but again were compelled to fall back in disorder. Soon we were driven from the main thoroughfare into the minor streets, refuging in and fighting from the houses, whilst our foe steadily and angrily pursued and closed in upon us, dislodging us from our shelters and leaving few loop-holes for escape.

The carnage was awful; quarter was refused. It seemed as though our hope was a forlorn one; the general and ruthless massacre ordered by the Great White Queen had actually begun!

The loss of our barricade paralysed us. Yet we could hear the roar and tumult, and seeing the reflection of fires in other parts of the city, only hoped that our comrades there were holding their own valiantly as we had struggled to do. Ever and anon loud explosions sounded above the thunder of artillery, and it became apparent that the royal troops were engaged in blowing up any defences they could not take by assault.

From where I had sought shelter behind a high wall with a lattice window through which I continually discharged my rifle into the roadway, I saw massacres within walls and without. The troops had poured down upon us in absolutely overwhelming numbers, and no resistance by our weakened force could now save us. One fact alone reassured me and gave me courage. In the bright red glare shed by the flames from a burning building, among a party who made a sally from the opposite house I caught a momentary glance of the lithe, active figure of Omar, fighting desperately against a body of the Naya's infantry and leading on his comrades with loud shouts of encouragement.

"Do your duty, men!" he gasped. "Let not your enemies crush you!"

But the *mêlée* was awful. Once again our partisans were driven back, and the street was strewn with bodies in frightful array, left where they fell, uncovered, unattended.

The thick black cloud of smoke which hung over the City in the Clouds and on either side of it obscured the rising dawn and intensified the horrors of the awful drama. Fires raged in every direction, making the air hot; it was close through the smoke cloud above and the absence of wind, foetid with the odour of human blood that lay in pools in every street and splashed upon the houses. The sight was majestic, terrible, never-to-be-forgotten; in the midst of it the terror and stupefaction were almost beyond human endurance. On all sides were heard the roar of flames, the breaking of timbers and the crashing in of roofs and walls. Fire and sword reigned throughout the magnificent capital of Mo; its people were being swept into eternity with a relentless brutality that was absolutely fiendish.

Into the hearts of the survivors of the gallant force who had so readily constructed our barricade and so valiantly defended it, despair had entered. There was now no hope for the success of our cause. The forces of tyranny, oppression and misrule were fast proving the victors, and in that fearful indiscriminate shooting down of men, women and children that was proceeding, all knew that sooner or later they must fall victims.

I had seen nothing of Kona or Goliba since the wrecking of our barricade, but Omar, I was gratified to observe, was stationed at a window of the opposite house from which he directed well-aimed shots at those below. A body of fully five hundred infantry were besieging the house wherein a large number of our comrades had taken shelter, determined to put them to the sword; yet so desperate was the resistance that they found it impossible to enter, and many were killed in their futile endeavours. At length I noticed that while the main body covered the movements of several of their companions the latter were preparing a mine by which to blow it up. With the half-dozen men beside me we kept up a galling fire upon them, but all in vain. The mine was laid; only a spark was required to blow the place into the air.

WILLIAM LE QUEUX

Knowing that if such a catastrophe were accomplished we, too, must suffer being in such close proximity to it, we waited breathlessly, unable to escape from the vicinity of the deadly spot.

Suddenly, as one man, more fearless than the others, bent to fire the mine, the soldiers, with one accord, rushed back, and scarce daring to breathe I waited, fearing each second to see the house and its garrison shattered to fragments and myself receive the full force of the explosive.

But at that instant, even as I watched, a loud exultant shout broke upon my ear, and looking I saw approaching from the opposite end of the street a great crowd of people rushing forward, firing rapidly as they came.

They were our comrades. Their shouts were shouts of victory!

"Kill them!" they cried. "Let not one escape. They have killed our brothers; let us have revenge! The Naya shall die, and Omar shall be our Naba!"

The man bending over the explosive sprang back in fear without having applied the fatal spark, and his companions, taken thus completely by surprise, stood amazed at this sudden appearance of so large a body of the populace. But the rifles of the latter in a few seconds had laid low several of their number, and then, making a stand, they lowered their weapons. A loud word of command sounded, and as if from one weapon a volley was fired full upon the victorious people. For a few moments its deadly effect checked their progress, but an instant later they resumed their onward rush, and ere a second volley could be fired they had flung themselves upon their opponents, killing them with bayonet, sword and pistol.

Their rush was in too great a force to be withstood. As in other parts of the city, so here, they compelled the troops to fly before them, and shot them down as they sped back up the hill towards the great stronghold.

In those few fateful minutes the tables had suddenly been turned. While we, fighting hard in that hot corner, had imagined that we had lost, our comrades in other parts of the city had won a magnificent victory, and had come to our rescue at the eleventh hour.

Truly it was everywhere a fierce and bloody fight.

XXVIII

The Fight for the Emerald Throne

Thrown into utter confusion by the great press of people well armed and determined, the soldiers, who had fought so desperately, and who intended to blow up the house that Omar and his companions had made their stronghold, fled precipitately up the hill, but so rapid and heavy was the firing, that few, if any, got out of the street alive.

On seeing the chances thus suddenly turned in our favour we poured forth into the street again, and joining our forces with those of our rescuers, rushed with them into the main thoroughfare leading to the palace, scrambling over the *débris* of our barricade and the heaps of bodies that blocked our passage. A hurried question, addressed to a man rushing along at my side, elicited glad tidings. So fiercely had the people fought that the troops sent out to quell the rising had been utterly routed everywhere, while many of the regiments had turned in our favour and had actually held several of the barricades, winning brilliant victories.

"It is yonder, at the palace, where the resistance will be greatest," the man cried excitedly, blood streaming from a ghastly wound on his brow. "But our cause is good. The Naya shall die!"

"To the Palace!" screamed the infuriated mob. "To the Palace!"

And forward the frantic dash was made at redoubled pace until we came to the pile of fallen masonry, which had, a few hours ago, been the great impregnable gateway that closed each day at sunset, and opened not till sunrise, save for the Great White Queen herself.

Here the place seemed undefended until we came close up to it, when without warning we were met with a withering rifle fire that laid low dozens of our comrades. The man who had been so enthusiastic a moment before and who had told me of our successes, was struck full in the breast by a ball and fell against me dead.

For a moment only did we hold back. Dawn was spreading now, but the heavy black smoke obscured the struggling daylight. Suddenly there sounded just at my rear Omar's well-known voice, crying:

"Forward! Forward, my brethren. I, Omar, your prince, lead you into the palace of my father. To-day there commenceth a new and brighter era for our beloved land. Falter not, but end the struggle valiantly as ye have commenced it. Forward!"

His words sent a sudden patriotic thrill through the great concourse of armed men, who instantly sprang forward, and regardless of the blazing lines of rifles before them climbed the ruins and engaged the defenders hand to hand. It was a brilliant dash and could only have been accomplished by the courage inspired by Omar's words, for the odds were once more against us, and the rapid fire from behind the ruins played the most frightful havoc in our ranks. In the midst of the crowd I clambered up, sword in hand, over the huge masses of masonry and rubbish, and springing to earth on the other side, alighted in a corner where the picked guards of the Naya were making a last desperate stand.

At first the struggle had been a hand-to-hand one, but they had retreated, and were now firing heavy volleys that effectively kept us at bay.

Almost at the same moment as I sprang down I heard behind me fiendish yells and the clambering of many feet. In an instant I recognised it as the savage war cry of the Dagombas, and next second a hundred half-naked blacks, looking veritable fiends in the red glare, swept down headlong to the spot where I stood and, headed by Kona brandishing his spear, dashed straight upon the defenders. The effect of this was to cause the others to spring forward as reinforcements, and quicker than the time occupied in relating it, this position, an exceedingly strong one, fell into our hands. So infuriated were the Dagombas by the excesses committed by the soldiery in various parts of the city, that they vented their savage wrath upon the defenders until the butchery became awful, and I doubt whether a single man escaped.

The soldiers holding the next court, seeing this disaster, placed, ere we could prevent them, two field-pieces behind the closed gate wherein holes had been hacked, and with the walls crowded with men with rifles they began to pour upon us a deadly hail of shot and shell. Once, for a moment only, Niaro, the provincial governor I had met at Goliba's, fought beside me, but after exchanging a few breathless words we became again separated. Little time elapsed ere one and all understood that to remain long under this galling fire of the palace guards would mean death to us, therefore it required no further incentive than an appeal from Omar to cause us to storm the entrance to the court.

"Well done, friends," he shouted. "We have broken down the first defence. Come, let us sweep away the remainder, but spare the life of the Naya. Remember I am her son. Again, forward! Zomara giveth strength to your hands and courage to your hearts. Use them for the purpose he hath bestowed them upon you."

In the forward movement in response to these loudly-uttered words fearful cries of rage and despair mingled with hoarse shouts of the vanquished. Rifles flashed everywhere in the faint morning light, bullets kept up a singing chorus above our heads, and about me, in the frightful tumult, gleamed naked blood-stained blades. At first the guards, like those in the outer court, made a desperate resistance, but soon they showed signs of weakness, and I could distinguish in the faint grey dawn how gradually we were driving them back, slowly gaining the entrance to the court, which, I remembered, was a very large and beautiful one with cool colonnades, handsome fountains and beautiful flowering trees of a kind I had never seen in England.

At last, after a fierce struggle, in which the defenders very nearly succeeded in driving us out or slaughtering us where we stood, the field-pieces were silenced, a charge of explosive was successfully placed beneath the gate and a loud roar followed that shook every stone in that colossal pile.

The ponderous door was shattered and the defenders disorganised by the suddenness of the disaster. Almost before they were aware of it we had poured in among them. Then the slaughter was renewed, and the scenes witnessed on every hand frightful to behold.

Kona and his black followers fought like demons, spearing the soldiers right and left, always in the van of the fray. Omar and Kona were apparently sharing the direction of the attack, for sometimes I heard the voice of one raised, giving orders, and sometimes the other. But, however irregular the mode of proceeding might have been from a military standpoint, success was ours, for half an hour later the two inner courts, strenuously defended by the Naya's body guard, were taken, and judging from the fact that the firing outside had become desultory it seemed as though hostilities in the streets had practically ceased.

At this juncture some man, a tall, powerful fellow who was distinguishing himself by his valiant deeds, told me that the military down in the city, finding the populace so strong, had, after a most terrific fight, at last ceased all opposition and declared in favour of the Prince Omar. This, we afterwards discovered, was the actual truth. The carnage in the streets had, however, been appalling, before this step had been resolved upon, but when once the declaration had been made, the remnants of the Naya's army were, at the orders of the leaders of the people, marched without the city wall on the opposite side to the great cliff, and there halted to await the progress of events.

Meanwhile, we were still hewing our way, inch by inch, towards the centre of the palace of the Great White Queen. So desperate was the conflict that the perspiration rolled from us in great beads, and many of my comrades fell from sheer exhaustion, and were trampled to death beneath the feet of the wildly-excited throng.

Soon, driving back the final ring of defenders, and shooting them down to the last man, we dashed across the central court, where the polished marble paving ran with blood, and battering down the great gilded doors, that fell with a loud crash, gained our goal, entering the spacious Hall of Audience, in the centre of which, upon its raised daïs, under the great gilded dome, stood the historic Emerald Throne.

The magnificent hall was deserted. The bloodshed had been frightful. The courts were heaped with dead and dying. Several chairs were lying overturned, as if the courtiers and slaves had left hastily, and even across the seat of royalty one of the Naya's rich bejewelled robes of state had been hastily flung down. This, snatched up by one of the Dagombas, was tossed away into the crowd, who gleefully tore it to shreds as sign that the power of the dreaded Naya was for ever broken.

To the exultant shouts of a thousand wild, blood-bespattered people, the great hall echoed again and again. The faint light showed too plainly at what terrible cost the victory had been won. Their clothes were torn, their faces were blackened by powder, from their superficial wounds blood was oozing, while the more serious consequences of sword-cuts and gun-shots had been hastily bound by shreds of garments. Flushed by their victory, they were a strange, forbidding-looking rabble. Yet they were our partisans; a peaceful, law-abiding people who had been oppressed by a tyrannical rule and long ripe for revolt, they had seized this opportunity to break the power of the cruel-hearted woman who was unworthy to hold sway upon that historic throne.

"Let us seek the Naya! She shall not escape! Let us avenge the deaths of our fathers and children!" were the cries raised when they found the Hall of Audience deserted. Apparently they had expected to find the Great White Queen seated there, awaiting them, and their chagrin was intense at finding her already a fugitive.

"She dare not face us!" they screamed. "All tyrants are cowards. Kill her! Let us kill her!"

But Goliba, whom I was gratified to see present and unharmed, sprang upon the daïs, and waving his arms, cried:

"Rather let us first place our valiant young prince upon the Emerald Throne. Let him be appointed our ruler; then let us seek to place the Naya in captivity."

"No," they cried excitedly. "Kill her!"

"Give her alive to Zomara!" suggested one man near me, grimly. "Let her taste the punishment to which she has consigned so many hundreds of our relatives and friends."

Heedless of these shouts, Goliba, stretching forth his hand, led Omar, whose torn clothes and perspiring face told how hard he had fought, towards the wonderful throne of green gems, and seating him thereon, cried:

"I, Goliba, on behalf of these, the people of our great kingdom, enthrone thee and invest thee with the supreme power in place of thy mother, the Naya."

Loud deafening cheers, long repeated, rose from the assembled multitude, and the soldiers dying in the courts outside knew that the revolt of the people had been successful; that right had won in this struggle against might. Then, when the cries of adulation became fainter, and with difficulty silence was restored, Omar rose, and raising his sword, upon which blood was still wet, exclaimed in a loud, ringing voice:

"I, Omar, the last descendant of the royal house of Sanom, hereby proclaim myself Naba of Mo."

Again cheers rang through the vaulted hall, and presently, when the excitement had once more died down, he added, gazing round with a regal air:

"About me here I see those who have borne arms in my cause, and to each and every one I render thanks. How much we may all of us deplore the loss of so many valuable lives death is nevertheless the inevitable result of any recourse to arms. At least, we have the satisfaction of knowing that our cause was a just one, and by the sacred memory of our ancestors I swear that my rule shall be devoid of that cruelty and tyranny that have disgraced the later pages of my beloved country's history. I, Omar, am your ruler; ye are my people. Obey the laws we promulgate and the good counsels of our advisers, and security both of life and property shall be yours. From this moment human sacrifices to our great god Zomara—to whom all praise be given for this victory of our arms—are abolished. But our first and foremost word from this, our

WILLIAM LE QUEUX

seat of royalty, is that the life of the Naya shall be spared. Your Naba hath spoken."

A visible look of disappointment overspread the countenances of those around me. All had, in their wild enthusiasm, desired to wreak their vengeance upon the unjust queen, but this royal decree forbade it. There even went forth murmurs of disapproval, and Omar, hearing them, said in a loud, serious voice:

"A Sanom hath never allowed his kinsman to be murdered, therefore although the Naya hath plotted to take my life, she shall be held captive, and not die. Let not a hair of her head be touched, or he who lifteth his hand against her shall be brought before me, and I will not spare him. Enough blood hath been already shed since the going down of the sun; let not another life be wasted."

Then calling Goliba, Kona, Niaro, and myself up to his side upon the royal daïs, he continued:

"These, my friends, who have assisted me to gain this, my kingdom, are deserving of reward, and this shall at once be given them. Goliba, whom all know as a sage and upright man—"

Cheers, long and ringing, here interrupted his words. When quiet had been restored he continued:

"Goliba shall retain his position as chief of our royal councillors, and shall be also Grand Vizier of Mo. Niaro, a trusty governor to whom all who have appealed have met with justice, is appointed Custodian of the Gate of Mo, in place of Babila, for whom we all mourn. To Kona, head man of the Dagombas of the forest, I owe my life, and he shall be chief of our army and of our body-guard, and his native followers shall themselves be the principal members of the guard. And Scarsmere," he said, turning towards me, "Scarsmere hath been my friend and companion across the great black water; he knoweth not fear, for together we have been held by Samory and Prempeh, and have yet managed to preserve our lives. Since I, your Naba, left Mo by the Way of the Thousand Steps, and entered the land of the white men, Scarsmere hath been my friend and companion, therefore all shall treat him with due respect, for although he cometh from the wonderful land afar he shall be Governor of this our city and Keeper of our Treasure-house. He is the trusted and faithful friend of your Naba, and all shall regard him as highest in favour."

"We greet thee, Goliba!" enthusiastically cried the surging crowd. "We greet thee, Niaro, Custodian of the Gate! We greet thee, Kona, a savage but great chieftain! Thou art head of our army! We greet thee, Scarsmere, the friend of our royal Naba, and Governor of Mo! We, the people, accept you, and have confidence in your rule. Ye are all great, and are worthy of the offices to which ye have been raised. May your names be exalted above all others, and your faces be as beacons unto us!"

And they shouted themselves hoarse in cheering, seeing in the enthronement of the young Naba the dawn of a just and beneficent rule. Their adulations became louder, and even more profuse, when Omar proceeded to appoint others, well known and popular, to various offices connected with the palace.

"Happy," cried the white-bearded sages who had taken their places behind the throne—"happy is the prince whose trust is in Zomara and whose wisdom cometh from the King of the River."

"Happy," cried the people, humbling themselves—"happy is our Naba, the favourite of the Crocodile-god, the one from whose wrath all flee."

"That," replied Omar, "O people, is too much even for the Naba of Mo to hear. But may Zomara approve of my thoughts and actions! So shall the infernal powers destroy the wretches that employ them, and the arrows recoil upon those who draw a bow upon us. But, O sages, though your numbers are reduced your integrity is more tried and approved; therefore let Omar, your Naba, partake of the sweetness of your counsels and learn from aged experience the wisdom of the sons of earth. Ye shall tell me from time to time what the peace and sincerity of my throne requireth from me, for human prudence alone is far too weak to fight against the wiles of the deceitful."

I stood beside the royal seat, deep in thought, silently gazing upon the thousand upturned, grimy faces. It had indeed been a curious turn of events that had conspired to place my friend upon the throne of an autocrat, and also to give, into my own unaccustomed hands, the rule and control of this most magnificent and extensive capital, and all the wondrous treasures of the royal house of the Sanoms.

WILLIAM LE QUEUX

XXIX

A Mystery

From the glittering Hall of Audience a forward movement was soon made to the inner rooms that formed the private apartments of the Naya. Carried onward by the press of people, I was amazed at the magnificence and luxury everywhere apparent. The walls were mostly of polished marble inlaid with gold and adorned with frescoes, the ceilings ornamented with strange allegorical paintings, and the floors of jasper and alabaster. But as the irate crowd dashed onward through the great tenantless chambers they tore down the rich silk hangings and trod them underfoot, broke up the tiny gold-inlaid tables, and out of sheer wantonness hacked the soft divans with their swords.

The discovery that the Naya had fled increased the indignation of the mob, and were it not for the urgent appeal of Kona, who had at once assumed the commandership, the whole of the magnificent rooms would no doubt have been wrecked. As it was, however, the good counsels of the Dagomba head-man prevailed, and wanton hands were stayed from committing more serious excesses.

Whither the Great White Queen had fled no one knew. To every nook and corner search parties penetrated; even the sleeping apartment, with its massive bed of ivory and hangings of purple, gold-embroidered satin, was not held sacred. Yet nowhere could the once-dreaded ruler be discovered. Some cried that she had escaped into the city in the guise of a slave, others that she had descended into the cavern where stood the gigantic Temple of Zomara.

Another fact puzzled us greatly. From our elevated position we could see afar off a fierce conflict proceeding near the city gate on that side where access could be gained only by the steep flight of steps. Once, when I had looked, I saw that the city was comparatively quiet; now, however, this conflict had broken out again suddenly, and judging from the smoke and tumult it must have been terrific. All were surprised, and stood watching the clouds of grey smoke roll up into the bright morning air. But soon it died away, and believing it to be an outbreak by the conquered troops subdued with a firm hand by the victorious people, we thought no more of it.

The hours that succeeded were full of stirring incidents, and it was long before the least semblance of order could be restored in the city. With Kona I went forth into the crowded, turbulent streets, and the sight that met our gaze was awful. Bodies of soldiers and civilians were lying everywhere, the faces of some, to whom death had come swiftly, so calm and composed that they looked as if they slept, while upon the blood-smeared countenances of others, hideously mutilated perhaps, were terrible expressions, showing in what frightful agony they had passed into eternity. The road-ways were strewn with heaps of corpses; the gutters flowed with blood.

At such terrible cost had the tyrannical reign of the Naya been terminated; by such a frightful loss of human life had Omar been raised to the Emerald Throne.

Greater part of that eventful day was spent by Niaro, Kona, Goliba and myself in restoring order, while the people themselves, assisted by the troops, who had already sworn allegiance to their young Naba, cleared the streets and removed, as far as possible, all traces of the deadly feud. But to us there came no tidings of the Naya, although the strictest watch was kept everywhere to prevent her escaping.

The people were determined that if she might not pay the penalty of her evil deeds by death, she should at least be held captive in one of the foul dungeons beneath the palace, where so many of their relatives had rotted and died in agony or starvation.

A blazing noontide was succeeded by a calm and peaceful evening. Through many hours I had endeavoured, as far as lay in my power, to assume the command given me, and assisted by a number of quaintly-garbed officials enthusiastic in Omar's cause, I found my office by no means difficult. Order again reigning in the streets and the bodies removed, the city had quietly settled down, though of course not to its usual peacefulness. Crowds of the more excited ones still surged up and down the broad thoroughfares, calling down vengeance upon the once powerful queen, but all voices were united in cheers for the Naba Omar, their chosen ruler.

Save for those required to preserve order, the survivors of the troops were back in barracks long before sunset, and the palace-guard had been reorganised under Kona's personal supervision. The Dagombas alone comprised Omar's body-guard, and I found on my return to the palace that they had exchanged their scanty clothes of native bark-cloth for the rich bright-coloured silk uniforms of those who had acted in a

WILLIAM LE QUEUX

similar capacity to the Naya. With their black happy shining faces they looked a magnificent set of men, though for the first few hours they appeared a trifle awkward in gay attire that was entirely strange to them. It was amusing, too, to watch how each stalked by, erect and proud, like a peacock spreading its brilliant plumage to the sun.

That night, when the bright moon rose, lighting up the great silent court, until yesterday occupied by the terrible queen and her corrupt *entourage*, Omar and I sat together discussing the events of those fateful hours since midnight. We had eaten from the gold dishes in which the Naya's food had been served; we had quenched our thirst from the jewel-encrusted goblets that she was wont to raise to her thin blue lips. By Omar's side I thus tasted, for the first time, the pleasures of royalty.

My old chum had sent away his attendants, the host of slaves with the twelve Dagombas who acted as the body-guard on duty, and we sat alone together in the moonlight, the quiet broken only by the distant roll of a drum somewhere down in the city, and the cool plashing of the beautiful fountain as it fell softly into its crystal basin. Kona, Goliba and Niaro were all away at their duties, and now for the first time for many hours, we had a few minutes to talk together.

"Do you know, Scars," Omar said, moving uneasily upon the royal divan that had been carried out into the court at his orders, while, tired out, I reclined upon another close to him—"do you know there is but one thing I regret, now that I have succeeded to the throne that was my birthright?"

"Regret!" I exclaimed. "What regret can you have? Surely you were entirely right in acting as you did? The people were anxious for a just and upright ruler, and having regard to the fact that your mother plotted your assassination in so cold-blooded a manner, her overthrow is justly deserved."

"Yes, yes, I know," he answered, rather impatiently. "But it is not that—not that. One thing remains to complete my happiness, but alas!"—and he sighed heavily without finishing his sentence.

"Why speak so despondently?" I inquired, surprised. "As Naba of Mo all things are possible."

"Alas! not everything," he said, with an air of melancholy.

"Well, tell me," I urged. "Why are you so downcast?"

"I—I have lost Liola," he answered hoarsely. "Truth to tell, Scarsmere, I loved Goliba's daughter."

"She is absolutely beautiful," I admitted. "No man can deny that she is handsome enough to share your royal throne."

"Indeed she was," he said with emotion, his chin upon his breast.

"Was!" I cried. "Why do you speak thus?"

"Because she is dead!" he answered huskily. "Ah! Scars, you don't know how fondly I loved her ever since the first moment we met. I loved her better than life; better than all this honour and pomp to which I have succeeded. Yet she has been taken from me, and my life in future will be devoid of that happiness I had contemplated. True I am Naba of Mo, successor to the stool whereon a line of unconquered monarchs have sat throughout a thousand years, yet all is an empty pleasure now that my well-beloved is lost to me."

"Have you obtained definite news of her death?" I asked sympathetically.

"Yes. When we were captured in Goliba's house, she, too, was seized by the soldiers. While held powerless I saw her struggling with her captors, for they had somehow obtained knowledge of the part she had played in our conspiracy against their queen. The Naya had, it appears, ordered her guards to bring us all before her, dead or alive. With valiant courage she resented the indignity of arrest, and as a consequence she was brutally killed by those who held her prisoner."

"How have you ascertained this?" I asked, shocked at the news, for I myself had admired Liola's extraordinary beauty.

"To-day I have had before me the three survivors of the guards who captured us, and all relate the same story. They say that a young girl, taken prisoner with us, while being dragged up the roadway towards the palace was in danger of being released by the people, and one of their comrades, remembering the Naya's orders that none of us were to escape, in the *mêlée* raised his sword and plunged it into her heart."

"The brute!" I cried. "Is the murderer among the survivors?"

"No. All three agree that the mob, witnessing his action, set upon him and literally tore him limb from limb."

"A fate he certainly deserved," I said. "But has her body been recovered?"

"A body has been found and I have seen it. But the limbs are crushed, and her face is, alas! trampled out of all recognition, although the dress answers exactly to one that Goliba says his daughter possessed, and in which I myself saw her. There is, alas! no doubt of her fate. She has been brutally murdered, and at the instigation of the Naya, who sent forth her fiendish horde to kill us."

"I knew from the manner you exchanged glances with Liola that you loved her," I said, after a pause, brief and painful.

"Yes," he answered sadly. "Surreptitiously I had breathed into her ear words of affection, and had been transported to a veritable paradise of delight by the discovery that she reciprocated my love. But," he added, harshly, "my brief happy love-dream is now ended. I must live and work only for my people; they must be to me both sweetheart and wife. I must act as my ancestors have done, indulging them and loving them."

Never before, even in the moments when as fellow-adventurers things looked blackest, had I seen him in so utterly dejected an attitude. The light had died from his face, and he had suddenly become burdened by a monarch's responsibilities; prematurely aged by a bitter sorrow that had sapped all youthful gaiety from his buoyant heart.

With heartfelt sympathy I endeavoured to console him, but all was unavailing. That he had loved her madly was only too apparent, and it seemed equally certain that she was dead, for shortly afterwards Goliba entered, and in a voice full of emotion told us how he had been able to identify the body, and that his tardy attendance upon his royal master was due to the fact that he had been superintending her burial.

The old sage's words visibly increased Omar's burden of sorrow, for in the moonlight I saw a tear trickle down his pale cheek, glistening for an instant brighter than the jewels upon his robe. Liola had fallen victim to the inhuman brutality of the Naya's guards, and Mo had thus been deprived of a bewitchingly handsome queen.

The *dénouement* of this stirring story of a throne was indeed a tragic one; Goliba had lost his only daughter, the pride of his heart, and Omar the woman he loved.

The silence that followed was broken by a hasty footstep, and the tall dark figure of Kona approached.

"A strange fact hath transpired, O Master!" he cried breathlessly, addressing Omar.

"Speak, tell me," the young Naba exclaimed, starting up. "Is it of Liola that thou bearest news?"

"Alas! no. That she was murdered in the first moments of the conflict is only too certain," he answered. "The news I bring thee is amazing. While we were engaged in the struggle for thy throne, thine enemies, the people of Samory, entered the city and fought side by side with the military!"

"Samory's people here!" we all three cried, starting up.

"They were, but they have departed no one knows whither. Their numbers were not great, but they sacked and burned several large buildings near the city-gate and fought desperately to join their allies the troops of Mo, but were at last prevented and driven back by the people in a fierce bloody conflict that actually occurred after thou wert enthroned."

Then I remembered having noticed the smoke of the encounter, and how with others, I had been puzzled.

"But how could they enter our country, and unseen approach the city?" Omar exclaimed astounded.

"I know not the intricacies of the approaches to Mo save the perilous Way of the Thousand Steps," Kona replied. "The force may have been the rear-guard of the army that attacked Mo, and were defeated in the great chasm known as the Grave of Enemies. If they approached by that means they must have followed closely in our footsteps, and through the treachery of spies, been admitted to the city at a time when the alertness of the guards was diverted by the popular rising."

"Were their losses great in the fight?" Goliba asked.

"Terrible. Whole streets and market-places in the vicinity of the entrance to the city were found strewn with their dead," the black giant answered. "Apparently the people discovered the identity of their enemies and took no prisoners. With the exception of about two hundred survivors all were killed."

"And the survivors have escaped!" Omar observed thoughtfully.

"Yes. Owing to the lax watch kept at the gate during those momentous hours, they were enabled to descend the steps to the plain and get clear away."

"They must nevertheless be still in Mo. They must be found," Omar cried excitedly. "While they are among us our country will be in jeopardy, for they will act as spies. Samory hath set his mind upon conquering this our land; his plot must be frustrated."

"Already have I given orders for a search from the land's most northerly limits even to the Grave of Enemies, O Master," Kona answered. "All the men who could be spared from guarding the city I have dispatched on expeditions with orders to attack and destroy the fugitives."

"They cannot have travelled far," the young ruler said. "They have only about twelve hours' start of your men."

"To a man our troops are now loyal to thee," the newly-created chief of the army answered. "They are alive to the fact that Samory's fighting-men are their bitterest foes, therefore if the survivors of that intrepid force are within our boundaries, they will assuredly be overtaken and killed."

"I would rather that they were captured and held as hostages," Omar said. "Enough blood hath been already shed to-day."

"The order to capture them is not sufficient incentive to thine army to rout them from their hiding-place," Kona replied. "They have had the audacity to make a dash upon thy city and burn some of its most renowned and beautiful structures, therefore in their opinion if not in thine, death alone would expiate their offence."

"I would wish their lives to be spared," Omar repeated. "But the army is under thy control, and I leave the final annihilation of the band of freebooters unto thee. Hast thou obtained any tidings of the Naya's flight?"

"None. My Dagombas have searched every nook and corner of this thy palace, each prison dungeon hath been entered by detachments of soldiers, while enthusiastic parties have descended to the subterranean Temple of Zomara, but found only the dwarf priests there. The Naya hath disappeared as completely as if Zomara had crushed her between his jaws."

"Her disappearance is amazing," Omar observed. "Even her personal attendants whom I have questioned are ignorant of the direction she hath taken. They declare that she escaped within ten minutes of the blowing up of the palace-gate. The catastrophe alarmed her, and she saw in the fall of these defences the instability of her throne."

"All is being done that can be done to secure her arrest," Kona said. "It is absolutely necessary that we should hold her captive, or, like the deposed queen of the Nupé, she may stir up strife and form a plot to reascend the stool."

"To thee, Kona, I look to guard me from mine enemies," my friend exclaimed. "We must elucidate the mystery of the sudden descent of this weak force of Samory's, the rapidity with which they struck their blow, and the means by which they have, within twelve hours, so completely eluded us."

"News of them hath been flashed even unto the furthermost limits of thy kingdom, O Great Chief," Kona assured him. "No effort shall be spared by thy servant in executing thy commands. I go forth again, and sleep shall not close my eyes until the men of Samory have been overtaken."

With these words he made deep obeisance to the newly-enthroned sovereign, and lifting his long native spear, which he still retained, he swore vengeance most terrible upon the enemies of Mo, who had, with such consummate strategic skill, entered and attacked the city at the moment when it remained undefended.

"There is some deep mystery underlying this, Scars," Omar said, when Kona had stalked away into the darkness, and Goliba had risen and crossed the moon-lit court in response to a message delivered by a black slave. "I am scarcely surprised at Kona's failure to capture the Naya; indeed, personally, I should only be too happy to know that she had got safely beyond the limits of Mo. But the sudden attack and rapid disappearance of this marauding band of Samory proves two things; first that our country, long thought impregnable, may be invaded, and secondly that through Kouaga Samory is in possession of certain of our secrets."

"What secrets?" I asked.

"Secrets upon the preservation of which the welfare and safety of my country depend," he answered mysteriously. Then, with a sudden air of dejection, he added: "But there, what matters after all, now that Liola is dead and my life is desolate? At the very moment when the greatest honour has been bestowed upon me and I am enthroned Naba, the saviour of my people, the greatest sorrow has also fallen upon me."

After a moment's silence he started up in sudden desperation, crying: "Slave have I been to evil all the days of my life! I have toiled and earned nothing; I have sown in care and reaped not in merriment; I have poisoned the comfort of others, but no blessing hath fallen into my own lap. Blasted are the paths whereon I trod; my past actions are ravenous vultures gnawing on my vitals, and the sharpened claws of malicious spirits await my arrival among the regions of the accursed."

"Yes," I observed with a sigh, for the remembrance of that bright, beautiful face was to me likewise one of ineffable sadness. "Yes," I said, "Fate has indeed been unkind. What she has bestowed with one hand, she has taken away with the other."

Then we were silent. Above the cool plashing music of the fountain could be heard the distant roar of voices in great rejoicing, while upon the starlit sky was still reflected a red ominous glare from the fires raging in the city that no effort of man could subdue. At the gate leading outward to the next court stood two sentries with drawn swords gleaming in the moonbeams, mute and motionless like statues, while echoing along the colonnade was the measured tramp of the soldier as he paced before the entrance of the gilded Hall of Audience, the scene of so many stirring dramas in the nation's history. From the divan whereon I sat I could see the great Emerald Throne glittering green under a brilliant light, with its golden image of the sacred crocodile and its banner bearing the hideous vampire-bat, while around it were still grouped the officials of the household, the body-guard of faithful Dagombas, the slaves ready with their great fans, and Gankoma, the executioner, with his bright double-edged *doka*, all standing in patience, awaiting the coming of their royal master.

The Court of Mo was, I reflected, a strange admixture of European civilization and culture with African superstition and barbarity. On the one hand the buildings were of marble or stone, magnificent in their proportions, with decorations in the highest style of Moorish art, the arms were of the latest pattern surreptitiously imported from England and many of them faithfully copied by skilful, enlightened workmen; electricity was known and used, and the tastes of the people showed a refinement almost equal to that of any European state. Yet in religion there prevailed the crudest and most ignorant forms of superstition, one of which was the horrible practice of burying alive all sick persons, while the custom of the executioner accompanying the reigning monarch everywhere, ready to obey the royal command, was distinctly a relic of savage barbarism.

"A few moments ago you spoke of secrets that must be preserved," I said presently, turning to Omar.

"Yes," he answered slowly. "But my heart is too full of poignant grief to think of them. To-night the secrets are mine alone; to-morrow you shall be in possession of at least one of them. I have, however, much yet to do, I see, before I rest," he added, glancing over his shoulder into the brilliant hall where stood the empty throne.

Then rising wearily, he sighed for Goliba's dead daughter, and weighted by his rich robes, slowly strode across to the arched entrance from which the light streamed forth, and as he set foot upon its threshold every proud head bowed to earth in deep, abject obeisance.

XXX

Treasure and Treason

At Omar's request a few days later I accompanied him alone through a private exit of the palace, and ere long we found ourselves unnoticed beyond the ponderous city walls, where two horses, held by a slave, were awaiting us. Mounting, we rode straight for the open country, and not knowing whither we were going or what were my companion's intentions, we soon left the great city far behind. For fully three hours we pressed forward, my companion avoiding any answer to my questions as to our goal, until about noon we came to a rising mount in the midst of a beautiful country with palms and scattered orange-groves.

The scene was a veritable paradise. Beautiful fruits peeped from between the foliage, and every coloured, every scented flower, in agreeable variety intermingled with the grass. Roses and woodbines, very much like those in England, appeared in beauteous contention; while beneath great trees were rich flocks of birds of various feather. At the foot of the hill ran a clear, transparent stream, which gently washed the margin of the green whereon we stood. On the other side a grove of myrtles, intermixed with roses and flowering shrubs, led into shady mazes; in the midst of which appeared the glittering tops of elegant pavilions, some of which stood on the brink of the river, others had wide avenues leading through the groves, and others were almost hidden from sight by intervening woods. All were calculated to give the ideas of pleasure rather than magnificence, and had more ease than labour conspicuous.

"Beautiful!" I cried, gazing entranced upon the scene.

"Yes. From the moment we left the city and passed through the ancient gateway that you admired, we have been riding in my private domain. Here, as far as the eye can reach, all is mine, the garden of the Sanoms. But let us hasten forward. It was not to show you picturesque landscapes that I brought you hither. We have much to do ere we return."

Skirting the stream, where flocks and herds stood gazing at their own images and others drinking of the transparent waters, we found the river, growing wider, opened into a spacious lake which was half surrounded by a rising hill. From the lake, higher than the river, ran a

WILLIAM LE QUEUX

glittering cascade and over the pendant rocks fell luxuriant vines and creeping plants. At the opposite extremity of the lake, which by its pure waters exposed the bright yellow pebbles on which it wantoned, two streams ran towards the right and left of the hill and lost themselves amidst the groves, pasture and hillocks of the adjacent country. The prospects around us were beautiful and enchanting. Lofty trees threw a delightful, welcome shade, and the hill-side seemed covered with flowering shrubs, which grew irregularly except where a torrent from the summit, now dry, had during ages worn out a deep hollow bed for its rapid passage and descent.

There were no roads or beaten paths in this secluded portion of the royal domain, neither could there be seen any traces of habitation.

"Deep in yonder lake," said Omar, drawing up his horse suddenly and swinging himself from his saddle near the spot where the waters, springing from beneath some green, moss-grown rocks, fell with gentle music into the river—"deep in yonder lake there lies a hidden mystery."

"A mystery!" I cried. "What is it?"

"Have patience, and I will reveal to you a secret known only to myself and to the Naya; the secret that I told you must be preserved."

"But you say it is buried beneath these waters!" I exclaimed, puzzled. "How will you reveal it?"

"Watch closely, so that if occasion arises you will remember how to exactly imitate my movements," he answered, and when we had tethered our horses, he led me away from the edge of the lake up the hill-side some distance to where a number of points of moss-grown rock cropped up out of the turf.

After searching among them for some minutes he suddenly stopped before one that rose from the ground about three feet and was perhaps ten yards in circumference, examining it carefully, at last giving vent to an ejaculation of satisfaction.

"You see this rock, Scars!" he cried. "Does anything about it appear to you remarkable?"

I bent, and feeling it with both my hands, carefully examined its side, top and base.

"No," I answered, laughing. "As far as I can detect it is the same as the others."

"You would never guess anything hidden there?" he asked, smiling.

"No."

"Well, watch and I'll show you." And with these words the Naba of Mo approached the rock at a point immediately facing me, and placing his hands upon the side, about two feet from the ground, drew out bodily a portion of its lichen-covered face about eighteen inches square, that had been so deftly hewn that when in its place none could detect it had ever been removed.

Peering into the cavity thus disclosed I saw, to my surprise, what appeared to be a small iron lever, thickly rusted, descending into some cog-wheeled mechanism of a very complicated character.

"Now, watch the lake while I reveal to you its mystery," my companion said, placing his hands upon the lever. With a harsh, grating noise it fell back beneath the weight he threw upon it, and the harsh jarring of cog-wheels revolving sounded for a few moments beneath our feet. Then, as he set the mechanism in motion, my gaze was fixed upon the lake and I stood aghast in wonderment.

As the lever was drawn and the rusty cogs ran into one another, the whole mass of rock damming the lake above the small cascade where it fell into the river, gradually rose, like a great sluice gate, allowing the waters to escape and empty themselves, roaring and tumbling, into the winding river beside which we had journeyed. It was an amazing transformation, as imposing as it was unexpected. A few seconds before, the river, shallow and peaceful, fed by its tiny cascade, rippled away over its pebbly bed; now, however, with the great volume of water from the lake it rose so rapidly that the swirling, boiling current overflowed its banks, sweeping everything before it.

Nor was this the only result of pressing the lever, for at the opposite end of the lake a similar outlet opened, and as I looked I saw the water falling with a rapidity that was astounding. Hydraulic power was evidently known to these strange semi-civilized people, yet the actual means by which the lake was so rapidly emptied I was unable to discover, all the machinery being hidden away in some subterranean chamber.

"By what cunning device is this accomplished?" I inquired of Omar, who stood regarding the disappearing flood with satisfaction.

"This mechanism was invented ages ago by one of my ancestors," he answered. "Its exact date no man can tell. But here water is given mastery over itself, and so careful was its constructor to preserve the secret of its existence that the slaves and workmen, all criminals, were kept close prisoners during the whole time they were at work, and on its completion they were all, without a single exception, killed, in order that none should know the secret save the reigning Naba and his heir."

"They were murdered then!"

"They were all criminals who for various serious crimes had been condemned to death. It is said they numbered over two hundred," Omar answered.

But even as he had been speaking the water of the lake had so drained away that its clean stony bottom was now revealed, the pebbles being exposed in large patches here and there, while the deeper pools remaining were alive with water-snakes and fish of all kinds. There seemed but little mud, yet in the very centre of the great basin was a patch of pebbles and rock higher than the remainder, standing like a small island that, before the lever had been touched, had been submerged. Leading the way, Omar descended to the edge of the lake, skirted it for some little distance, until he came to a long row of flat stones placed together, forming stepping-stones to the miniature island.

"Come," he said. "Follow me," and starting off we were soon crossing the bed of the lake, being compelled to advance cautiously owing to the slippery nature of the weeds and water-plants that overgrew the stones. On gaining the island, however, a fresh surprise awaited me, for Omar, halting amid the mud in the centre, exclaimed:

"Watch carefully, Scars. You may some day desire to act as I am acting; but always remember that here any undue hurry means inevitable death."

"Death! What do you mean?"

"Wait, and you shall see," he replied, as stooping suddenly he turned up the sleeves of his royal robe and groping with his hand in the mud, at last discovered an iron ring, green with slime, which, grasping with both hands, he slowly twisted many times. A hissing sound was emitted, as if the action of untwisting the ring relieved some heavy pressure, admitting air to a chamber that had been hermetically sealed. This surmise was, I afterwards learned, correct. The unscrewing of this ring caused the sides of a plate embedded in the mud to contract, and air, so long excluded, entered the mysterious place below.

In a few moments, having paused to wipe the perspiration from his brow, Omar, again grasping the slippery ring, gave it a sudden jerk and by that means lifted the covering from a circular hole descending into an impenetrable darkness, but bricked round like a cottage well in England, and having projecting pieces of iron, forming steps.

"Now," exclaimed Omar, as together we peered into the mysterious opening. "To descend at once would mean certain death."

"How? Is the air below foul?"

"Not at all. The ingenuity of my ancestor who constructed this place made arrangements to avoid all that. The danger arises from a contrivance he devised by which any person attempting to explore it and being unaware of the means to guard against death, must be inevitably swept into eternity. Now, in order to give you an illustration of this danger I will show you the result of any adventurous person stepping down."

Taking from the mud a long iron bar, which he observed incidentally was kept there for the purpose of guarding against death, he reached down the shaft and placing the end of the bar upon the third step, threw his whole weight upon it, saying:

"We will suppose you have descended until your feet stand upon this step. Now, watch."

As the weight fell upon the step it gave way so slightly as to be almost imperceptible, but suddenly from hidden cavities around the well-like shaft there came six rings of long, sharp steel spikes, set inwards, three above and three below, which, contracting as they came forward, met and interlaced. In an instant I recognised what terrible fate would be the lot of any adventurer who dared to enter that dark shaft. The action of stepping upon that fatal projecting iron released hydraulic pressure of irresistible power, and the unfortunate one, unable to ascend or descend by reason of the danger being above and below, must be impaled by a hundred cruel spikes, sharp and double-edged like spears, while the bands whereon they were set must crush his bones to pulp.

I looked at this terrible device for producing an agonizing death and shuddered. The precautions taken to prevent anyone entering the place were the most elaborate and ingenious I had ever seen. Even if any person learnt the secret of draining the lake, the shaft leading to the mysterious subterranean place was unapproachable by reason of this extraordinary mechanical device.

During five minutes the spikes remained interlaced, then automatically they disengaged themselves, and slowly fell back into the cavity running round the brickwork, wherein they remained concealed.

Thrice again did Omar repeat this action of pressing the bar upon the step, each time with an exactly similar result, chatting to me the while. Then, when for the third time the spikes had fallen back into their places, he said:

"Now the secret to avoid this and lock the mechanism is to turn back this little lever and place it in this catch, so. This cannot, however, be done unless the step has been pressed three times."

And bending over he showed me another tiny lever thickly encrusted with rust, secreted behind a movable brick in the first tier below the lake's bottom. This he placed in position, securing it in a niche so that it became immovable.

"Now," he said, "we may descend without fear," and with these words knelt down, and after lighting a torch he had brought with him, commenced the descent into the cavernous gloom. I quickly followed, my feet resting for a brief instant upon the fatal iron projection, but no spikes came forward, for the terrible mechanism was now locked. Deep down into this circular shaft we went, the smoke and sparks from Omar's torch ever ascending into my face as I lowered myself from rung to rung, until at last, at considerable depth, we found ourselves in a kind of natural cavern. The place seemed damp and full of bad odours, to which submitting with patience we, by a long passage, sometimes crawling under rugged arches, sometimes wading in mud and dirt, attained the end of the cavern, where we stumbled on some narrow steps; but the torch shed little light, and we became nearly suffocated by the noisome vapours.

"I thought you said the air was fresh here," I exclaimed good-humouredly to my companion.

"So I did," he answered. "I cannot make out why it has become so foul. The air-holes must have become accidentally stopped up."

The widening ascent was so intricate and clogged with dirt and rubbish that we worked like moles in the dark; nevertheless, by diligent industry we gained ground considerably, yet as we endeavoured to mount, the slimy steps slipped from under us, and ever and anon we would come tumbling down with a weight of dirt upon us.

After various labours, however, we suddenly entered a great cavern, quite dry. From its roof hung great stalactites that glittered and sparkled in the torch's uncertain light, while around the rough walls of this natural chamber were heaped in profusion great heavy chests of iron and adamant.

With the torch held high above his head Omar rushed across to the pile and bending, examined one chest after the other. Then, raising himself as the truth suddenly dawned upon him, he cried in a hoarse, excited voice:

"By the power of Zomara, we have been tricked!"

"Tricked! How?" I gasped in alarm.

"Cannot you see?" he wailed. "This, the Treasure-house of the Sanoms, has been entered and its contents, worth a fabulous sum, have been extracted! See! Each trunk has been forced by explosives!"

I gazed eagerly where he directed, and saw that the trunks of iron and stone had been blown open by gunpowder, for on each remained a blackened patch, showing plainly the means used to force the strong chest wherein reposed the magnificent jewels, the vessels of gold, and the historic gem-encrusted and invulnerable armour of the Nabas of Mo.

"Then this is the place the secret of which the villainous old Arab, Samory, endeavoured to wrench from you by torture," I exclaimed, gazing round the grim, weird cavern.

"Yes," he answered. "This is the Treasure house of my ancestors. Since the days of King Karmos each Naba or Naya has added to the great store of treasure amassed for the purpose of the emancipation of our country in the day of need. Only the reigning monarch and the heir have, in any generation, ever known the secret of how the Treasure-house can be approached—the secret I have to-day revealed to you as Keeper of the Treasure."

"But if you alone knew the secret, who could have ransacked the place?" I asked. "The chests seem to have been recently opened."

"True," he answered, and pointing to a heap of bejewelled swords, breastplates and helmets, that had apparently been hastily cast aside as the least valuable of the great treasure, he added: "All the most historic and beautiful jewels have been taken, and the gold vessels and things of minor value left. See! It is plain that the theft was accomplished in all haste, for there was scarce time to sort the gems that are unique from those rivalled by others."

"It certainly looks as if the jewels were secured in feverish haste," I said, at the same time picking up from the uneven floor a bronze oil lamp lying overturned and discarded.

Together we set about making a systematic examination of the various chests, numbering nearly one hundred. Those fashioned from single stones were of great age, looking like coffins, while those of iron were ponderous caskets bound with huge bands, studded and double-locked, with great antique hinges of marvellous workmanship. With perhaps half a dozen exceptions the lid of each had yielded to the charge

WILLIAM LE QUEUX

of explosive placed beneath it, while in many cases the whole side of the casket had been blown completely out, injuring or destroying some of its valuable contents. Jewellery and gems, set and unset, had been strewn about and trodden into the dust by hurrying feet, and a few that I recognized at once as of fabulous value had been overlooked. Stooping, I picked up from the dirt a marvellously-cut ruby, almost the size of a pigeon's egg. But the majority of the treasure-chests had been emptied. The place had been visited, and the vast wealth of a nation stolen.

"For the first time in the long, glorious history of my land has the Treasure-house been entered by thieves," Omar said, as if to himself. "No mere adventurer can have been here; this great robbery is the result of some base conspiracy. The treasure of the Sanoms, renowned through the whole world as the most wondrous collection of magnificent and unsurpassable gems, has been cleared out and the entrance re-closed in a manner little short of marvellous. To-day is indeed a sad one for Mo, and for me. My inheritance has been taken from me."

"By whom?" I inquired, continuing my way, examining one of the few chests that had apparently not been tampered with. But, as in the gloom I hastened from one casket to another, my foot suddenly struck against some object, causing me to lose my balance, and thus tripped, were it not for the fact that I clutched at the corner of the great chest, I should have fallen upon my face.

Bending to examine what it was, I was amazed to discover the body of a male slave, still dressed in the uniform of the servants of the palace, but rapidly decomposing. It was the faint sickening odour emitted from the corpse that had greeted our nostrils when we entered the place.

We both bent and looked at him, astounded at discovering, still imbedded in his back, a long keen knife. He had been struck down from behind and murdered, while in the act of securing some of the treasure, for his brown withered fingers still grasped a beautiful necklet of magnificent pearls, an ornament worth several thousand English pounds.

"That is one of the Naya's personal attendants," observed Omar, recognizing the dress, but unable to distinguish the features of the murdered man, so decomposed were they. "He perhaps participated in the plot, and to secure his silence, or his portion of the booty, his fellow-conspirators struck him to earth."

"But to whom is due the chief responsibility in this affair?" I asked. "Surely you have some suspicion?"

"I know not," he answered. "Besides myself only the Naya knew the secret means by which the treasure might be reached."

"Then in all probability she secured it before her flight!" I cried.

"That may be the truth," he answered in a tone of suppressed agitation. "Immediately she obtained knowledge through her spies of my intention to disobey her, she may have secured the most valuable of the jewels and had them packed ready to take them with her if compelled to flee. Yet somehow I cannot believe she has done this, for their removal must have attracted attention. No, I believe we shall have to look in another quarter for the thief." Then, bending again to examine the hilt of the knife embedded in the body of the unfortunate slave, he added: "That poignard was hers. She carried it always in her girdle, and it seems, after all, as though this man was her confidant and assistant, and that here alone she closed his lips by murdering him. Yet to her, life was more valuable than the treasure, and I cannot believe that she risked detection and capture in order to secure what she might afterwards obtain by the assistance of hirelings."

"A dark tragedy has certainly been enacted," I said, glancing around the gruesome place with its gloomy corners and crevices where the blackness was impenetrable. "The theft has been accompanied by a secret assassination at some coward's hand."

"Yes," he exclaimed, standing with folded arms and chin sunk upon his breast. "The great treasure, belonging not only to our family but to our nation, has been stolen, and I swear by Zomara's power that I will seek out the thief and recover it. I am Naba, and it is my duty to my people to restore their wealth to its hiding-place. Each successive ruler has enriched his country by making additions to the store of jewels, and it shall never be recorded that on finding the most valuable of our possessions stolen, I made no effort to trace and recover them. True, they have been abstracted in a manner almost miraculous for ingenuity and rapidity, but from this moment I will not rest until they are recovered. And you, Scarsmere, as Keeper of the Treasure-house, shall assist me."

"I am ready," I answered, excited at the prospect of this new task before us. "We will spare no effort to seek the thief and recover the Treasure of the Sanoms. It is, as you declare, a duty, and I am ready and anxious to commence the search."

XXXI

A Spy's Startling Story

We remained fully two hours in the noisome Treasure-chamber of the Sanoms, the early history of which was lost in the mist of legendary lore, then after careful and minute examination of the rifled chests, worked our way to the base of the shaft, and, having ascended, let down the tiny concealed lever, thereby allowing the pressure to increase, and place in position the ingenious contrivance for causing death to the venturesome. Replacing the iron plate that closed the mouth of the well-like aperture, we screwed it down, rendering it water-tight, and, crossing the stones, regained the bank of the lake. Then, having turned back the lever, the flood-gates slowly closed down again, and, ere we mounted our horses to ride back to the city, the waters, fed by the many torrents, had already risen sufficiently to hide the slime-covered entrance to the secret chamber.

One of the greatest thefts in the world's history had been committed, and the question that puzzled us was the identity of the thief. Our first suspicions had fallen upon the Naya, but calmly discussing the question as we rode back, we both became convinced that so critical was the deposed ruler's position, that she would never have undertaken all the risks in removing the treasure. She knew she was in deadly peril of her life, and that every moment lost was of vital importance, therefore it was hardly probable that she would have delayed her departure to secure the wealth of her ancestors.

Omar argued that if compelled to fly she might have afterwards entrusted the secret of the Treasure-house to spies, who could have returned and secured the jewels. That she had not done this was certain, for the time that had elapsed since her flight was insufficient.

I suggested that the detachment of Samory's men who had entered the city during the revolt might have had knowledge of the secret and secured the treasure, but Omar pointed out that none in Samory's camp could have been aware of the means by which the place could be entered, Kouaga himself being in ignorance.

"Then the thief was the Naya herself," I said, decisively.

"No; after all, I am not actually positive that such is the case," he answered. "There are facts connected with the affair, trivial in themselves, that lead me to believe otherwise."

"What are they?"

"One is that the wonderful ruby necklet, an ornament of matchless gems that belonged to King Karmos and is one of the talismans of the Sanoms, has been left. I found it flung aside and discarded. Had the Naya committed the theft she would have secured this first of all, because of our family tradition that no reigning Sanom can live longer than three moons without it is in his or her possession."

"But you retain it," I said. "You, at least, are safe."

"Yes," he replied thoughtfully. "Yet if the Naya had intended to secure the treasure for herself she would most certainly have taken this first of all. It is one of the most historic and valuable ornaments of the royal jewels of Mo, besides being one in which most superstition is centred. In her flight she would entertain the bitterest ill-feeling towards me and desire my rule to be brief. Therefore, she must have stolen the necklet; she would have secured that, if nothing else."

I was compelled to agree with this view, especially as he added that one of the most firm beliefs of the Sanoms had ever been that Zomara would send vengeance most terrible upon any who removed the treasure from its chests without the sanction of the people. No, it seemed evident that some third person had been in possession of the secret. Who, we knew not, but were determined to discover.

On returning to the palace I stood, as usual, beside the Emerald Throne while its occupant gave audience to those who came to make obeisance and offer congratulations. The Court of the Naba Omar was even more brilliant than that of his mother had been, and at evening, under the bright lights, was, indeed, a glittering assembly, where the gems worn by officials and courtiers almost dazzled one's eyes by their profuseness.

Days passed—bright, peaceful days succeeding the brief period of feverish excitement and deadly hatred. Mo had become herself again; her people assured that an era of liberty and prosperity had recommenced, her ruler leaving no effort unspared to act in the best interests of his beloved nation. By day the great sunny courts of the palace, with the bright flowers and fruit-laden vines, rang with the tramp of armed men and tall, stately officials; by night the sounds of revelry, music and dancing awakened the echoes of the great moon-lit colonnades, and was wafted on the sweet-scented air afar beyond the grim, frowning outer walls.

Yet the burden of kingship seemed to press heavily upon the young Naba. Though wearing no diadem, his brow soon became furrowed, as if by its weight, and his air was one of constant preoccupation. His change of manner puzzled me. His mind appeared overshadowed by some gloomy foreboding, the nature of which I could by no amount of cautious questioning elicit. During each day he attended assiduously without relaxation to affairs of state, and when night drew on and the inmates of the great luxurious palace, a veritable city within a city, gave themselves up to reckless enjoyment, he was seldom present, for he would withdraw to one of his small private apartments, and there sit, pretending to read, but in reality brooding in silence. One poignant sorrow had transformed him from a bright, happy youth, to a man sad-eyed, dull, morose. Sometimes, as I watched, I noticed how he would suddenly sigh heavily, and set his teeth as a bitter relentless expression would flit for an instant across his countenance, and I knew that at such moments there entered into his heart the contemplation of a fierce and terrible revenge.

Even to me, his constant companion, whose opinion he sought almost hourly, he made no mention of his heart's sorrow, yet from close observation through many days, I knew the cause of his overwhelming grief was the loss of Liola. He never mentioned her, for the day after we had ascertained the truth about her tragic end, he had taken me aside and asked me never to allow her name to pass my lips in his presence.

"Memories are painful, you know, Scars," he had said. "I must try and forget, try and live down my sorrow if I can, although I fear I shall carry it with me to the grave."

These words I often remembered when, alone with him, I watched the look of ineffable sadness upon his face. In the Hall of Audience, the centre of his brilliant court, his face was always pleasant, smiling and full of good-nature, as it had ever been; but, alas! it was only a mask, for alone, in the privacy of his chamber, he cast it aside and gave himself up to debauches of melancholy painful to behold.

Thus weeks lengthened into months. He had wished me to keep from the people the great loss sustained by the robbery from the Treasure-house, believing that in the circumstances silence was best, and I had not breathed a word to a soul, not even to Kona or Goliba. The city had resumed its old look of prosperity, its markets were crowded daily, and its populace were content in the knowledge that under the reformed *régime* they were free. Although once every week, Omar, with his court, descended to the Temple of Zomara, and there adored the Crocodile-god, human sacrifices had been discontinued, and the worship of the giant idol was devoid of those revolting practices introduced by the Naya. Of the latter, no tidings had been gleaned. Although every effort had been made to trace her, she had disappeared. Of the treasure of the Sanoms, too, nothing had been heard. How it had been conveyed out of Mo remained an inscrutable mystery.

I confess to being astonished that Omar seldom, if ever, spoke of either of these matters, which had at first so seriously agitated him. Whether he had relinquished all thought of recovering the jewels collected by his ancestors, or whether he was endeavouring to formulate some plan of action I knew not, yet his unwillingness to speak of them was, to say the least, noteworthy.

"Niaro has to-day returned from the gate of Mo," I observed one evening when we were sitting alone together in one of the smaller courts, the night air stirred by the distant sound of stringed instruments and the thumping of Moorish tam-tams. "He has sent messengers by the Way of the Thousand Steps far into the lands beyond, but no word have they been able to gather regarding the Naya."

"She has escaped the mad vengeance of our people, who would have killed her," he said, calmly. "For that I am thankful."

"You seem to have no desire that she should be captured," I said.

"None. She has escaped. After all it is best."

"But the treasure," I said, dropping my voice so that no eavesdropper might overhear. "Its hiding place, like the thief, is still unknown."

"Yes," he answered. "Unknown at present, but ere long some discovery must be made. When it is, I anticipate it will be a startling one."

Our conversation was interrupted at that moment by the approach of a slave who, bowing low until his brow touched our carpet, said:

"One of thy servants, O Master, desireth to have speech with thee. He hath sped from afar upon the wings of haste and beareth tidings."

"Of what?" cried Omar, starting up.

"I know not, O Master. The name of thy servant who awaiteth audience with thee is Makhana, who cometh from beyond the great black water."

"Makhana!" we both cried, and Omar ordered that he should be admitted immediately, and without ceremony. Then, turning to me, he explained that on ascending the throne he had sent a message to Makhana in London ordering him to return at once.

A moment later the secret agent of Mo, a tall, sparse figure, attired in shabby European clothes, entered, and, snapping fingers with his master, greeted and congratulated him. Then, casting himself upon the mat near us, he began to tell us what had occurred after our flight from Eastbourne, and relate the latest news from the civilised land we had left so many months before. I also told him how we had been enticed away by Kouaga, and the order of the Naya for Omar's assassination.

"Much has happened since I returned," Omar observed, when I had concluded. "As you have no doubt already heard, my mother has been deposed, and I have been enthroned in her stead."

"Yes," the secret agent answered. "I have already heard all this, and although I wish you every peace and prosperity, I have, I regret, to make a startling announcement."

"What is it?" gasped Omar, with wide-open eyes.

"Our enemy, Samory, is upon us!"

"Samory!" we both cried.

"Yes. Not much longer than a moon past I was crossing the mountains of Niene, near the confines of his country, on my way hither from the sea, and learnt the truth. Two moons ago, accompanied by twenty thousand armed men, Kouaga marched out of Koussan to obtain savage allies for an expedition, having for its object the conquest of Mo."

"The conquest of our country!" Omar cried astounded. "Only a week before we returned hither one of his expeditions was utterly routed and slaughtered in the Grave of Enemies. Now another has been dispatched! What route has it taken?"

"On learning the news I at once reassumed native dress, crossed into our enemy's country and acted as spy," Makhana answered, his fierce-looking eyes glistening in the moonlight. "In Koussan I ascertained that the expedition, led by Kouaga, the man who was once our Grand Vizier, had gone northward one moon's journey towards the Niger, his intention being to skirt the country of the Aribanda and to enter our territory from the north by crossing the Hombori Mountains."

"You have done well to ascertain this and hasten on," Omar answered. "But there is only one pass by which the Hombori can be crossed."

"That is known to Kouaga, for three years ago he led our army through it to the successful conquest of the border tribes of the Massina.

He is now a formidable enemy, for he knows all the secret approaches and the whereabouts of our hidden defences."

"We must dispatch an army at once to meet them," Omar said, after a thoughtful pause.

"No time should be lost," Makhana urged. "Already they are due at the Hombori, and it will occupy our expedition fully two weeks to reach there. Yet Samory's hordes may be delayed, and if so, we shall be able to hold the pass successfully and sweep them down as they advance. I have brought with me from England the ten additional Maxims ordered by the Naya."

"Excellent, let them be given into Kona's charge," Omar exclaimed, explaining briefly that the Dagomba head-man was now in command of the troops, and then turning to the slave who stood in waiting he ordered that Kona should be fetched immediately, and that the council and principal officers should be at once summoned.

In a few minutes we saw upon the clear night-sky long beams of light, and knew that signals were being flashed from Mo to the furthermost limits of the kingdom, summoning the officers from their various posts to a council of war. Twenty thousand men, with a similar number of savage allies, under a leader who was well acquainted with all the intricacies of the secret way were advancing upon Mo, and the faces of the officers and members of the council became grave when, on arrival at the palace, they heard the astounding news.

That Mo was threatened by a serious calamity was recognized by everyone. The news spread through the city quickly, and throughout the night the streets were agog. Only by swift vigorous defence, by pushing a great force forward night and day to the point of attack, could a catastrophe be averted. This was the unanimous opinion of the Naba's advisers, and ere the sun rose the first detachment of the defending army was already on its way to meet the Arab invaders.

Kouaga evidently meant making a sudden descent upon the mysterious country, and if his force once accomplished the passage through the mountain pass they would then no doubt make a rapid dash towards the capital itself, and would approach it at its only vulnerable point.

If this occurred, then the slaughter must be terrible and the catastrophe complete.

XXXII

WAR

Twelve days later I found myself accompanying Kona who, at the head of a great force of over eighteen thousand men, was crossing the treacherous quicksands by the Way of the Thousand Steps. The critical position of Mo had been fully discussed by Omar, his officers and sages, and it had been decided to send, in addition to the force of twenty thousand men to the Hombori Mountains on the northern frontier, a second expedition to travel with all swiftness across the sandy plain and make a dash upon Samory's stronghold at Koussan in the absence of its picked troops.

Within two days after Makhana had brought news of the coming invasion, the whole of the twenty thousand men, with Omar himself at their head, had marched out of the capital on their way to defend the pass. I had expressed a wish to accompany them, but my friend had requested me to go with the expedition to Samory's capital because, having been there in captivity, I could act as guide. To this I made no objection, and bidding farewell to Omar, Goliba and Niaro at the city gate, I had watched them ride away at the head of a brilliant cavalcade, and the same evening at sundown descended the face of the cliff by the long flight of steps, and jumping into the saddle of a horse held ready for me, rode with all haste to catch up Kona who, as leader of our expedition, had already started for the gigantic precipice known as the Gate of Mo.

To Niaro, an excellent officer, the leadership of the defending force had been entrusted, as he had already had experience of fighting in the Hombori country, having been second in command of Kouaga's expedition when he conquered the tribes of Massina, while Kona, who had with him his valiant Dagombas, had orders to enrol another thousand men of that tribe when passing through their territory, prior to our dash upon Samory's country.

The passage to the desert by the Way of the Thousand Steps was a brilliant feat, for of our great force not a single life was lost, and so rapidly did we travel, that within two weeks of the day we left the palace, our Dagombas, who preferred their native spears and arrows to firearms, were enrolled and we were well on our way to the Great Salt Road, a mere native path notwithstanding its imposing designation, towards Samory's great fortress-city.

Heedless of the noontide heat we pushed forward over stony desert and green grass-land, now plunging into those gloomy dismal forests of eternal darkness where the stench of decaying vegetation sickened us, only to emerge again into the open plain devoid of shade, scorched by the pitiless rays of the fiery sun. Snatching brief rests, and pushing for ever onward our great host of armed men and carriers, with the vigilant Kona at their head, pressed forward, entering at last the land of our enemies.

The Dagomba scouts, travelling before us, splendid fellows, all eyes and ears, who could detect the slightest indication of an enemy's presence far or near, whether it were the broken twig at one's feet or the sudden rising of a bird in the distance, kept us well informed of all transpiring on every side. For a hundred miles we marched through the Arab chieftain's land without any of its inhabitants dreaming of the presence of a hostile force, and it was only by our sudden descent one night upon the small walled town of Torola, which we sacked and burned, that they were awakened to the truth.

But ere the news could spread to Koussan, about forty English miles distant, we, by a forced march, had already reached the capital. Making a dash upon the place by night with our Maxim and Hotchkiss guns, the garrison were completely taken by surprise, nevertheless so well were its high white walls defended, that our forces were driven back with severe loss.

Undaunted however, Kona, who placed himself at the head of our Dagomba allies, backed by the well-armed soldiers of Mo, made a second assault upon a point that had been indicated by our spies as weaker than the others. The fighting was desperate, and the sight, viewed from where I was standing with the reinforcements, was one of exceeding grandeur. Night was rendered almost bright as day by the constant flashing of guns, and the noise of the tumult ever increasing sounded high above the constant roar of artillery. Suddenly, as I gazed across the plain to where the sharp conflict was proceeding, a brilliant blue flash blinded me and an instant later a deafening explosion caused the ground to tremble, while the red light of the guns gleamed through the increasing veil of smoke, and I saw that our men had successfully placed a mine beneath that portion of the fortifications near where they were fighting, and it had been fired, effecting a great breach through which they next moment poured, engaging the defenders hand to hand.

Soon afterwards a signal light flashed thrice, as had been agreed, and six thousand men, including myself, sped over the plain to reinforce our comrades. Soon, clambering over the fallen masonry where the enormous breach had been made, I found myself with my sword, the one I had used in the conquest of Mo, hacking right and left, endowed with a strength that only came to me in moments of intense excitement.

The dash we made was indeed a brilliant one. The Arab defenders were, we found, fully equal to us in numbers and were withal magnificent soldiers, for in the broad squares of the city their cavalry, with their white flowing robes and heavy curved swords, committed frightful havoc in our ranks, yet in such numbers had we clambered into the great chieftain's stronghold that they became gradually hampered in the streets and, unable to manoeuvre, were compelled to dismount and engage us in combat. The fight proved an even more desperate and bloody one than that which resulted in the dethronement of the Naya. So equally matched were the forces, that the struggle raged with frightful ferocity, each side determined to secure the victory. In the old Moorish-looking streets, so narrow that two asses could scarce pass abreast, there were encounters more desperate than any I had ever witnessed, for the soldiers of Samory and the fighting-men of Mo, the two most fierce and valiant forces in the whole of the African continent, were pitted against each other.

Cutting our way forward, I found myself at last beneath the high whitewashed wall of the great Djamäa Thelatha Biban, or Mosque of the Three Gates, one of the most ancient in the city. I recognised it by its fine dome standing out white against the flame-illumined sky, and remembered that when a captive in the hands of the brutal Arab ruler, Omar had translated to me the fine Kufic inscription on its handsome façade, recording its construction by Mohammed Ibn Kheiroun el-Maäferi in the second century of the Hedjira. For a moment I paused under its handsome entrance of black and white marble, when suddenly Kona rushed towards me, crying:

"Quick, Master! Fly for thy life, here, across the square!" and as he tore away as fast as his long black legs would carry him, I followed wondering.

Scarcely had we reached the opposite side of the great market-place when a deafening roar sounded, and an instant later, as I turned, I saw the great dome crack, tremble and collapse, together with the high white minaret, while the whole of its façade fell out with a terrific crash in the opposite direction. Our men had blown up the principal mosque in Samory's capital, an action which increased tenfold the rage of our fierce fanatical enemies.

With loud yells they fell upon us from every quarter, when a few minutes later they realised what had been done, and during the next hour the conflict became terrific. Hundreds were struck to earth by bullets and swords, and it appeared to me, striving as I was in the midst of the smoke and heat of battle, that the longer we fought the more numerous became the defenders, and the less our chance of success. Yet slowly we had succeeded in cutting our way from the city wall up the hill crowned by the great white Kasbah, or fortress, which constituted Samory's palace, and were now actually within sight of it. Fiercely exerting every muscle we fought to attain our goal, but so desperate was the defence, that time after time our forward movement was prevented, and we were compelled to fall back bleeding and frustrated. In these valiant attempts to reach the walls of the Kasbah there fell, at a low estimate, fully five hundred of that portion of the force to which I had attached myself. With reinforcements we might have flung back the defenders, yet separated as we had been into small bodies during the earlier manoeuvres, fighting was now taking place in every part of the city, no two bodies being able to unite their forces.

To thus cut us off one from another had, no doubt, been the tactics of the defenders, for we afterwards learnt that in many instances the smaller of our gallant little bands had been slaughtered literally to a man.

At last, however, my worst fears began to be realized, for the defenders, receiving reinforcements, swooped suddenly down upon us, and with their swords and those sharp double-edged knives they carried in their belts, wrought frightful havoc among us everywhere, while upon us another body poured a terrible fire from their long-barrelled rifles.

As result of this, although we made a spirited stand, once again we were compelled to fall back in confusion, leaving many dead and dying upon the stones. Suddenly I heard Kona's well-known voice behind me uttering the fierce war yell of the Dagombas, and next instant we found to our satisfaction that a great body of his dark oily-faced warriors had come to our relief. The reckless and savage manner in which they fought a few moments later was astounding, and it was certainly due to their courage and strength that the Arabs were first forced back and then cut to pieces and utterly routed.

This, however, did not carry us much further towards the Kasbah, for when within an ace of gaining its walls, another body of Arabs swept across the great square with its clump of date-palms, and with cries of rage attacked us vigorously with rifle and sword. The combat again became terrible, and in it I received from a big, raw-boned Arab a severe sword-cut over the left wrist that caused me excruciating pain. Still I fought on, although half fearing that our expedition was ill-fated. We had believed Samory's capital practically denuded of troops, and of such strenuous opposition as that offered we had never dreamed.

But the assertion of the West Coast tribes that the soldiers of the mystic land of Mo know not fear is certainly true, for never once did they falter, although the citadel seemed absolutely unassailable by reason of the fierceness and strength of its defence.

Through the dark night hours we had fought on revengefully, and when dawn spread the grey glimmering light disclosed the terrible result of the deadly fray. Dead and wounded lay everywhere, and through the suffocating smoke the fire of the rifles now seemed yellow where in the darkness it had appeared blood-red. By some means the Arabs rallied their forces, and I confess that the sight of the overwhelming numbers opposing us caused my courage to fail. Swiftly and unrelentingly the attack upon us was delivered, and with such vigour that our van fell back, weak and decimated. Suddenly, without warning, a sound above the din broke upon our ears, startling us.

The rapid cackling was unmistakable, and involuntarily I burst into a good old-fashioned English cheer. One of our Maxims had been tardily brought into play!

Ere a few moments had elapsed the Arabs, having already had a taste of the terrible effect of the deadly weapon during the recent campaign against the French and English, stood panic-stricken. Their hesitation proved fatal. Under the hail of lead they were mowed down, and ere the remainder could recover from their astonishment a second weapon was brought into play, riddling their ranks with showers of death-dealing missiles.

XXXIII

The Harem Slave

A dozen times were we driven back by overwhelming numbers of Arabs, but as many times we dashed forward again, determined to strike a fatal, irrisistible blow at the power of the egotistical and fanatical chieftain whose depredations had earned for him the appelation of "The Pirate of the Niger." Every nation in Western Africa, save the dwellers in the mystic land of Mo, existed in daily fear of raids by his ruthless armed bands, who, travelling rapidly across desert and forest, devastated whole regions, seizing cattle, laying waste prosperous and fertile districts, burning towns and villages, and reducing their weaker neighbours to slavery. Indeed, no bodies of armed men throughout the whole of the great African continent, including even the Tuaregs, were so reckless in their attacks, or so fiendish in their wholesale butchery of those who resented the ruin and devastation of their homes. It was therefore scarcely surprising that this brigandish horde, whose power even European nations failed to break, should throw themselves into the conflict with reckless enthusiasm, and repel our attack by the exertion of every muscle.

In point of numbers we were much inferior; our superiority existed only in our arms. Their old-fashioned bronze field-pieces, flint-lock pistols and long-barrelled Arab guns, although deadly weapons in the hands of such expert shots, proved no match against such irresistible appliances as the Maxim, the Hotchkiss, or the modern English-made rifle. This fact very soon became apparent, for although the fierce battle raged for many hours, and Samory himself, in yellow robe, and mounted upon a snow-white stallion, gorgeously caparisoned, could be seen urging on his hordes to valiant deeds, we nevertheless everywhere made a firm stand at various points of vantage, and by no effort were they able to dislodge us.

When the sun rose, red and fiery through the veil of smoke, the increasing weakness of the defence was visibly demonstrated by the manner in which the entrance to the Kasbah was guarded. The great doors of iron were closed and barred securely, and on the walls the crimson fezes of the defenders showed in profusion, but presently Kona, as we drove back the soldiers of Al-Islâm almost for the hundredth time, shouted the order to storm the citadel. With one accord we made a mad, reckless rush an instant later, and carried on by the thousands of my comrades behind, I found myself slashing to right and left under the high, sun-blanched walls of the enormous fortress. Kona, appearing a giant even among his tall Dagombas, gave one the impression in those critical moments of a veritable demon, filled as he was with a mad excitement and knowing that upon the success of our assault depended the result of the expedition. Towering above his fellows, his long spear in hand, he seemed to lead a charmed existence, swaying to and fro among whistling bullets, whizzing arrows, flashing swords and whirring spears. His own weapon he dyed in the blood of his adversaries times without number, for where he struck he never failed to kill. His aim was unerring, and his courage that of a lion of his native forest.

In those furious moments I escaped death only by a miracle. As I dashed forward to seek shelter beneath the ponderous wall, a tall Arab, with long brown hairy arms, swung his curved sword high above his head and brought it down with such force that had I not dodged him just in time, he would have smashed my skull. Lowering my rifle quickly till its muzzle almost touched his flowing garments, I fired, but unfortunately the bullet passed beneath his arm-pit, and flattened itself against the wall. Again, muttering some fearful imprecation in Arabic, he raised his gleaming blade, and, unable to fire at such close quarters, I was then compelled to use my rifle to ward off his attack. For an instant we struggled desperately, when suddenly he gave his sword a rapid twist, jerking my weapon from my hands and leaving me unarmed at his mercy.

His features broadened into a brutal grin as, noticing me fumbling for my pistol, he again raised his razor-edged Moorish blade, and holding it at arm's length, gave one vigorous slash at me. Pressed forward towards him by men engaged in mortal conflict behind me, I could not evade him, and was about to receive the full force of what my adversary intended should be a fatal blow, when suddenly a savage spear struck him full in the throat, and stuck quivering there.

Instantly his sinewy arm fell, the heavy sword dropped from his nerveless fingers, and he stumbled backward and fell to earth like a log.

"Thou art safe, O Master!" a voice cried cheerily behind me, and turning, I saw that the man who had thrown his spear and saved my life was Kona.

Shouting an expression of thanks I bent, and, unable to recover my lost rifle in the frightful *mêlée*, snatched up the dead Arab's sword that had so nearly caused my death, then fought on by my deliverer's side. His wounds were many, for blood was flowing from cuts and gashes innumerable in his bare black flesh, yet he appeared insensible to pain, striving forward, gasping as he dealt each blow, determined to conquer.

The fight continued with unabated fury—the bloodshed was horrible. The open square before the gate of the Kasbah was transformed into a veritable slaughter-yard, the stones being slippery with blood, and passage rendered difficult by the corpses that lay piled everywhere. At last, however, while engaged in another warm corner, the shrill, awe-inspiring war cry of the Dagombas again sounded above the tumult, and turning, I saw that by some means our men had opened the great gate, and that they were pouring into the spacious courtyards that I so well remembered.

Our assault, though fiercely and savagely repelled, was at last successful. We were entering the stronghold of Samory, and had achieved a feat that the well-equipped expeditions of the French and English had failed to accomplish.

The Arabs during the next quarter of an hour struggled bravely against their adversity and fought with a dogged courage of which I had not believed them capable. Soon, however, finding themselves conquered, they cried for quarter. Had they known the peculiar temperament of the Dagombas and the soldiers of Mo, they would never thus have implored mercy. But they cried out, and some even sank on their knees in the blood of their dead comrades, uttering piteous appeals. But the Arabs of Samory had never shown mercy to the Dagombas or the people of Mo, and consequently our army, in the first flush of their victory, filled with the awful lust for blood, treated their cries with jeers, and as they advanced into court after court within the great Kasbah walls, they fell upon all they met, armed or unarmed, men or women, and massacred them where they stood.

The appeal shouted time after time by Kona to view our victory in temperate spirit and spare those who submitted, was disregarded by all in this wholesale savage butchery. The scene within the Arab chieftain's stronghold was, alas! far more horrible than any I had witnessed during the revolt in Mo. Guards, officials and slaves of Samory's household were indiscriminately put to the sword, some of the men being hunted into corners and speared by the Dagombas, while others were forced

WILLIAM LE QUEUX

upon their knees by the soldiers of Mo and mercilessly decapitated. The door of the great harem, long ago reputed to contain a thousand inmates, including slaves, was burst open, and in those beautiful and luxuriant courts and chambers the whole of the women were butchered with a brutality quite as fiendish as any displayed by the Arabs themselves. The handsome favourites of Samory in their filmy garments of gold tissue and girdles of precious stones were dragged by their long tresses from their hiding places and literally hacked to pieces, their magnificent and costly jewels being torn from them and regarded as legitimate loot. Women's death-screams filled the great courts and corridors; their life-blood stained the pavements of polished jasper and bespattered the conquerors. The Dagombas, finding themselves inside this extensive abode of luxury, where beautiful fountains shot high into the morning sunlight, sweet-smelling flowers bloomed everywhere and sensuous odours from perfuming-pans hung heavily in the air, seemed suddenly transformed into a demoniac horde bent upon the most ruthless devastation. They remembered that times without number had the Sofas of Samory burnt their villages and towns, and carried hundreds of their tribesmen away as slaves; they were now seeking revenge for past wrongs.

As, nauseated by the sight of blood, I witnessed these awful atrocities, I reflected that the curse of Zomara, uttered solemnly by Omar when Samory had sold us to the slave-dealers, had at last fallen upon the Arab chieftain.

Omar had prophesied the downfall of Samory, and his utterance was now fulfilled.

Screams, piercing and heart-rending, sounded everywhere, mingled with the fierce war-shouts of our savage allies, as, time after time, some unfortunate woman in gorgeous garb and ablaze with valuable gems was discovered, dragged unceremoniously from her hiding-place to the great court wherein I stood, her many necklets ruthlessly torn from her white throat and a keen sword drawn across it as a butcher would calmly despatch a lamb. Then, when life had ebbed, her body would be cast into the great basin of the fountain, where hundreds of others had already been pitched.

In other parts of the Kasbah a similar massacre was proceeding, none of those found therein being allowed to escape; while an active search was everywhere in progress for Samory himself.

From where I stood I witnessed the breaking up of the Arab ruler's throne, and the tearing down of the great canopy of amaranth silk under which Samory had reclined when, with Omar, I had been brought before him. The crescent of solid gold that had surmounted it was handed to Kona, who broke it in half beneath his heel as sign of the completeness of his victory. Then, when the destruction of the seat of the brutal autocrat was complete, the *débris* with the torn silk, and the long strips of crimson cloth, whereon good counsels from the Korân were embroidered in Kufic characters of gold, that had formed a kind of frieze to the chamber, were carried out into the court by fifty willing hands, heaped up and there burnt.

While watching the flames leaping up consuming the wrecked remains of the royal seat of the powerful Arab ruler, a woman's scream, louder than the rest, caused me to look suddenly round at the latest victim of the Dagombas' thirst for vengeance, and I beheld in the clutches of half-a-dozen savages, a young woman, dragged as the others had been by her fair, unbound hair towards the spot where each had, in turn, been murdered. She was dressed in a rich, beautiful robe of bright yellow silk, embroidered with pale pink flowers, but her garments were bedraggled with water and blood, and her bleeding wrists and fingers showed with what heartless brutality her jewels had been torn from her by her pitiless captors. She struggled frantically to free herself, but without avail, and one of the savages, noticing a magnificent diamond bangle upon her ankle, bent, and tried to force it off.

Just at that moment, in endeavouring to twist herself free from their clutches, her fair face became turned towards me and her deep blue, terrified eyes for an instant met mine.

Next second I uttered a cry of recognition. Yes, there was no mistake about that flawless complexion, those handsome features or those wondrous eyes, the mysterious depths of which had enthralled me, as they had done Omar.

It was Liola!

With a bound I sprang forward, tearing at the knot of savages and shouting to them to release her. At first they only grinned hideously, no doubt thinking that I desired her as a slave, and as they had decided that all should die without exception, in order that their conquest should be rendered the more complete, they were in no way disposed to obey my command. At last I succeeded in arresting their progress, when the man who had attempted to wrench from her ankle the diamond ornament shook his long, keen knife threateningly at me, while the others yelled all kinds of imprecations. Not liking his fierce attitude, and knowing that in the heat of victory they were capable of turning upon friends who attempted to thwart them, I drew back, and as I did so he flung himself upon one knee and raised his knife over Liola's foot.

Instantly I saw his intention. He meant to hack off her foot in order to secure the bangle, a horrible proceeding that had been carried out more than once before my eyes within the past hour. There was, I knew, but one way to save her, therefore without hesitating I drew my revolver and fired at him point blank.

The ball pierced his breast. With an agonized cry he clutched for a moment wildly at the air, then fell back dead.

My action, as I fully expected it would, aroused the intense ire of his companions and all released Liola, now insensible, and sprang at me, their ready knives flashing in the sunlight. I was compelled to fly, and had it not been for Kona, who, standing some distance off watching the reduction of Samory's throne to ashes, took in the situation at a glance, sped in their direction, and ordered his men to stop and tell him the cause, I should undoubtedly have lost my life. As their head-man his word was law. Then, glancing at the inanimate form of Liola, who, having fainted, had been left lying on the blood-stained pavement, he recognized her as Goliba's daughter, and in a dozen words told his men that she was the betrothed of the young Naba of Mo, and that I, his friend, had saved her.

The savages, aghast at this statement, and recognizing how near they had been to murdering the beloved of the Naba Omar, rushed towards me penitent, urging that they might be forgiven, and declaring that their conduct, under the circumstances, was excusable. They had, they said, no idea that they would find in the harem of their enemy Samory the betrothed of Mo's ruler, and I also was compelled to admit myself quite as astounded as themselves. Therefore in brief words explanations and forgiveness were exchanged and I rushed across, and with the ready help of Kona and his men endeavoured to restore her to consciousness.

The dread of her horrible fate had caused her to faint, and it was a long time ere we could bring her back to the knowledge of her surroundings. Tenderly the Dagombas, who a few minutes before would have brutally murdered her, carried her into one of the small luxuriantly-furnished chambers of the harem, and at my request left me alone with her. Kona, though fierce as a wild beast in war, was tender-hearted as a child where undefended women were concerned, and would have remained, but as commander of the forces now engaged in sacking the palace many onerous duties devolved upon him. Therefore I was left alone with her.

Her eyes closed, her fair hair disarranged, her clothing torn and blood-stained, she lay upon a soft divan, pale and motionless as one dead. I chafed her tiny hands, and released her rich robe at the throat to give her air, wondering by what strange chain of circumstances she had come to be an inmate of the private apartments of our enemy Samory. At last, however, her breast heaved and fell slowly once or twice, and presently she opened her beautiful eyes, gazing up at me with a puzzled, half-frightened expression.

"Liola," I exclaimed softly, in the language of Mo. "Thou art with friends, have no further fear. The soldiers of thy lover Omar have wreaked a vengeance complete and terrible upon thy captor Samory."

"But the savages!" she gasped. "They will kill me as they massacred all the women."

"No, no, they will not," I assured her, placing my arm tenderly beneath her handsome head. "The savages are our Dagomba allies who, not knowing that thou wert a native of Mo, would have butchered thee like the rest."

"And thou didst save me?" she cried. "Yes, I remember, thou didst shoot dead the brute who would have cut off my foot to secure my diamond anklet. I owe my life to thee."

"Ah! do not speak of that," I cried. "Calm thyself and rest assured of thy safety, for thou shalt return with us to the land of thy fathers. Thou shalt, ere a moon has run its course, pillow thine head upon the shoulder of the man thou lovest, Omar, Naba of Mo."

She blushed deeply at my words, and her small white hand still smeared with blood, gripped my wrist. Her heart seemed too full for words, and in this manner she silently thanked me for rescuing her from the awful fate to which she had so nearly been hurried.

Soon she recovered from the shock sufficiently to sit up and chat. Together we listened to the roar of the excited multitude outside, and from the lattice window could see columns of dense black smoke rising from the city, where the fighting-men of Mo, in accordance with their instructions from Omar, having sacked the place, were now setting it on fire.

In answer to my eager questions as to her adventures after her seizure by the soldiers of the Great White Queen, she said:

"Yes. It is true they captured me, together with my girl slave, Wyona, and hurried me towards the palace. Wyona fought and bit like a tigress, and one of the men becoming infuriated, killed her. Just at that moment the attack was made upon us by the populace, and they, witnessing his action, tore him limb from limb. Then, in the fierce conflict that followed, I escaped from their clutches in the same manner as Omar and thyself. Knowing of the attack to be made upon the palace I fled for safety in the opposite direction, and remained in hiding throughout the night in the house of one of my kinswomen away towards the city-gate. At last the report spread that the people had taken the palace by assault, the Naya had been deposed, and Omar enthroned Naba in her stead. Then, feeling that safety was assured, I ventured forth, but ere I had gone far I met a body of strange fighting men. They were Arabs, and proved to be men from this stronghold of our enemy Samory. After a strenuous attempt to cross the city they had been repulsed by the people, leaving many dead, and in their retreat towards the city-gate they seized me and bore me away in triumph here."

"How long hast thou been in Koussan?"

"Twenty days ago we arrived, after fighting our way back and losing half our force in skirmishes with the hostile savages of the forest. I was brought here to Samory's harem as slave, attired in the garments I now wear, loaded with jewels torn from the body of one of his favourites, who, incurring his displeasure, had been promptly strangled by the chief of the negro eunuchs, and placed in an apartment with three other slaves to do my bidding, there to await such time as it should please my Arab captor to inspect me. I was contemplating death," she added, dropping her deep blue eyes. "If your attack upon the Kasbah had not been delivered I should most assuredly have killed myself to-day ere the going down of the sun."

"It was fortunate that I recognized thee, or thou wouldst have been hacked to pieces by the keen blades of our savage allies," I said.

"Take me hence," she urged panting. "I cannot bear to hear the shout of the victor and the despairing cry of the vanquished. It is horrible. Throughout the night we, in the women's quarters, have dreaded the fate awaiting us if the invaders, whom we thought were savages of the forest, should gain the mastery and enter the palace. From the high windows yonder we witnessed the fight, knowing that our lives depended upon its issue, and judge our dismay and despair when, soon after dawn, we saw the Arabs overwhelmed and the Kasbah fall into the hands of their conquerors. Many of my wretched companions killed themselves with their poignards rather than fall into the hands of the blacks, while the majority hid themselves only to be afterwards discovered and butchered. Ah, it is all terrible, terrible!"

"True," I answered. "Yet it is only revenge for the depredations and heartless atrocities committed by these people upon the dwellers in thy border lands. Even at this moment Samory hath a great expedition on the northern confines of Mo, making a vigorous attempt to invade thy country, so that he shall reign upon the Emerald Throne in the place of thy lover Omar."

"An expedition to invade Mo?" she cried surprised. "Hath Samory done this; is it his intention to cause Omar's overthrow?"

"Most assuredly it is," I answered. "The reason of our presence here in such force was to assault Koussan in the absence of its picked troops, twenty thousand of whom were we ascertained on their way northward, with the intention of forcing a passage through Aribanda and the Hombori Mountains into Mo. Niaro hath led our fighting-men to repel their attack, and he is accompanied by Omar and thy father, while we are here, under Kona's leadership, to punish Samory for his intrepidity."

Then she asked how Omar fared, and I explained how it had been believed that she had died, and that all were mourning for her.

"My slave Wyona must have been mistaken for me," she answered. "And naturally, as I had given her one of my left-off robes only the day before."

"Omar believeth thee dead. Thy presence in Mo will indeed bring happiness to his eyes, and gaiety to his heart," I exclaimed happily.

"Doth he still mourn for me?" she inquired artlessly. I knew she wanted to ask me many questions regarding her lover, but her modesty forbade it.

"Since the fatal night when thou wert lost joy hath never caused a smile to cross his countenance. Sleeping and waking he thinketh only of thee, revering thy memory, reflecting upon the happy moments spent at thy side, as one fondly remembers a pleasant dream or adventures in some fair paradise, yet ever sad in the knowledge that those blissful days can never return. His is an empty honour, a kingship devoid of all pleasure because thou art no longer his."

Her lips trembled slightly, and I thought her brilliant eyes became brighter for a moment because of an unshed tear.

"I am still his," she said slowly, with emphasis. "I am ready, nay anxious, to return to him. Thou hast saved me from death and from dishonour; truly thou art a worthy friend of Omar's, for by thy valiant deed alone thou restorest unto him the woman he loveth."

I urged her to utter no word of thanks, and pointing to the sky, rendered every moment more dark by the increasing volumes of smoke ascending from the city, said:

"See! Our men are busy preparing for the destruction of this palace that through many centuries hath been a centre of Mohammedan influence and oppression. Time doth not admit of thanks, for we both have much to do ere we start forth on our return to Mo, and—"

My words were interrupted by a terrific explosion in such close proximity to us that it caused us to jump, and was followed by a deafening crash of falling masonry. From the lattice we saw the high handsome minaret of the palace topple and fall amid a dense smoke and shower of stones. Our men had undermined it and blown it up.

Liola shuddered, glancing at me in alarm.

"Fear not," I said. "Ere we leave, the city of Koussan must be devastated and burned. Samory hath never given quarter, or shown mercy to his weaker neighbours, and we will show none. Besides, he held thee captive as he hath already held thy lover Omar and myself. He sold us to slavers that we might be sacrificed in Kumassi, therefore the curse of thy Crocodile-god Zomara placed upon him hath at last fallen. The flood-gates of vengeance now opened the hand of man cannot close."

The great court of the harem, deserted by the troops, had become filled with volumes of dense smoke, showing that fire had broken out somewhere within the palace, and ever and anon explosions of a more or less violent character told us that the hands of the destroyers were actually at work. The sack of the Kasbah was indeed complete.

The loot, of which there was an enormous quantity of considerable value, was being removed to a place of safety by a large body of men told off for the purpose. Although Samory was a fugitive, yet the treasures found within his private apartments were of no mean order, and ere noon had passed preparations were being made for its conveyance to Mo, the greater part of the city being already in flames. The fire roared and crackled, choking smoke-clouds obscured the sun, and the heat wafted up was stifling. All opposition to us had long ago ceased, but whenever an Arab was found secreted or a fugitive, he was shot down without mercy. To linger longer in the harem might, I judged, be dangerous on account of the place having been fired, therefore we went together out into the court, and stepping over the mutilated bodies of its beautiful prisoners, entered the chamber where Samory had held his court. Empty, dismantled and wrecked, its appearance showed plainly how the mighty monarch had fallen. Even the great bejewelled manuscript of the Korân, the Arab book of Everlasting Will, that had reposed upon its golden stand at the end of the fine, high-roofed chamber, had been torn up, for its leaves lay scattered about the pavement and after the jewels had been hastily dug from their settings, the covers of green velvet had been cast aside as worthless. Every seat or divan had been either broken or slashed by swords, every vessel or mirror smashed, every ornament damaged beyond repair.

Thinking it best to leave her, a woman, in care of a guard of our armed men, while I went forward, I made the suggestion, but she would not hear of it.

"No," she answered smiling. "I will remain ever at thy side, for beside thee I fear not. Thou art my rescuer, and my life is thine."

"But some of the sights we may witness are not such as a woman's eyes should behold," I answered.

"It mattereth not. That thou wilt allow me to accompany thee, is all I ask."

"Very well," I replied, laughing. "Thou art welcome. Come."

By my side she hurried through the chamber wherein had stood the throne, and thence through several handsome courts, wandering at last into another smaller chamber at the side of which I noticed an alcove with a huge Arab bed surrounded by quaint lattices, so dark that my gaze could not penetrate to its recesses.

As we passed, the movement of some object in the deep shadow beside the bed attracted my attention. Advancing quickly I detected the figure of a man, and, fearing a sudden dash by one of our lurking foes, I again drew my sword.

Liola, seeing this, gave vent to a little scream of alarm and placed her hand upon my arm in fear, but next second the fugitive, anticipating my intention to attack him, sprang suddenly forward into the light.

The bearded face, the fierce, flashing eyes, the thick lips and bushy brows were all familiar to me. Although he wore the white cotton garb of the meanest slave, I recognised him in an instant.

It was the great Arab chieftain Samory!

XXXIV

Liola's Discovery

With a sudden bound I left Liola's side and sprang upon the leader of our enemies, clutching him fiercely by the throat and shouting for assistance. No one was, however, near, and for a few moments we struggled desperately. He was unarmed, and I, having unfortunately dropped my sword in the encounter, our conflict resolved itself into a fierce wrestle for the possession of the weapon which must give victory to the one into whose hands it fell. Once Samory, wiry and muscular like all Arabs, notwithstanding his age, stooped swiftly in an endeavour to snatch up the blade, but seeing his intention, my fingers tightened their grip upon his throat, and he was compelled to spring up again without obtaining possession of the weapon. For several minutes our struggle was desperate, for he had managed to pinion my arms, and I knew that ere long I must be powerless, his strength being far superior to my own.

Liola screamed for help, but no one seemed within call, when suddenly the thought seemed to suggest itself to her to snatch up my weapon and hold it.

I turned to take it from her, but by this action my grip upon my Arab foe became released, and with a desperate spring he forced himself from my grasp, bounding away, leaving a portion of his white *jibbeh* in my hand. But, determined that he should not escape, I dashed after him headlong across the chamber, and out by the opposite door. In the court beyond a knot of our soldiers were standing discussing the events of the day, and I shouted to them; but the sight of me chasing a single fugitive slave did not appeal to them, and they disregarded my order to arrest his progress. Nevertheless I kept on, feeling assured that sooner or later I must run him to earth, but never thinking of the intricacies with which all such palaces abound, intricacies which must be well-known to the Mohammedan ruler.

Suddenly, after endeavouring to elude me by ingenious devices innumerable, and always finding himself frustrated, he entered a chamber leading from the Court of the Eunuchs, and had gained on me sufficiently to disappear ere I reached the entrance. I rushed through after him, believing that he had crossed the deserted court beyond, but was surprised to find that I had utterly lost him. I halted to listen, but could hear no footsteps, and after a careful examination of all the outlets, presently returned in chagrin to the chamber into which he had suddenly dashed, before escaping.

Standing in its centre I looked wonderingly around. Then, for the first time, I discovered that our soldiers, obeying their instructions, had been pouring inflammable liquids everywhere throughout the Kasbah, and a great burst of blood-red flame in the outer court told me that the place had been ignited. At that moment, Liola, with white scared face, believing that she had lost me, entered the chamber, but I recognized our imminent peril, surrounded as we were by a belt of fire.

"Fly!" I cried, frantically. "Fly! quick, back across yonder court to save thy life! In a few moments I will join thee. I must examine this chamber ere I depart."

"I will not go without thee," she answered with calm decision.

"Why riskest thou thy life?" I cried in excitement. "Fly, or in a moment it may be too late, we may both be overwhelmed or suffocated."

But she stirred not. She stood by me in silence, gazing in fear at the red roaring flames that, raging outside, now cut off our retreat by either door. The cause of my hesitation to rush away at first sight of the flames, was the suspicion that somewhere in that chamber was a secret exit. The sudden manner in which the Arab chieftain had eluded me could only have been accomplished by such means. The chamber, well furnished and supported by three great twisted columns of milk-white marble, had its floor covered with costly rugs and its walls hung with dark red hangings, bearing strange devices and inscriptions in long thin Arabic characters. Few rooms in the Kasbah were decorated in this manner, and it had instantly occurred to me that, concealed somewhere, was one of those secret ways which, whether in the Oriental palace, or the mediæval European castle, are so suggestive of treachery and intrigue.

Although one horse-shoe arch of the place led into the Court of the Eunuchs, the other, I noticed, was in direct communication with Samory's private apartments. With consummate skill he had led me here by such a circuitous route that I had not at first noticed that it joined a kind of ante-room to his pavilion.

But the roaring flames that every moment leaped nearer, crackling furiously and fanning us with their scorching breath, allowed me no time for further reflection. Escape was now entirely cut off; only by discovering the secret exit could we save ourselves. In breathless haste I rushed around the walls, tapping them with my sword; but such action proved useless, as I could hear nothing above the roaring and crackling on either side. With my hands I tried to discover where the door was concealed, rushing from side to side in frantic despair, but the exit, wherever it existed, was too cunningly hidden.

So dense had the smoke become that we could not see across the chamber; tongues of fire had ignited the heavy silken hangings, and the whole interior was alight from end to end.

"We are lost—lost!" shrieked Liola in despair "We have fallen victims to our own terrible vengeance upon our enemies."

Within myself I was compelled to admit this, for it seemed as though Samory had led us into a veritable death-trap that the soldiers of Mo had themselves prepared. Suddenly, as a last chance, I remembered I had not examined the three great marble columns, each of such circumference that a man could not embrace them in his arms. I dashed forward, and in the blinding smoke, that caused my eyes to water and held my chest contracted, I tried to investigate whether they were what they appeared to be, solid and substantial supports. The first was undoubtedly fashioned out of a single block of stone, the lower portion polished by the thousands of people who during many centuries had brushed past it. The second was exactly similar, and the third also. But the latter seemed more chipped and worn than the others, and just as I was about to abandon all hope I made a sudden discovery that thrilled me with joy. As I grasped it a portion of it fell back, disclosing that the column was hollow.

The hole was just sufficient to admit the passage of one's body, and without an instant's hesitation I drew Liola forward, and urged her to get inside. The flames were now lapping about us, and another moment's delay would mean certain death. Therefore she dashed in, and as she did so sank quickly out of sight, while the portion of the marble column closed again with a snap.

The rapidity with which she disappeared astounded me, the more so, when, after the lapse of about a minute the platform whereon she had stepped rose again, and with a click returned to its place. Only then was I enabled to re-open the cavity. Apparently it worked automatically, and being balanced in some way, as soon as Liola had stepped off it, had risen again. Instantly I stepped upon it, and with hands close to my sides, sank so swiftly into the darkness that the wind whistled through my garments and roared in my ears. The descent was, I judged, about two hundred feet, but in the pitch darkness I could not discern the character of the shaft. Of a sudden with a jerk it stopped, and finding myself in a strange dimly-lit chamber bricked like a vault, with Liola standing awaiting me, I stepped off, and as I did so the platform shot up again into its place.

"We have, at all events, escaped being burned alive," my fair companion exclaimed when she recovered breath. "But this place is weird and dismal enough."

"True," I answered. "There must, however, be some exit, or Samory would not have entered it. We must explore and discover it."

Glancing around the mysterious vault I saw burning in a niche, with a supply of oil sufficient to last several weeks, a single lamp that had apparently always been kept alight. Taking it up I led the way through the long narrow chamber. The walls, blackened by damp, were covered with great grey fungi, while lizards and other reptiles scuttled from our path into the darkness. At the further end, the vault narrowed into a passage so low that we were compelled to stoop when entering it. In this burrow, the ramifications of which were extraordinary, Liola's filmy garments came to sad grief, for catching upon the projecting portions of rock, they were rent from time to time, while the loss of one of her little green slippers necessitated some delay in recovering it. Yet groping along the narrow uneven way in search of some exit, we at length came into a larger chamber, bricked like the others, and as we entered it were startled by a sudden unearthly roar.

We both drew back, and Liola, in fear, clutched my arm.

"Listen!" she gasped. "What was that?"

Again the noise was repeated, causing the low-roofed chamber to echo, and as I peered forward into the darkness, my gaze was transfixed by a pair of gleaming fiery eyes straight before us.

Similar noises I had heard in the forest on many occasions, and the startling truth at once flashed across my mind. Confronting us was a lion!

I stood in hesitation, not knowing how to act, while Liola clung to me, herself detecting the gleaming eyes and being fully aware of our peril. Yet scarcely a moment passed ere there was a loud rushing sound in the darkness, and the animal, with a low growl, flew through the air in our direction. We had no time to elude him, but fortunately he seemed to have misjudged his distance, for he alighted about half-a-dozen paces short of us. So close was his head that the two gleaming orbs seemed to be rivetted to us. We felt his breath, and unable to draw back, we feared that each second must be our last.

Next moment I heard a clanking of chains, a sound that gave me instant courage.

"Hark!" I cried joyously. "At present we are safe, for the brute is chained!"

Such we ascertained a few minutes later was actually the case, and as I stood there, lamp in hand, my foot struck something. Glancing down I saw it was a human thigh-bone. The animal had already tasted the blood of man, and, straining at his chain, was furious to spring upon us. I then became puzzled to know the reason why this fierce king of the forest should be kept in captivity at this depth if not to guard some entrance or exit. For a few moments I reflected, and at length arrived at the conclusion that during our progress we had slowly ascended towards the earth's surface, and that through the lion's den was the exit of that subterranean way. Again, we had neither seen nor heard sign of the fugitive chieftain. By some means or other he must have succeeded in passing the ferocious brute, and if he had accomplished it, we surely could also.

With my words half drowned by the continuous roar of the fiery-eyed guardian of the secret burrow, I explained briefly to Liola the result of my reflections, and then set about to ascertain the length of the chain holding the animal. After several experiments, allowing it to spring forward at me half-a-dozen times and narrowly escaping its ponderous paws more than once, I ascertained that the chain was just short enough to allow a person to cross the chamber flattened against the opposite wall.

Holding the lamp still in my hand and urging Liola to brace her nerves and watch me closely, I essayed the attempt, creeping cautiously with my back against the roughly-hewn side of the underground lair, and drawing my garments about me to prevent them being hooked by the cruel claws that followed me within a yard during the whole distance. Before my eyes the big shaggy head wagged continuously, the great jaws with their terrible teeth opened, emitting terrific roars of rage and closed again with a dull ominous click, while the chain was strained until I feared it might be rent asunder.

Through several minutes mine was a most horrible experience, for I knew not whether the wall was even; if not, I must have fallen beneath the ferocious claws. However, I managed to successfully cross the brute's den, and shouting to Liola that the passage was perfectly safe, providing she kept her garments closely about her and did not remove her back from the wall, held up the light to her.

With reassuring words she commenced to follow my example, and when the brute saw me in safety and noticed her approach, he left me and sprang towards her. But again he fell short, almost strangled by the pressure upon the iron collar that held him. With an awful roar, his jaws snapping in rage, and his paws constantly clutching at her, he followed her closely just as he had followed me. I feared that she might suddenly faint from the terrible strain upon her nerves, but having witnessed my safe passage she preserved a calmness that was amazing. Twice as the animal, after crouching, leapt suddenly forward I feared the chain must give way, but beyond a low frightened scream escaping her, she preserved a cool demeanour, and a few moments later I was gratified to find her standing panting but unharmed at my side.

"There is an exit somewhere near," I exclaimed a moment later, while she rearranged her torn, blood-stained garments and smoothed her hair with her hands. "Come, let us search."

On proceeding we soon found ourselves in a small passage, drier than the former, and descending rather steeply for some distance, suddenly entered another spacious chamber hewn from the solid rock. Immediately we were inside some peculiarity of its walls attracted my gaze, and I noticed, in addition, that we were in a *cul-de-sac*.

There was, after all, no exit!

The rocky walls, however, rivetted the attention of both of us, for let into them at frequent intervals were large square plates of iron. These I examined carefully, quickly arriving at the conclusion that they had been placed there to close up hewn cavities. With this opinion, Liola, assisting me in my investigations, fully agreed. Each plate, looking curiously like the door of an oven, had apparently been fitted deeply into grooves sunk in the hard rock, for although I tried one after the other, seeking to remove them, they would not budge. By tapping upon them I ascertained that they were of great thickness, and I judged that each must weigh several hundredweight. They were not doors, for they had no hinges, yet beneath each one was a small semi-circular hole in the iron into which I could just thrust my little finger. These were certainly not key-holes, but rather, it seemed, intended to admit air.

In the course of our eager investigations we suddenly came upon a

WILLIAM LE QUEUX

great pile of strongly-bound loads, each wrapped in untanned cow-hide and bound tightly with wire. From their battered appearance they had evidently rested upon the heads of carriers throughout a long march.

"I wonder what they contain?" Liola exclaimed, as we both looked down upon them.

"Let us see," I said. Handing her the lamp, I knelt upon one of the packages, and after considerable trouble succeeded in unbinding the wire. Then as I tore away its thick covering, we both uttered cries of amazement. The sight that met our gaze was bewildering.

From the package there rolled out into the dust a profusion of magnificent glittering jewels.

"Ah! What diamonds!" Liola cried, with admiration for the iridescent stones that was particularly feminine. Then, picking up a splendid bracelet and slipping it upon her wrist, she added, "Look! Isn't this marvellous? The gems are larger than I have ever before seen."

"Beautiful!" I cried gleefully, for by sheer good fortune we had discovered Samory's hidden treasure, and I reflected that our conquest would be rendered absolutely complete by its removal in triumph to Mo.

After a cursory examination of the first pack we together undid them one after another, eagerly investigating their glistening contents, and finding them to consist of a collection of the most wonderful and valuable precious stones it was possible to conceive. There were a few heavy gold ornaments of antique pattern, but in most of them jewels were set, and those only of the most antique and magnificent character. Every known gem was there represented by specimens larger, and of far purer water, than my eyes had ever before beheld. Upon her knees, Liola, with a cry of pleasure, plunged both hands into the glittering heap of jewels, drawing out one after another and holding them up to the glimmering light, her bright eyes full of admiration. The examination of nearly forty great packages took us a long time, but so fascinating proved our task that we were heedless of how the hours sped in our determination to ascertain the true extent of our discovery.

While still upon her knees I had opened almost the last package and spread it before her, when, with a sudden ejaculation she withdrew a magnificent necklet of emeralds of huge size in quaint ancient settings, and with a gay laugh held it up to me for a moment, then clasped it about her own white neck. In the centre hung a pendant consisting of a single emerald of enormous size and brilliant lustre, and as I regarded it in the half light, its shape struck me as distinctly curious. I snatched up the lamp, and bending, examined the quaintly-cut gem more minutely. Then, next instant, I cried excitedly:

"See! The shape of the pendant proves the origin of the necklet!"

With a quick movement she tore it off and looked. Then, in amazement, she gasped:

"It is a representation of Zomara, our god!"

We both scrutinized it closely. Yes, there was no mistake, the emerald had been fashioned into the form of a perfect crocodile, with open jaws, even the teeth being finely chiselled, a veritable marvel of the lapidary's art. While we were both looking at it puzzled, Liola's eyes suddenly became attracted by sight of something in the package I had just opened, and stooping swiftly, picked out of a mass of ornaments a magnificent diadem of some strange milk-coloured, opaque crystals of a character entirely strange to me. The stones were beautifully cut and polished, and although they glittered, even in the sickly rays of our lamp, they had no transparency.

"Behold!" she cried in a voice full of awe, her clear eyes wide open in astonishment. "See what we have discovered!"

I gazed at it, failing at first to notice what I afterwards recognised.

"It is a crown," I said laughing. "A crown fit to grace thy brow!"

"It is the great Rock Diadem of the Sanoms of Mo!" she answered. "See! It is surmounted by the vampire, our national emblem!"

Then, I saw that upon the crest of the diadem was a single great diamond wonderfully chiselled to represent a bat with outspread wings, the device upon the banners of the mystic realm.

"This," she continued, "is without doubt the historic crown of the first Naya. Though it hath never been seen for ages by the eyes of man, it was always popularly supposed to be preserved in the secret Treasure-house of the Sanoms, among the royal jewels. Many are the beliefs and superstitions regarding it. The stones are said to be the first pieces of rock chipped during the foundation of our City in the Clouds, which, as thou art aware, was her work a thousand years ago. Among the possessions of our royal house no relic hath been more venerated than this Rock Diadem of the Naya. How it came hither I know not. It is assuredly a mystery."

"No," I answered, endeavouring to subdue my excitement. "We have now elucidated the mystery. The Treasure-house of Mo hath been entered by thieves, and the most valuable of the royal treasures stolen. The matter hath been kept secret from the people, but by our discovery the identity of the robbers is established beyond doubt, and we have thus recovered the wealth of a nation that was believed to be irretrievably lost."

"But is all of this Omar's lost treasure?" she inquired, astounded at my statement, glancing at the huge heap of gold and jewels nearly as high as ourselves, and of such great value as to be utterly beyond computation.

"Without doubt," I answered, stooping and picking up several jewelled trinkets, girdles and other ornaments, each bearing the sacred reptile or the vampire crest of royalty. "The recovery of these will, at least repay thy nation for the expedition sent against their enemy. Retain possession of the Rock Diadem of Mo, for thou hast discovered it, and with thine own hands shalt thou deliver it into the possession of the ruler who loveth thee."

Then, carefully wrapping the ancient badge of regal dignity in a piece of hide and binding it securely with wire as the carriers' loads had been, I gave it back to her. In half an hour we had completed our examination of the wondrous accumulation of treasure, finding among it many quaint and extraordinary ornaments, some no doubt dating from the earlier days of the foundation of the mysterious isolated kingdom, and others manufactured during recent centuries. The gems were unique in size and character. Truly the thieves in the employ of the Arab chief had taken care to secure the most valuable portion of the royal jewels and leave behind only those of least worth.

With the secret of their concealment in our possession we were both full of eagerness to get back to the light of day and take steps for their removal, yet I confess that the mystery of what was contained behind those strange plates of iron puzzled me.

Leaving Liola to continue her inspection of our discovered treasures, I crossed to the wall and examined one of the plates again, trying with both hands to force it out, but being compelled to relinquish the attempt as hopeless. I was about to give up all idea of discovering how they might be opened, when Liola suddenly uttered an exclamation, and in turning to glance at her, the flame of the lamp I held came into contact with the wall close to the plate that had defied my exertions to remove it.

In an instant a bright flash ran around the chamber, lighting it up as bright as day; a puff of grey smoke was belched in our faces, and a report like thunder deafened us.

An explosion had occurred, great pieces of rock and other *débris* being flung in all directions.

Its terrific force hurled me heavily against the wall, while Liola was flung face downward upon the pile of jewels. Fortunately, neither of us sustained any injury beyond a few bruises, but when I had assisted her to rise, and gazed around, I was amazed to discover that a strange thing had occurred. The whole of the iron plates had been torn from their sockets, and a dark cavity behind each disclosed.

The small sealed cells had been wrenched open simultaneously, as if by a miracle.

But upon careful examination there was, I found, nothing miraculous in the manner in which they had thus been forced. The suffocating smoke that filled the place was of itself sufficient evidence of the agent to which the explosion had been due, and when I looked at the first cavity I saw that right around the chamber, from plate to plate, there had been laid a train of gunpowder, communicating with a charge of powder placed behind each of the semi-circular holes that had so puzzled me. Apparently it had been deemed by Samory wiser to seal the cells entirely rather than secure them by locks, and the train of powder had been placed in position in the event of any reverse of fortune requiring him to secure his treasure quickly before flight. A single spark, as I had accidentally proved, was sufficient to open every cell simultaneously.

Fortunately our lamp was not blown out by the concussion, therefore as soon as the smoke cleared, we together made another tour of inspection around the cavities, finding each of them crammed to overflowing with treasure of every description. Five of the cells, apparently freshly sealed, contained a portion of the stolen jewels of Mo, but all the remainder were evidently the spoils of war, much of it of enormous value. It amused me, too, to discover in one of the cavities, among a great collection of costly bejewelled ornaments, such European articles as a pair of common scissors in a pasteboard case, several penknives of the commonest quality, an India-rubber squeaking doll, a child's toy train in tin, and a mechanical mouse. All were, no doubt, considered as treasures by the Arab potentate, yet I reflected that nearly every article in the whole of that miscellaneous collection had been acquired by the most ruthless and merciless bloodshed.

When at last we became convinced of the necessity for finding some exit, we left the chamber by the way we had entered. The discovery of the wonderful treasure of the Sanoms made it plain to me that there must be an exit somewhere, for the packs were far too ponderous to have been lowered from the Kasbah by the way we had entered. On reflection I saw that the lion was evidently kept there to guard the entrance to the store of treasure, therefore it was not surprising that there was no outlet in that direction.

No, we should be compelled to repass the brute. This fact I explained to Liola, but it in no way disconcerted her, for she crept past the snapping jaws of the furious beast calmly, holding the treasured Rock Diadem close beside her. Presently, on making a diligent search, we discovered a long dark tunnel running at right angles to the path we had traversed, and following this ascended to where a faint but welcome glimmer of light showed. Soon we were in a small natural cavern, and a few moments later struggled upward to the light of day, amazed to find ourselves on the bank of a beautiful river. At our feet the clear cool water ran by, placid and peaceful, but away across the grass-plain about half a mile distant was the once-powerful city of Koussan, enveloped in black smoke that ascended to the clear blue heavens, mingled with great flames, the fierce roar of which reached our ears where we stood.

The vengeance of Mo had indeed overtaken her Arab enemy, and completely crushed him.

XXXV

Into the Mist

Our troops had, we found, withdrawn from the burning city and were encamped about a mile away, taking a well-earned rest, and watching with satisfaction the destruction of the once powerful capital of the "Pirate of the Niger." The presence of Liola, together with the announcement of the discovery of the treasure of the Sanoms, that we made to Kona secretly, caused him the wildest delight. His barbaric instinct overcame him, and seizing his spear he executed a kind of war-dance around us, bestowing upon us the most adulatory phrases of the Dagomba vocabulary. Afterwards he addressed the assembled soldiers, omitting at my desire all mention of the jewels of Mo, and three days later, having secured all the gems and golden ornaments, together with Samory's hidden wealth, we set forth on our triumphant return to the mysterious far-off land.

Rapidly and pleasantly we accomplished the long journey, re-crossing the treacherous Way of the Thousand Steps without a single mishap, and ascended to the lofty plateau of Omar's kingdom until, high up in the grey morning mist, we saw looming before us with almost spectral indistinctness the gigantic battlements and domes of the City in the Clouds. On ascending the rope steps at the Gate of Mo a few days previously we had ascertained that the expedition to the Hombori Mountains had been entirely successful, for the enemy had been met in the pass by the defenders and mercilessly overwhelmed and slaughtered. Against the lightweight Maxim guns, weighing only about twenty-five pounds each and firing 600 to 700 shots per minute with an effective range of two miles, the old-fashioned rifles and field-pieces of the force under the traitor Kouaga had been powerless, hence the whole expedition had been utterly routed, followed up after their flight and massacred almost to a man, Kouaga himself being shot dead by Niaro while strenuously endeavouring to rally his men for a final onslaught. Omar, at the head of his victorious army, had re-entered the city only the day before our arrival, therefore on our return we found ourselves in the midst of feasting and merry-making of a most enthusiastic character.

Little wonder was it that when the news of the complete victory we had secured spread through the city the joy of the people knew no bounds, for especially welcome was the information that, in addition to utterly destroying Samory's city we had secured the whole of his treasure. Kona, Liola and myself held back the fact that we had also recovered the stolen jewels, and we also took elaborate precautions that the knowledge of Liola's safety should not be conveyed prematurely to Omar.

During the formal welcome that the young Naba, resplendent in his magnificent bejewelled robes of state and surrounded by his sages and officers, accorded us at the great palace-gate, now fully restored, Liola held back, hiding herself. Not until evening, when I was sitting with Omar in his luxurious private pavilion after eating a sumptuous meal served on the royal dishes of chased gold, I told him confidentially of the recovery of the lost jewels.

"Impossible, Scars!" he cried in English, starting suddenly to his feet. "Where did you find them? How?"

Brief words were required to explain how I had discovered them hidden in Samory's secret cavern beyond the lion's lair.

"I understood that only the wealth of the old Arab's Kasbah was hidden there," he exclaimed quickly. "This news is indeed as astounding as it is welcome."

"Your subjects are unaware that your treasure has ever been removed from Mo, therefore I have not enlightened them," I answered. "Come with me and see if you recognize any of the jewels."

Eagerly he followed me into a small adjoining apartment where the loot had been deposited, and as we opened pack after pack he uttered ejaculations of surprise and complete gratification, recognizing in the recovered gems the wonderful incomparable heirlooms of his royal house.

He turned to thank me when we had finished, and as he did so I placed my hand firmly on his arm, saying in a serious voice:

"In addition to these, Omar, I have also recovered a jewel of even far greater worth than all this magnificent collection; one that will shine as the brightest and most beautiful gem in the diadem of Mo."

A genuine look of bewilderment crossed his pale refined features for an instant, as he answered:

"I really don't understand, Scars. No jewel can be of greater intrinsic value than the Treasure of the Sanoms. What is it?"

For answer, Liola, a veritable vision of classic beauty in her loose white robe, gold-embroidered at the hem, and broad girdle of fiery rubies, stepped from behind the heavy curtain of blue silk where she had been concealed, and stood before him.

Rigid in speechless amazement he stood for a moment, then recognizing that his lost love was actually present, alive and well, he bounded towards her, and with a loud cry of joy embraced her, brushing back her soft hair and covering her white open brow with passionate kisses.

It was indeed a joyous reunion, but as I turned intending to withdraw discreetly and leave them alone together to continue their exchange of confidences, my friend promptly called me back, saying:

"Stay, Scars, old fellow! Let me hear from your own lips the solution of this mystery of the return of the dead to life. Truly you have recovered a jewel worth to me a hundred times all the treasures of Mo."

Crossing again towards him I described briefly the revolting circumstances in which I had discovered her, a harem slave of our Arab enemy; how we had both narrowly escaped being burned to death, our subsequent adventures in the damp subterranean burrow, and the finding of the secreted treasure.

"Liola herself also made one discovery," I said in conclusion, laughing and turning towards her.

Gently disengaging herself from her lover's fond arms she went behind the curtain where she had hidden, and on coming forth again held in her slim white hands a round package still securely wrapped in untanned hide, which she handed to Omar.

"The Rock Diadem of the Naya!" he cried in joy, when his trembling, eager hands had opened it. "The most valued of all our possessions!" Then, turning towards Liola, he tenderly placed upon her head the historic mark of royalty, saying in his own tongue:

"Now that the days of our sorrow have passed like the shadow of a cloud upon a sunlit sea, we will be wed as soon as it is meet for us so to do, and upon thy brow thus shalt rest the diadem of the first Naya, the upright queen to whom Mo oweth her magnificence, her power, and her present prosperity. Thou shalt sit beside me upon the Emerald Throne; thou shalt be known as the Naya Liola."

Again he embraced her with ineffable tenderness, and with her handsome head pillowed heavily upon her shoulder her breast heaved, and from her deep blue fathomless eyes there fell tears of joy.

At last, having received the warmest thanks from my old companion through many misfortunes and from the woman he loved, I turned and sought the sage Goliba, to whom I told the good news of his daughter's safety and betrothal to Omar.

Three days later the marriage took place amid the most gorgeous pomp and the wildest popular rejoicings, the strange ceremony being performed by the high-priest of the Temple of Zomara beneath the golden figure of the Crocodile-god that hung suspended above the Emerald Throne. Feasts and merry-making continued throughout a whole moon, and the mystic city, decorated with flags and flowers, was agog by day and brilliantly illuminated by night. Never in the long history of the ancient kingdom had such costly banquets been served; never had the royal entertainments been on such lavish scale; never had the sounds of revelry contained such a true genuine ring, for never before had the people been so happy and content. Though on the day of the marriage Liola was solemnly crowned with the wonderful Rock Diadem of Mo, I, as keeper of the royal treasure, allowed no word to go forth regarding the theft and recovery of the Sanom jewels, which had already been deposited in their original hiding-place beneath the lake. Samory's treasure was, however, given to Liola by Omar, and she ordered half of it to be distributed to the poor, an act of generosity that won for her intense popularity.

Her action was, she told me in confidence, a thank-offering to Zomara for her timely rescue from a terrible fate.

CONCLUSION

S amory, the truculent old Arab, escaped. By some means he eluded us in the dark intricacies of that subterranean way, and groping along in a similar manner to ourselves, he evidently fled to the forest, for he has since collected the scattered remnant of his nomadic bands, and although he has never since troubled us, yet he now and then commits depredations on the borders of the English and French spheres of influence. Ere long he will overstep the bounds, and one Power or another will certainly send a punitive expedition to crush and humiliate him, as they have crushed the arrogant Prempeh of Ashanti.

During many months the means by which the theft of the Treasure of the Sanoms had been effected remained an inscrutable mystery, and it was only on the day previous to my departure from the mysterious land for England, or rather more than six months ago, that the problem was solved and in a manner entirely unexpected.

In preparation for the annual feast in honour of the Crocodile-god I had occasion to go secretly and alone to the submerged Treasure-house, in order to obtain certain jewels which tradition decreed should be worn on that day by the reigning sovereign. I had emptied the lake, unsealed the cover of the well-like aperture, locked the mechanism fatal to intruders, descended and obtained what I sought, when on ascending I was dismayed to find water pouring in upon me in increasing volumes. Upwards I climbed, struggling desperately against the inrushing flood thundering down upon me, and was aghast to find, when I gained the surface, that the sluice-gates that held back the waters feeding the lake had been opened, and that it was rapidly refilling. Instantly it occurred to me to replace the cover, and in breathless haste I succeeded in screwing it down and dashing for my life back to the bank, the water being up to my arm-pits ere I reached it.

When next second I glanced upward to the mound where the mechanism was concealed, I saw standing thereon the wild-looking figure of a woman with her soiled, tattered garments fluttering in the wind.

Her long scraggy arms were raised high above her head, and she was crying aloud to me.

Without a moment's hesitation I dashed forward up the hill to secure the person who had apparently discovered the secret of the

Treasure-house, but on approaching her closely I suddenly halted in astonishment.

The wretched, fiendish-looking virago, upon whose face were the most hideous distortions of insanity I had ever witnessed, was none other than the once-powerful tyrannical autocrat, the Great White Queen!

Across her narrow, withered brow, brown almost as a toad's back, a single wisp of thin grey hair strayed; in her eyes was the unmistakeable light of madness, while the nails of her outstretched fingers were as sharp and long as the talons of some beast of prey. So weird and repulsive-looking was she that I stood before her dumbfounded.

"Ah!" she shrieked to me exultantly, in a harsh, rasping voice, "I have killed them—drowned them all, the accursed spies and renegades! The traitor Kouaga captured me as I fled for life from the city-gate, and promising me release and safe escort from this land of evil spirits in return for the secret of the Treasure-house, I recklessly gave it to him, on condition that his armed men should assist me to recover my lost position as Queen of Mo. I promised to forget the past and take him back into my favour. But, securing my jewels, he conveyed them to his Arab master at Koussan, and left me alone, deposed and ruined. May Zomara crush and torture him, the traitor!" Then, turning with wild gesture towards the lake, now a great sheet of placid water, her hands clutched convulsively, her eyes starting as if she saw, in her disordered imagination, a host of her enemies, she cried: "This, at last, is the hour of my revenge! I have drawn the lever, and while they were below with you they were drowned like rats in a hole!" And she gave vent to a short, dry laugh, exclaiming: "They refused to assist me to tear the usurper from the Emerald Throne, so I have killed them. My work is finished! I have reigned and have been deposed; I have striven for the people, and have been rewarded by their curses; I have—"

At this moment, determined to carry her back to the city, I sprang forward and gripped her lean, bony arms. With colossal strength, engendered by insanity, she fought and bit, shrieking and showering imprecations upon me, it requiring all my strength to hold her; but presently she became quiet again, uttering long strings of rapid incoherent words that plainly showed the hopeless state of her mind.

Thus walking, we gained the edge of the lake, and having passed the cascade were skirting the river when, with a suddenness that took me completely by surprise, she slipped from my grasp, and with a wild exclamation dashed towards the warm, oozy bank.

Next second I noticed that the waters were alive with the sacred reptiles, but ere I could reach her she threw up her long, thin arms, and uttering an unearthly yell, plunged in.

A dozen hideous, hungry jaws snapped viciously as she cast herself amongst them, and an instant later where, with a shriek of horror, she disappeared for ever beneath the waters, the swiftly-flowing current was tinged red by long streaks of human blood.

In an excess of religious fervour she had sacrificed herself to her god Zomara.

THIS IS NO APOLOGUE. LITTLE there remains to tell. Under the beneficent rule of Omar and Liola power, prosperity and contentment have now returned to the mysterious ancient realm, within which I have been the first stranger to set foot. As principal official of the ruler of the land that, although familiar to me, is still a mystery to the Royal Geographical Society, I left for England a few months ago on a mission to the greatest White Queen, Victoria, offering her assistance in her effort to crush the cruel sway of our mutual enemies the Ashantis. Our offer was cordially accepted, and the successful issue of the campaign which caused the downfall of Prempeh is now well known. Before returning to resume my duties as Governor of Mo, the far-off spectral City in the Clouds, into which no stranger may enter, I have, however, written down, at the instigation of the publishers whose name this volume bears upon its title-page, this plain tale of travel, treason and treasure as a record of the first successful journey to the high-up, inaccessible land of the Naya, the once-dreaded Great White Queen.

THE END

A Note About the Author

William Le Queux (1864–1927) was an Anglo-French journalist, novelist, and radio broadcaster. Born in London to a French father and English mother, Le Queux studied art in Paris and embarked on a walking tour of Europe before finding work as a reporter for various French newspapers. Towards the end of the 1880s, he returned to London where he edited *Gossip* and *Piccadilly* before being hired as a reporter for *The Globe* in 1891. After several unhappy years, he left journalism to pursue his creative interests. Le Queux made a name for himself as a leading writer of popular fiction with such espionage thrillers as *The Great War in England in 1897* (1894) and *The Invasion of 1910* (1906). In addition to his writing, Le Queux was a notable pioneer of early aviation and radio communication, interests he maintained while publishing around 150 novels over his decades long career.

A Note from the Publisher

Spanning many genres, from non-fiction essays to literature classics to children's books and lyric poetry, Mint Edition books showcase the master works of our time in a modern new package. The text is freshly typeset, is clean and easy to read, and features a new note about the author in each volume. Many books also include exclusive new introductory material. Every book boasts a striking new cover, which makes it as appropriate for collecting as it is for gift giving. Mint Edition books are only printed when a reader orders them, so natural resources are not wasted. We're proud that our books are never manufactured in excess and exist only in the exact quantity they need to be read and enjoyed.

bookfinity™

Discover more of your favorite classics with Bookfinity™.

- Track your reading with custom book lists.
- Get great book recommendations for your personalized Reader Type.
- Add reviews for your favorite books.
- AND MUCH MORE!

Visit **bookfinity.com** and take the fun Reader Type quiz to get started.

Enjoy our classic and modern companion pairings!

Printed in the USA
CPSIA information can be obtained
at www.ICGtesting.com
JSHW022327140824
68134JS00019B/1339

9 781513 280868